MW01267758

Other Books by Tom Hooker

<u>Fiction</u>

The War Never Ends
(with Gary Ader)

<u>Non-fiction</u>

Calvary's Child: The Life of Amanda Carol Hooker
Season of Shadows: A Father's Grief

Praise for The War Never Ends

"The War Never Ends . . . is a beautifully written novel.
I fell in love with the characters almost on the first
page."
—*Mensa Bulletin*

"A very compelling story! Fits nicely on the top shelf
with real page-turners!"
—Amazon Customer Review

"Truly original perspective of our recent history. Fast
reading - 'cause one wants to read what comes next."
—Amazon Customer Review

Twenty-Five Angels

by

Tom Hooker

Published by Escarpment Press

Published by Escarpment Press
Indian Land, SC

www.escarpmentpress.weebly.com
Indian Land, SC

Dedication

This book is dedicated to the men and women who have served in the Eighth Army Air Corps, or the Eighth Air Force. Thank you for the sacrifice you've made to protect our life, liberty and freedom.

This book is also in memory of those who have rejoined the angels, having completed their final mission.

Author's Note

When I was a young boy in North Mississippi, I often visited my neighbors, Lee and Joe Sewell. They had a tri-level tree house, and were every bit as imaginative as I was. We turned the tree house into a B-17 Flying Fortress.

Lee, the oldest, always piloted the aircraft on our missions. When he grew older and finished high school, Lee joined the Army and completed two tours of duty in Vietnam as a combat helicopter pilot.

Joe (the youngest) and I alternated between the roles of bombardier and top-turret gunner. We downed so many ME-109s and dropped payloads on so many targets, if they had been real, it would have put the real Eighth Army Air Corps to shame. But, of course, they were not real. The true heroes of the European skies had done their jobs fifteen years before our flights of imagination in North Mississippi.

Nevertheless, these games served as the impetus for *Twenty-Five Angels*. The daydreams of my youth never ended, you see. James Thurber's Walter Mitty has nothing on me.

I'm sure you know this is a work of fiction, and, as such, makes no claim to any real life events except as can be referenced in the general rather than the specific.

For example, I've tried to imbed the Reba Jean and its crew into real missions flown by the Eighth Air Corps. Any discrepancies between what really happened and what is recounted herein may be attributed to my ignorance, which I've tried to camouflage under the aegis of dramatic license.

My British friends probably already know that the title of Earl of Arundel is real, but not in the sense used here. My research indicates it is a subsidiary of the Dukedom of Norfolk, and is used by his heir apparent as a courtesy title. If I have offended, please accept my apology.

I hope you enjoy reading *Twenty-Five Angels* as much as I enjoyed writing it.

Twenty-Five Angels

The Pilot's Tale

17 August, 1943
Schweinfurt, Germany

The light from a small flashlight, what the Brits called a "torch," shone in Raymond Bishop's eyes and a soft voice said, "Oh-three hundred, sir. Time to get up."

"Thanks," Ray said, and the seemingly disembodied voice and light moved on to one of the other three bunks in his small quarters.

After showering, shaving and dressing, he joined the parade of shadowy figures making its way along the network of crushed rock walkways to the officer's mess. Ray was surprised at the mild temperature, given the RAF base lay roughly on the same latitude as Newfoundland. Even in the dark, he could see that a heavy fog surrounded the place. "Probably scrub today's mission," he muttered to himself. The butterflies in his stomach didn't know whether to be happy or sad. At the mess, he filled a tray with bacon and eggs and sat at one of the long tables.

A brown-haired second lieutenant sat beside him. He looked a bit frayed around the edges. "New here?" he asked.

Ray extended his hand. "Ray Bishop. How can you tell?"

The other guy shook his hand. "Steve Knighton. You look too fresh. Your eyes aren't jumpy enough. Who's your flight leader?" He shoved a mound of food into his mouth.

Bishop looked at the eggs on his fork and gently placed the utensil back on his plate. "Captain Blaylock."

"Good man," Knighton said.

"Where we going?"

"Won't know until the mission briefing."

"Heavy fog out there. Think we'll get scrubbed?"

Knighton canted his head at an angle, thinking. "Too early to tell. Sometimes the fog burns off. We'll know by 0900."

Bishop scanned the room, listening to the burble of voices and the clatter of pewter and tin, and sighed.

The parade resumed, as the ghostly figures continued from the mess hall to the officer's briefing room. Ray sat in a rickety wooden chair, Knighton on his right. Warren Lowery, Bishop's co-pilot, sat on his left.

"Ready to go?" Lowery asked. Bishop only offered a thin smile.

A slender man, with a bit more gray in his hair and a bit more brass on his collar, stepped onto a small raised platform at the front of the room. The mass of officers jumped to attention. "As you were," the man said, and everybody returned to their seats.

He stood before a cloth-covered board fastened to the wall, and waited for the hubbub of voices to die down.

Knighton leaned over and whispered, "Colonel Stephens."

Bishop knew that. He had met Kermit Stephens briefly last evening when he and his crew checked in. As commander of the First Bomb Wing, of which Bishop's 303rd Bomb Group was a part, Stephens ran the show at RAF Molesworth.

Stephens nodded toward a clerk standing at the corner of the covered board, and the assistant removed the cloth to reveal a map of Southeastern England and Western Europe. A silver thumb tack pinned one end of a length of red yarn at a spot Bishop identified as their air base. The yarn extended from there to a second tack in the heart of Germany.

"Schweinfurt," Stephens intoned.

The wave of groans circling the room told Bishop that his more experienced cohorts were familiar with the target.

"The manufacturing facilities at Schweinfurt make fifty percent of the ball bearings used by the German military," Stephens continued. "If today's raid is successful, it will shorten the war by six months." He paused to survey the men in the room. "If every pilot in this group were to dive his ship, fully manned and loaded with bombs, into the center of the target area, the mission would still be considered a success."

"He's not serious, is he?" Bishop whispered to Steve.

Knighton grinned and gave a minute shake of his head.

"You will fly twelve hundred miles round trip. You will spend five hours over enemy territory. Most of it without fighter escort." Stephens consulted his notes, giving the new wave of grumbling time to fade. "Takeoff is at 0700. Cross the Dutch coast at 0830. Drop at 1015. Return and land at 1500. You will have a headwind on your return, so it will take a little longer." He surveyed the room again. "Colonel Curtis LeMay will lead a simultaneous strike at Regensburg, near Schweinfurt. Our pronged attack will force the Luftwaffe to divide their fighters, and diminish their effectiveness."

Colonel Stephens stepped down, to be replaced by a major who gave the officers the meteorology report. "You should have clear skies over Europe. Unlimited ceiling. The trick will be to get you airborne. We expect this ground mist to burn off by departure."

He was followed by another staff officer. With the help of an aide operating a slide projector, the officer showed aerial photos of the target. Ray didn't know where Doug Cannon sat, but he knew his bombardier closely studied the images, picturing what they would look like through his bombsight.

Stephens returned to the platform. He placed his hands behind his back. "I don't have to tell you not to share this information with anyone not flying with you today. Not with your orderly, not with the cook, not with anyone." He lifted his chin. "Good luck. Dismissed."

The officers rose and began to file out. A priest set up a table along one wall, and the Catholic officers lined up to receive absolution. Being Southern Baptist, Bishop didn't go in for the priest thing, but he figured he'd be doing his share of praying between now and tonight.

He joined his other three officer crewmen, second lieutenants all, in the jeep that would take them to the flight line and the *Reba Jean*, their B-17 Flying Fortress — the Boeing Corporation's pride and joy. The corporal who drove the jeep must have had dreams of piloting his own plane, because he drove way too fast, considering how nobody could see a blasted thing. And there were a bunch of other jeeps making the same trip.

They reached their aircraft safely — a miracle — and clambered out of the vehicle. Bishop clapped the driver on the shoulder and said, "Thanks, Corporal."

"Good luck, sirs," the soldier responded.

Sergeant Butler, the ground crew chief, sketched a light salute. "We're almost ready, Captain." He and his crewmen would have been up at midnight, and working on the plane since 0130. The ordnance crew would have been on duty even before that, hauling the bombs from the ordnance depot, known as "boom city," and loading them into the belly of the aircraft.

Although it would be a while before takeoff, and although he could see only a few feet of the plane at a time because of the fog, Ray performed a walk-around. He made sure all the wing edges and flight control surfaces were clean and free of anything that could impede the flow of air and render the craft unstable in flight.

A B-17 Flying Fortress was a huge beast that carried ten crewmen, five double-barreled, fifty caliber machine guns and ammunition, three smaller machine guns and their ammunition, and up to twelve, five hundred pound bombs, not to mention the aviation fuel necessary to fly all that weight twelve hundred miles. The fog prevented Bishop from admiring the whole craft this morning, but he'd seen it enough times. It sat on two large wheels which descended from beneath the wings, with a shorter third wheel supporting the tail section. That made the long, cigar-shaped fuselage angle upward from tail to snout, and he knew the *Reba Jean* sat with her nose pointed skyward, as if she were anxious to get up there.

He paused at the front of the plane and studied the nose art. The image was rather chaste compared to some on other bombers, at least those he'd seen in yesterday's fading daylight. Ray had given the artist a picture of Reba Jean Carwyle, his fiancé, and the artist made a passable rendition of her image from the photo. Her face stared back at him. Strawberry blond hair and freckles. He ran a hand through his own brown mop, and wondered what color their kids' hair would be. The artist also had thrown in a little cheesecake. Reba's likeness sat on a bale of hay, wearing skin-tight dungarees and a clinging plaid shirt. Her torso was turned to the side to accentuate the shape of her breasts. Country girl all the way.

Ray figured his crew would have preferred something more racy, but they respected him, and said nothing.

Warren Lowery, Doug Cannon, and Aaron Hoffman loitered around the front of the aircraft. Ray sauntered up to them.

"Think we'll fly today?" Cannon asked.

Ray looked at the gray fog. It felt like being inside a pillow. "You know as much about this Limey weather as I do, Mr. Cannon. But if I had to guess, I'd say no. I don't see how this can burn off before 0700."

A bus pulled up and the six sergeants who comprised the rest of his crew hopped off. They exchanged "Good mornings" and salutes with the officers, and wandered off to putter around the bomber. Each loaded the barrels of his dual-fifty caliber gun, checked his ammunition supply, stashed a few bars of chocolate or other snacks near his flight station, and generally killed time, waiting for takeoff.

At 0645, Captain Blaylock rode up in a jeep driven by another corporal.

"Here we go," Bishop called to his crew. The fog seemed as thick as ever, maybe a lighter shade of gray, as the sun struggled to break through.

"Gentlemen," said the captain. Scott Blaylock looked to be a couple of years older than Ray, maybe twenty-six to Bishop's twenty-four. His hair color was what Reba Jean would call towheaded.

"Captain," Bishop saluted. "Are we scrubbed?"

Blaylock shook his head. "No. Only postponed. The brass really has a hard-on for this target." He

7

hopped into his jeep and moved on to the *Rack'em Up*, the next B-17 in the flight line.

"Hurry up and wait," Aaron Hoffman grumbled.

"Tell me about it," Doug Cannon added.

Ray pulled a blanket from the aircraft, spread it on the paved hardstand under the *Reba Jean*, and lay down hoping in vain for a nap.

Blaylock returned at 0830. "We're still on hold. The fog cleared a bit at Mildenhall, and Colonel LeMay got permission to launch his wing. They're on their way to Regensburg."

"But . . . I thought we were supposed to attack simultaneously," Bishop sputtered.

"That was the plan, but it's been changed." Blaylock wiped his hand across his mouth. "There'll be no double-whammy. The German fighters will be able to hit LeMay's Regensburg wing, then land, refuel, rearm, and have time to come after us."

The *Reba Jean's* crew was silent. Thinking about what lay ahead.

"Ah, hell," Blaylock said. "We'll probably get scrubbed anyway."

At 1100, Sergeant Mike Hilton, one of the waist gunners, said, "I've eaten about all my snacks. Permission to make a resupply run, Boss?"

Bishop studied the fog for about the thousandth time. It did look a little thinner. He scratched his chin. He would not be the cause of a delay if they were green-lighted. "Mr. Hilton, if you keep eating like that, the

Reba Jean won't be able to lift off. If we go, you can have some of my stash."

Hilton looked glum. "It's just that I eat when I get nervous."

Bishop glanced around at the other crew members, then leaned in close and whispered, "Lucky you. I haven't been able to eat a thing this morning."

Hilton smiled, and Bishop, who'd feared the revelation of his own little bit of weakness, smiled back.

Blaylock's jeep roared up to the *Reba Jean's* hardstand. He didn't dismount. "We go at 1200 hours." Then his driver launched the vehicle down the row.

"Okay, girls," Bishop yelled. "Let's get this show on the road."

Everyone gathered the blankets and gear they'd lounged on for the past four hours and stowed it in the plane. Then they policed the area, picking up gum wrappers and other litter.

By 1145, the ten crewmembers were aboard and at their posts. Ray and Warren had completed their final walk-around with the ground crew chief, and had completed the cockpit pre-flight checklist.

Ray slid the cockpit's left side window back and shouted, "Clear left!" while Lowery did the same on the right. Ray hit the button to engage the Bendix starter on engine number one. The engine made a loud cough and the propeller began a slow rotation.

When Ray was satisfied the engine had caught and wouldn't stall, he repeated the process for numbers two, three, and four. As the engines spooled up to idle speed,

Ray thumbed his throat mike, "Okay, Davis. Check us off. Pilot is on board."

"Roger, Cap'n," Gary Davis, the tail gunner, responded. While Bishop was only a second lieutenant, he was commander of this airship. The Army Air Corps followed the Navy protocol. It was customary to address the pilot by any title attributed to a ship commander: captain, skipper, boss.

"Bombardier," Davis intoned.

"Here," Doug Cannon answered.

"Navigator."

"That's me" Aaron Hoffman said.

"Co-Pilot."

"Yo!" Warren Lowery.

Davis continued down the list, verifying the presence of the engineer, radio operator, left and right waist gunners, and ball turret gunner.

"Cap'n, tail gunner reports crew complement present and accounted for," Davis said.

"Acknowledged," Bishop responded.

Warren Lowery looked out his side window. "There goes the *Rack'em Up*."

The fog had lifted considerably. Little more than a light haze covered the ground now.

Bishop gestured to the ground crewman waiting off the aircraft's nose, and he in turn motioned to the crewmen waiting behind the wings, well clear of the spinning propellers. They moved in a crouching run to the wheels, pulled the chocks clear, and moved back away from the wings. The crewman gave a thumbs up to Bishop, who advanced the throttles, and the *Reba Jean* rolled off its hardstand into a right turn onto the taxiway.

The first B-17 trundled down the runway, gaining speed as it went. Despite the clearing fog, the pilots still couldn't see the end of the airstrip, and the bomber seemed to fade into the mist as it proceeded toward takeoff. Thirty seconds later, the second aircraft followed.

"Geez," Lowery grumbled. "The brass really wants this mission to go off. We can't even see our takeoff point."

The *Reba Jean's* instrument panel clock read 1214 when Bishop shoved the throttles to the wall and the airship's four, twelve-hundred-horsepower, Wright Cyclone engines screamed. The craft gained speed rapidly. Bishop smiled when the wheels left the ground, and his stomach sent that familiar buoyant feeling to his brain.

The fog extended up so they had no visibility throughout their entire takeoff climb. They would survive the next few minutes only if Bishop followed the prescribed speed, turn rate, and angle of ascent, in order to avoid a mid-air collision with the other bombers.

A few minutes later, the B-17 broke through the clouds and into brilliant sunshine. Bishop and Lowery scanned their surroundings, checking for proper spacing with the other aircraft. Everything looked good.

Bishop had grown up in Taliposa County, Mississippi, a farm region with cotton as the main cash crop. As a little boy, he'd looked at the sky and marveled at how much the clouds looked like fluffy balls of the white stuff. When he'd first learned to fly, and first flown above heavy cloud cover, he felt as if he'd been transported to a world whose surface was made of pure, white, ginned cotton. He still got that feeling every time — like now.

He'd done his basic flight training at Eglin Air Base, near Pensacola, Florida. His primary aircraft there had been a stubby-winged, Stearman bi-plane that he'd nicknamed "The Bumblebee" because, by all known laws of physics, the thing should not have been able to fly. Bishop was convinced the instructor had assigned him the plane in an effort to wash him out. But the cotton farmer's son had spent his teen years muscling an iron-wheeled tractor around the loamy fields of his home, so Bumblebee had been a piece of cake in comparison.

But he couldn't dwell on the past. He searched for and spotted the *Suzy Q*, Captain Blaylock's plane. He was assigned to fly on his left wingtip, and he smoothly moved into that position. Meanwhile, the *Rack'em Up*, eased into the slot on Blaylock's right wingtip.

Donnie Stapleton, the flight engineer, climbed up the narrow passageway behind the pilot and co-pilot seats, and popped his head between the two men's shoulders. "Howdy, sirs," he said, in a Tennessee drawl.

For the next four hours (eight, counting the return trip), Bishop's attention would be devoted to station-keeping — maintaining the proper spacing within the squadron's formation. Stapleton would split his time between helping Lowery watch the gauges and attending to any equipment malfunctions. He glanced out the window and uttered a low whistle. "Would you look at that? We never had this many planes in formation on our training flights."

About that time, a flight of P-47 Thunderbolts, the smaller, single-engine fighters that would escort the bombers to the German border, joined the squadron and added to the spectacle. "And it just keeps getting better," Stapleton added.

"Two hundred-thirty-one, plus the fighters," Lowery said. "That's two thousand three hundred and ten souls. I wonder how many will come back?"

Nobody had an answer to that question.

They cleared the coast and entered the airspace over the North Sea.

"Permission to have the gunners test fire their weapons, Captain?" Stapleton asked.

"Granted," Bishop replied.

Stapleton descended the short ladder to the walkway—crawlway actually—that ran beneath the cockpit, and the length of the aircraft. A few minutes later, Bishop heard a series of throaty growls as each gunner fired a short burst from his weapon to make sure it was operating properly.

Bishop had been busy since takeoff, and that had allowed his butterflies to settle a bit. He thought he could eat something now. He retrieved his kit and grabbed a handful of shelled peanuts from a paper bag, chasing them with a swig of water from his canteen.

Thoughts of home floated to the surface of his mind. He'd been a first-year English teacher at the high school in Buttermilk Springs, his home community, when the

Japs hit Pearl Harbor. He went to visit his Lit professor at Ole Miss, where he'd gotten his degree just seven months before.

"I'm thinking of joining up," he had told his old professor.

They sat in Doctor Graham's small office, surrounded by students' work and pipe smoke.

"You should re-read *The Red Badge of Courage*," Graham said after a pause. "It won't all be honor and glory."

Bishop smiled. "I'm ahead of you." He stood and peered out the window at the green park across the street. "I'm not doing this out of some romantic notion. We are blessed to live in a country where brave men have died to give us freedom, and more have died to maintain it." He realized his little speech sounded rehearsed, but that was because he'd held this discussion in his head a hundred times already.

Graham met his gaze. "Are you willing to die to help preserve that freedom for someone else? Because that may happen."

"Yes."

"I'm not sure you understand what you're committing yourself to, but you're not alone." He gestured toward the deserted park. "The campus is almost empty. Young men are leaving school in droves to enlist."

Bishop said nothing. He'd spent four years in Graham's classroom, and knew he hadn't finished his thought.

"The Army, or Navy, will need officers to lead these troops. You have a degree, a keen analytical mind, and you're not afraid of hard work. You should talk to your recruiter about applying for officer's training." Graham extended his hand. "Godspeed."

* * * * *

"Ray," Warren Lowery's voice broke Ray's reverie. "We're crossing ten thousand feet."

"Right." Bishop thumbed his throat mike and spoke to his crew. "Listen up! We're at ten angels. Put on your oxygen masks. It's gonna get cold, too. Make sure you've got your cold-weather gear on."

The aircraft would eventually reach twenty-five thousand feet—twenty-five angels. Some boob had decided that high altitude made the bomber formation a harder target for the anti-aircraft guns. At that altitude, temperatures reached forty degrees below zero, and a man could easily freeze to death, or lose a finger, toe, or some other more important piece of flesh to frostbite. Most of the crew just wore leather overalls that resembled the hip waders worn by a fisherman, only these garments were lined with wool. They wore wool-lined leather jackets over that. Add a cap with wooly ear-flaps, leather gloves over silk gloves, and an oxygen mask to protect the face, and a crewman stood a chance—*if* he was careful.

"Enemy territory," Lowery intoned, as the formation crossed the Dutch coast.

"Occupied territory," Bishop corrected with a smile. "We won't be over enemy territory until we reach Germany."

"You say po-tay-to, I say po-tah-to," Lowery responded. "Either way, if we go down now, and survive, we'll win an all-expenses-paid vacation at the *stalag* of our hosts' choice."

"You're such a sad sack. We might get picked up by the Resistance. Then we'd have a chance to get out."

"One can always hope."

Bishop activated his interphone. "Okay, guys, this may be our first trip to the prom, but we've flown hundreds of training hours, so we know what to do. We're in bogey range now. Man your posts. Maintain radio discipline. Limit your interphone chatter to only what's necessary. Watch your firing lines. If you shoot at a Jerry who's between you and another B-17, you might shoot a buddy by mistake. That's a no-no."

The crew uttered short syllables of acknowledgement. Bishop mentally pictured them as they clambered into position.

The time was 1330. One-thirty PM in civilian time. Bishop had expected to be flying into an early morning sun, but the delayed departure changed that. German fighters liked to attack with the sun behind them, forcing the American gunners to stare into the blinding glare. They wouldn't be able to do that today. With an afternoon takeoff, the enemy would find it very hard to hide.

"There go our little friends," Donnie Stapleton reported. The smaller P-47s carried less fuel, and thus had a shorter range than the B-17s.

"Look sharp, gunners," Bishop said over the interphone. "We're on our own."

The crew was silent for a few minutes. Then, Stapleton sang out, "Bogies at two o'clock high!"

"I knew it," Cyrus Lisenbe complained. "The krauts were waiting for the Thunderbolts to leave."

The top turret gunner, Donnie Stapleton on the *Reba Jean*, and the ball turret gunner, Kyle Waits, were the only crew members with a full three-hundred-sixty degree view of the sky, and they had primary responsibility for calling the shots, although any gunner could, and should, sing out if he spotted a bogey before Stapleton or Waits.

The gunners called the angles of attack as if the airplane were sitting on the middle of a clock face. Straight ahead, the direction the nose pointed, was twelve o'clock. Straight behind, where the tail pointed, was six o'clock. "High" meant the bogey was above the plane, and told the gunners to look up. "Low" told the gunners to look down.

When Stapleton shouted "Two o'clock high," Bishop looked up and to his right, and was rewarded with the sight of the sun glinting off the windshields of three ME-109s.

The B-17 pilots had been trained to fly in a tight diamond formation. This allowed the gunners to protect each other with interlocking fields of fire. While Bishop's brain told him the German fighters were making a diagonal slash across the entire bomb wing, hoping to damage as many aircraft as possible, his gut said they were coming after him, personally.

Since the *Reba Jean* was slotted off and behind *Suzie Q*'s left wingtip, the '109s would have to fly over the top of the lead plane to get an angle on them. Bishop felt pride in his gunners' patience. They waited until they had a clear shot before opening up. The *Reba Jean* shuddered from the vibration of the fifties, as Doug Cannon fired from the nose, and Donnie Stapleton fired from the top turret. Both gunners had the angle of attack wrong. Red tracers from Cannon's gun trailed behind the German, while Stapleton's shots went high.

The German fighter flashed over the top of the cockpit, causing both Lowery and Bishop to duck.

"C'mon, guys," Lowery complained. "Can't you shoot any better than that?"

"You wanna come give it a try?" growled Stapleton.

The second German fighter made its run, and Cyrus Lisenbe, the right waist gunner, added his gun to the barrage. His tracers showed that he was firing just above the *Reba Jean*'s right wing.

"Careful, Lisenbe," Bishop warned. "Don't shoot your own propeller."

The third '109 made its run and Stapleton's tracers appeared to hit the aircraft, although it didn't falter in flight.

"I got him! I got him!" the top turret gunner exulted.

"More bogies, seven o'clock low," Kyle Waits sang, before anyone could comment on Stapleton's apparent victory. Then Waits cursed as one of the German planes flew way too close to his ball turret.

For the next half hour, the air was filled with stunting aircraft and tracers, as the slow, lumbering B-17s fought it out with German Messerschmitt Me-109s and Focke-Wulff FW-190s. Bishop envisioned the scene from a distance. The image made him think of a flock of geese being harassed by a bunch of hawks.

"One of ours just took a hit. The engine's on fire," Gary Davis shouted from the tail-gunner position. "He's dropping out of formation. I can't tell who it is."

Bishop tried to look out his side window, but the injured plane was behind him, and he couldn't see it.

"Hope he makes it home," Lowery whispered.

Bishop knew the odds weren't good. He was too busy to rubber-neck, but he knew that wasn't the only B-17 to have bought the farm.

As if on a signal, which it probably was, the German fighters peeled away and flew toward the horizon.

"Whew," Hoffman said over the interphone. "Did we scare them off?"

"You wish," Lowery answered. "We didn't scare them off. *That* did." He pointed out the cockpit window at the black puffs of smoke appearing just ahead of the lead aircraft.

"What? What?" Hoffman, in the nose compartment below the cockpit, couldn't see Lowery's hand.

"Tighten your chin straps, boys," Bishop said. "Ack-ack's coming."

Anti-aircraft fire. On the ground, twenty-five thousand feet below, eighty-eight-millimeter cannons were launching shells into the sky. When those shells reached a pre-set altitude, they exploded, sending hundreds of pieces of jagged, bullet-sized metal — shrapnel — into the air. Some of that metal found part of a B-17. Sometimes the shrapnel just punched through the thin aluminum wall of the aircraft and back out the other side, harmlessly. Other times it found an oil pump, or a fuel line, and occasionally it found human flesh.

The plane began to bounce like a truck on a bumpy road as the concussion from the anti-aircraft fire disrupted the air around them. Bishop heard squeaks and groans all around him, as the huge B-17 flexed.

"Two minutes to IP," Aaron Hoffman called out. Initial point, the beginning of the bomb run.

"All set, Mr. Cannon? Have you armed the bombs?" Bishop asked.

"Affirmative, Captain," the bombardier answered.

Once the bomb run began, the flight controls would be interlinked to the Norden bombsight, and the bombardier would fly the plane by making minute adjustments to the device's controls. During a bomb run, the aircraft had to fly straight and level, no deviation. Just like a toy duck in a shooting gallery.

"Standing by," Bishop said.

"On my mark," Cannon intoned.

Seconds passed.

"Mark," Cannon said. "Initiate bomb run."

Bishop flipped the bank of switches that engaged the link to the bombsight. "Bombardier has the plane," he said.

"I have the plane," Cannon acknowledged.

For the next few minutes, Bishop would have nothing to do but help Lowery watch the gauges—and sweat—*despite* the forty-below temperature.

"Opening bomb bay doors," Cannon announced.

Bishop heard the whine of the motors that controlled the hatch in the underbelly of the aircraft, and felt the increased drag on the bomber. Now there was a big hole in the belly of the plane.

Early on, the brass had decided that having each bombardier plot his bomb run and drop independently produced unreliable results. They found that having the lead bombardier, the one deemed the best, plot the run and make the drop, then having all the other bombardiers drop when he did, produced a more consistent result.

So, two hundred and thirty-one planes, minus the casualties that had already fallen to the Luftwaffe and ack-ack, would drop on the actions of one man.

While Bishop knew that Cannon had made his own computations and was prepared to make his own drop if called upon, at this moment he was watching the lead plane, with his finger on the bomb release.

The interphone grew silent, as the plane jounced through the rough air. Bishop found his eyes drawn to the space below the belly of the lead B-17. A line of small dots appeared.

The *Reba Jean* lifted a bit, and he knew the plane had lost six thousand pounds of weight. He didn't need to hear Cannon shout, "Bombs away," to know the *Reba*

Jean had completed her bomb run. Cannon closed the bomb bay doors.

Bishop reached down and flipped the switches which returned the aircraft to the pilot's control.

"I have the plane," he announced.

"Acknowledged," Cannon responded.

Bishop focused on the *Suzy Q*, and on keeping the *Reba Jean* in formation as the squadron made its turn to head home.

Cannon's head popped up between Bishop's and Lowery's. Above his oxygen mask, his eyes were teary. "I know this is my first run, Captain, but I'd swear the lead bombardier dropped too soon."

Lowery cursed. "We did all this for nothing?"

Bishop met Lowery's eyes, then he looked at Cannon. A ball of acid formed in his gut. "Okay, Doug. Thanks for keeping that off the interphone."

"Okay." Cannon returned to his station.

"Do you think we missed the target?" Lowery asked.

Bishop adjusted his oxygen mask. "We won't know that until we get the after-action report, probably tomorrow. But Doug knows his stuff. If he says we dropped early, we probably did."

"Seems like we went through a lot of grief for a miss," the co-pilot said, then grunted as the concussion from a flak burst near the aircraft slammed the plane. "And we're only halfway through the mission. We've still got to get home."

Bishop had no answer to that complaint, and the two turned their attention to their duties. Under

Bishop's guiding hand, the *Reba Jean* flew back through the gauntlet of ack-ack fire and Luftwaffe fighters before rendezvousing with another flight of P-47s that would escort them to Allied territory.

Ray watched the last of the Me-109s disappear over the horizon, then said," Take the yoke, Warren. I want to make a walk-through. See what kind of damage we took."

"You got it. No, actually, I've got it," Lowery said, and grasped the yoke, the steering-wheel-like device that was used to fly the plane.

Bishop switched to a portable oxygen tank, and clambered down to the walkway below the cockpit. With all the action he hadn't noticed the temperature. In the few seconds it took to switch from the built-in oxygen system to the portable tank, the cold air turned his cheeks numb. He found Lisenbe, Hilton, Waits, and Davis huddled behind the forward bulkhead. "Everybody okay?" he asked.

Four heads bobbed. The faces behind the oxygen masks were pale, but no blood was in evidence.

"Mr. Waits, how'd you make it in the ball turret?"

Kyle Waits' Adam's apple bobbed. "You know that '109 that flew under the plane?"

"Yeah."

"Well, the pilot had blue eyes."

Bishop laughed. "Got a close-up view, did you?"

"Oh, yeah," Waits nodded. "Sitting in that ball turret, with your butt hanging out over twenty-five thousand feet of nothing takes some getting used to. My asshole is puckered up so tight, I won't shit for a week."

That got everybody laughing. A good sign. Ray looked over the cylindrical tube that was the fuselage. He saw a bullet hole near the left waist gunner's window. He pointed to it and said, "Mr. Hilton, I do believe somebody was shooting at you."

Mike Hilton nodded. "Yes, sir. I got that impression, too."

Bishop finished his visual inspection of the fuselage. "Looks like we got off pretty light." He clapped his gloved hands together. "Okay, I'd better get back to the cockpit and wake up Lieutenant Lowery."

He couldn't see if the non-coms were smiling behind their oxygen masks, but the crinkled skin around the eyes made him believe they were.

As he turned, Lisenbe said, "Hey, Cap'n, the non-coms have a weekly boxing card in one of the hangars, and Donny's pretty good, you know. You might wanna put a few dollars down when he gets a bout scheduled.

Bishop paused, torn between agreeing to put down a bet in support of a crewmate and his innate reticence about gambling. Then there was the issue of possible resentment if he won money from airmen who were lower in rank. He shook his head. "I'm sure Stapleton's good, but I want to save all my luck for these joyrides. Just remind him to stay healthy so he can get his twenty-five missions in and go home."

"Will do, Cap'n," Lisenbe responded.

Bishop stopped by the bombardier's station before returning to relieve Lowery. The clear glass nose allowed him to see down to the ground, and gave him an idea of what Kyle Waits felt when he was in the ball turret hanging below the aircraft.

Doug Cannon was reading a novel. Aaron Hoffman sat in the navigator's station behind and to the left of the bombardier's station. Bishop nodded at Hoffman before speaking to Cannon. "Did you see the bombs hit?"

Cannon nodded. "They fell short. Like I said, we dropped early."

Bishop took a deep breath. "I guess we'll find out what happened when we get back to base." He returned to the cockpit.

The formation flew over the Dutch Coast and began to descend. When they reached ten thousand feet, the crew removed and stowed their oxygen equipment.

Upon reaching Molesworth, the B-17s lined up in the landing pattern. When the *Rack'em Up* began its landing approach, someone aboard fired a red flare into the sky.

Lowery grunted in surprise. "Somebody on Lovejoy's plane got hurt."

"Shrapnel, or a bullet, I guess," Bishop responded. "Hope it isn't serious."

Acting on the *Rack'em Up*'s signal, an ambulance left the control tower and drove down to the end of the runway, near where the aircraft with the injured crewman would roll out.

The *Reba Jean* touched down at 1815 and taxied to her hardstand. Bishop crawled out the hatch and stretched. "We've been up since 0300. I think I could sleep for a week."

"Not so fast, sir," the ground crew chief said. He inclined his head toward an approaching jeep. "You can go get some chow, but then you'll have to report for debriefing. So will your crew."

"Crap," Bishop grumbled. "I forgot about that."

After a tiring and stressful first mission, even though the *Reba Jean* and her crew had come through it relatively unscathed, Bishop would have enjoyed a leisurely dinner and a restful sleep. But the debriefing was still unexplored territory, and he wanted to get it over with. He rushed through his meal and reported to Major Blevins, who was assigned to debrief him.

He packed his pipe with tobacco and lit it while he walked the major through the events of the day. Blevins asked an occasional clarifying question, but otherwise just recorded Bishop's words. Not too bad.

"My bombardier thought we dropped too early," Bishop said. "Have you heard anything about that?"

Blevins lit a cigarette. "We won't see the reconnaissance photographs until sometime tomorrow, at the earliest. But the word is the lead bombardier took a piece of shrapnel in the belly. His finger jerked on the drop switch, releasing the bombs."

"Dear God." Bishop closed his eyes. "Was he hurt bad?"

Blevins smiled under his Clark Gable mustache. "You're the first person who asked about the man before cursing about the early drop. Good for you." He tapped the ash off the end of his cigarette. "He was wearing a flak jacket, so his injury isn't serious. Bet we'll be making another trip to Schweinfurt soon, though."

"My top turret gunner got a '109. How soon can we paint a swastika on the *Reba Jean*?" asked Bishop.

"Not so fast. We'll have to get confirmation from another crew before we can give you credit for a kill. If we counted kills just on individual reports, our records would show we shot down the entire German air force on each mission. You and your crew will be asked if you saw kills by other aircraft, too." Blevins drew on his cigarette. "Which raises the question, did you see any kills by other aircraft?"

Bishop shook his head. "I was too busy holding my position. Sergeant Hill kept a tally of any reported kills. I'll ask him. Anything else?"

"No, that's it."

Bishop rose and shook Blevins' hand. As he started out the door, the major spoke up. "Oh, one more thing. You've got a Jew on your crew, haven't you?"

"Aaron Hoffman. He's my navigator, and a good one. Why? Is that a problem?"

"Not for me, but I hear one of your crewmen has a problem with it."

Bishop's chin came up a notch. "Oh, really? Who?"

"Don't know. A non-com."

"Okay, I'll look into it."

The Left Waist Gunner's Tale

31 August, 1943
Amiens, France

After the *Reba Jean*'s initial mission to Schweinfurt, the crew flew two more raids. One was to Gilze Rijen, an airdrome in Holland, and another to Watten, to bomb a "special installation" in France. The grapevine said the "special installation" was where the Krauts were building a launching facility for their new V-2 rockets.

The veterans called both of these missions "milk runs," because they were short, easy trips just across the Channel. In Mike Hilton's book, though, an easy run was one where nobody shot at him, and he hadn't had one of those yet.

Donnie Stapleton claimed to have shot down a Me-109 on their first mission, but he hadn't gotten confirmation, so the *Reba Jean* was still a virgin. She had no swastikas painted on her nose to indicate having killed a German fighter. Hilton planned to change that situation, and soon.

On the days they weren't assigned to fly a mission, the gunners attended morning sessions on aircraft recognition. Along with the other gunners in their squadron, they sat in a darkened room while pictures of German, American and British fighters were projected on a white screen mounted against the wall.

"Oh, man," Gary Davis whined, "those Me-109s sure do look like Spitfires."

"Yeah, they do," Hilton agreed. "Good thing the Brits don't fly cover for us very much."

Most of the time American P-47s and P-38s provided air support. The blunt nose of the P-47 was much different from the '109's sleek snout, and *nothing* had the silhouette of the twin fuselage P-38 Lightning. Giles Drury, a boy from the Massachusetts coast, who flew tail gunner for the *Rack'em Up*, said it looked like a flying catamaran.

After lunch the boys played a few innings of baseball, breaking off when someone fired a flare from the control tower, a signal that the B-17s on that day's mission were on their way in.

The gunners and the ground crew guys lined up under the tower and counted aircraft as they touched down. Ground crew members cheered when the plane assigned to them landed safely. Eighteen planes came in, leaving a single plane to circle the airfield, a thin ribbon of smoke trailing from its number four engine. Normally the twin fifty-caliber gun barrels, which protruded from the ball turret under the belly of the plane, were pointed toward the tail to keep them from catching on the runway if the B-17 bounced while landing. In this case, the barrels were skewed off to one side.

"Why isn't that plane landing?" Mike Hilton asked of nobody in particular.

"Twenty-four planes left Molesworth this morning. Five are still unaccounted for," a non-com standing off to one side said to another sergeant standing beside him.

"There are usually some laggards. They may all get back yet," his buddy replied.

The plane with the smoking engine climbed for altitude and circled the field again. One by one, small dots fell from the belly of the aircraft, parachutes opening like blossoming flowers above each dot. Hilton counted eight chutes.

Hilton pointed at the circling aircraft. "That can't be good."

An officer sidled up from the direction of the tower. "The ball turret is jammed."

"What about the ball turret gunner?" Hilton asked.

"He's trapped inside."

"Shit. He's in for a scary ride."

"It gets worse." The officer squinted at the B-17, dark against the pale sky. "The landing gear is jammed, too. The plane will have to make a belly landing."

Hilton's jaw dropped, and he turned to stare at the officer. "You can't be serious. Sir."

The officer met his gaze. "I wish I wasn't."

Many of the observers, having heard the same news, began walking away. They didn't want to see this. Mike went looking for Kyle Waits, who was nervous enough about operating the belly gun of the *Reba Jean*. This would give him the willies for sure.

From the look on his pale face, the small man had already heard.

"C'mon, Kyle," Hilton said, "let's go to the barracks."

"Can't. I gotta watch."

"Don't torture yourself. This will never happen to you."

Kyle swallowed; his face was still turned to the sky. "Never say never. That's what Mama always told me."

Mike resolved to endure this with his buddy. The plane entered the downwind leg. A mist fell from the B-17 as the pilot jettisoned fuel from his wing tanks. Having just returned from a mission, there wasn't much to dump. That would reduce the chance of fire caused by sparks. The aircraft made its turn onto the base leg, then another turn, and began its approach. It flew just above tree-top level.

Several onlookers stayed with Mike and Kyle to watch. Mike figured some of those who'd left were also watching from less obvious positions.

Mike had grown up in Elk Mound, Wisconsin, a small community a few miles west of Eau Claire. His older brother, Paul, had loved to hide out in the cemetery, dressed as the headless horseman from the Washington Irving story. He'd talk Polly, their sister, into bringing Mike and one or two of his friends along the road bordering the graveyard after dark.

Paul wore an oversized dark shirt pulled up over his head to make him look, in dark silhouette, as if he were headless. He added a black cape that billowed in the breeze.

When Mike and his companions reached the proper spot, Paul stood up, threw a pumpkin that was supposed to be his head, and let go with his most blood-curdling roar. Mike and his friends shrieked and ran along the road away from the monster. Polly screamed and ran, too, to add to the sense of danger. Paul chased them.

Despite being scared near to fainting, and believing that his only chance to survive was to run as fast as his little feet could carry him, Mike felt compelled to peek over his shoulder at the crazed demon, who was bent on catching and eating him alive. He *had* to look.

Mike stumbled and fell, and peed his pants in fright. When Paul reached him, he had collapsed in gales of laughter. To this day, Mike couldn't walk past that cemetery alone.

Watching the heavy bomber cross the tree line at the end of the runway, wheels up, the ball turret a shiny wart on the abdomen of the fuselage, Mike felt in himself and in those around him that same morbid compulsion to watch this brutal disaster unfold. He put his arm around his crewmate's shoulders.

The pilot would be in the cockpit, flying the plane. The other eight crew men, not counting the belly gunner, had been under those parachutes that bailed out earlier.

The B17 descended so that the ball turret was mere inches above the paved surface. Mike imagined he could see the panicked face of the kid.

"What's his name?" Kyle asked the officer.

"Don't know," he answered.

The plane flared out—made the transition from flying to falling. If the landing gear had been deployed, here's where the wheels would've touched down. Instead the ball turret scraped against the tarmac and shattered. Mike thought he saw an arm or leg flail in that last second before the aircraft's underbelly smacked against the runway.

The four propellers struck the ground, and the forward motion of the plane bent them back around the engine cowlings. The plane's speed plummeted, but the inertia of tons of metal kept it sliding forward, scrubbing against the runway, gouging furrows in the pavement. *The runway maintenance crew will have to work all night to get this strip ready for use tomorrow*, Mike thought.

The Plexiglas nose of the B17 dissolved into shards. Smoke and dust surrounded the behemoth, as it finally ground to a stop. Sparks flew, but no flame.

Two ambulances rushed up to the aircraft. Mike looked back along the path of wreckage and saw jagged pieces of metal and glass, and a smeary reddish liquid— blood, or hydraulic fluid. Beside him, Kyle Waits bent over and vomited. The acidic stench forced Hilton's stomach to rebel, and he vomited, too.

After both had emptied their bellies and recovered a little of their equilibrium, they stood and stared at the wreckage. This B17 would never be repaired. It would never fly again. Too much damage. The ground crew would drag it over to the bone yard, and park it beside the hulks of other unrecoverable aircraft, where it would be cannibalized for parts to keep the flying B17s in the air.

One of the ambulance crews loaded an empty stretcher back into the vehicle. There wasn't enough of the belly gunner's body left to recover. The pilot, alive, walking, but clearly shaken, was helped into the second emergency vehicle.

"C'mon," Hilton clapped Waits on the shoulder. "Let's go."

As they walked away, a clerk spoke to the officer who'd stood near them. "Four of the five missing planes diverted to Archbury. We only lost one plane of the Molesworth contingent — two, counting this one."

Back to business as usual.

Many of the American air bases were newly carved out of the fields and pastures of East Anglia, the section of England located northeast of London and nearest the European targets the bombers went after. The barracks and offices at the new bases were metal Nissen huts that looked like huge pipes half-buried in the ground. Molesworth, however, was a converted RAF base. The buildings were made of wood: old, leaky, paint-peeled. The barracks building allotted for the crew of the *Reba Jean* and other aircraft of her squadron was no exception. Wooden bunk beds lined the walls on each side of a center aisle. The place smelled of the oil used to polish the wood, and of soot from the single, coal-fired stove used to heat the building; and heat was needed, even in August.

Waits and Hilton sat on the edge of Waits' bunk. The young belly gunner was so short he looked like a kid. That was why he had the job, he had to be tiny to fit into one of those ball turrets.

"Why don't you go to the doc?" Hilton said. "I bet he'll write you a medical certificate for a day off. You need a little time after that."

Kyle shook his head. "What if every belly gunner in the squadron made sick call?"

Hilton shrugged. "We'd fly without 'em, I guess."

"And lose twice as many planes. No, I've got to fly tomorrow, just like everybody else."

After dinner they went to the NCO club. With a mission scheduled for the next day, the bar's warm, weak beer was off limits. Mike drank soda, while Kyle had orange juice. Then both went to bed.

The *Reba Jean*'s crew got the next day off, anyway, along with the entire Eighth Air Force. All of Europe was under a dense cloud cover. All missions were scrubbed.

"We coulda had some booze last night," Cyrus Lisenbe said, running a hand through his oily black hair.

"I bet those Krauts love days like this. They get to breathe easy for a while," Gary Davis said.

"And you don't?" Nicky Hill, the *Reba Jean*'s radio operator, asked.

Mike noticed that Kyle Waits still looked pale, and breathed a prayer of thanks for the day off.

The boys, except for Hilton, settled in for a game of poker. Mike discovered early on that he couldn't bluff to save his life, or his money, so he usually passed on the card games. It was too easy to go broke.

The senior barracks crewman, an engineer from the *Suzy Q*, saw that Mike was unoccupied. "Hey, Hilton, whyn't you rustle up some coal? It's getting chilly in here."

"Ah, you don't know what cold is," Hilton responded. "In Wisconsin, we'd call this a heat wave." He grabbed the coal hod, anyway.

Each building, officers' quarters included, was issued only enough coal for four days use per week. The argument, beside the cost, was that the buildings didn't need to be heated while the crews were on a mission. Never mind that the guys were shooting at Krauts at twenty-five thousand feet, in forty-below temperatures, and were perfectly willing to crawl *in* the damn heater to get warm when they got back.

When missions were scrubbed and the crews stayed on base all day, the need for coal increased. They were making it okay for now. It was August. But in fall and winter, junior crewmen would be delegated missions of "midnight coal requisitions," to supplement their coal supply.

Captain Bishop walked up to Mike while he filled his bucket at the coal dump.

"Got a minute, sergeant?" he asked.

"Sure, skipper," Mike said. The two walked to a more secluded spot.

"What do you think of Lieutenant Hoffman?" Bishop asked.

Hilton scratched his chin. "Well, I don't know him very well, personally, you know. But as a navigator, he seems top notch. We were the only crew whose aircraft didn't get lost a single time during training, weren't we?"

"Yep," Bishop said. "Lieutenant Hoffman is the best navigator I've ever seen. But I've heard that somebody on the crew has it in for him."

Hilton immediately thought of the comments he'd heard from one of his crewmates. "Where'd you hear that?"

"A little bird told me."

"Well, it's not me."

"If you knew who it was, would you tell me?"

"Aw, Cap'n," Hilton ducked his head. "You're not asking me to rat on one of my buddies, are you?"

"Look, Mr. Hilton (Bishop's gaze was ice), "I can't have disharmony on my crew. I won't abide it."

"I wish I could help you, skipper, but I can't."

Bishop stared at him for a long moment. Then he turned on his heel and walked away.

Mike finished filling the coal bucket and trudged back to the barracks. He emptied his load, and went to stand over the card players.

"Go siddown, Hilton," Lisenbe complained. "You're makin' me noivous."

"Donnie," Mike said. "Cap'n wants to see you."

Donnie Stapleton looked up and frowned. "What for?"

"Didn't say."

Stapleton scooped up the small pile of cash in front of him. "Deal me out, boys. I'll catch you later."

Hilton walked out the door with Stapleton.

"Hold up, Donnie." Mike grabbed Stapleton's arm when they were outside the barracks and away from the walkway. "I lied. Cap'n didn't really ask for you, not directly."

"Well, then. Why'd you say so?"

"He's looking for the crewman who's bad-mouthing Lieutenant Hoffman."

Stapleton frowned. "You didn't say nothing, did you?"

"No, of course not. But, what've you got against him, anyway?"

"What do you think?" Stapleton pulled a pack of Lucky Strikes from his pocket, shook one out, and put it in his mouth. "He's a Jew."

"So what?"

"You don't have any 'Jew boys' around your home? Where you from?"

"Wisconsin. I suppose there are a few around."

"Well back where I'm from—Lawrenceburg, Tennessee—we've got a bunch of folks call themselves the Ku Klux Klan. If any Kike, or Nigger, or even a Papist tries to come around, the Klan makes them wish they hadn't. White is right, you get me?"

Hilton wrinkled his brow. "That sounds a lot like Old Man Hitler and his Aryan race bullshit."

Stapleton balled up his fists. "Say that again and you'll be shittin' and eatin' through the same hole."

"I just came to warn you," Hilton said. "The Captain knows somebody's trying to stir up trouble. The word came down. There's a mission on, but no early reveille."

One of the veterans clapped his hands. "That means another milk run."

The next morning, after a leisurely breakfast of bacon and powdered eggs, the squadron's enlisted crewmen gathered for the briefing, led by Sergeant Robert Lang, the senior non-com.

"Target is Romily-Sur-Seine," he said. Mike didn't think anybody could botch the town's pronunciation any worse.

"It's somewhere near Paris. That's all I know. The officers will have the specifics."

"Maybe we'll see the Eiffel Tower," Cyrus Lisenbe wisecracked.

"Just hope you don't get to see it too close," Lang responded, "like from underneath a parachute canopy."

The guys were getting used to the pre-mission routine. Mike carried his gun barrel through the belly hatch, and mounted it on the gun, and then mounted the gun on the pedestal attached to the *Reba Jean*'s airframe. He then stored the fifty caliber ammo belts he would use during the mission. Since his first mission he'd learned to pack extra snacks—Hershey bars, Cracker Jack and the like. He ate when he was nervous. Only problem was his trousers were getting tight in the waist.

The *Reba Jean* went wheels up at 1524, and she formed up with her squadron to begin her journey across the Channel.

Hilton snacked on a chocolate bar and watched Hill, Davis, Lisenbe, and Stapleton play cards until Captain Bishop's order came over the interphone. "Ten thousand feet. Begin oxygen protocol. Prepare for cold weather conditions."

"Hilton, you're from Wisconsin, aren't you?" Gary Davis asked, as he pulled on his oxygen mask. The device looked a lot like a hot water bottle. It had a bladder that hung below the chin that inflated and deflated each time the crewman exhaled and inhaled.

"Yeah," Hilton answered.

"What did you do there before you joined up?"

"My family ran a dairy farm. I helped."

"So," the skin around Davis's eyes crinkled, giving away the grin that was hidden by the oxygen mask, "you got to handle all the tits you wanted."

"Believe me," Mike gave an answering grin behind his mask, "handling those cows' teats was nowhere near as fun as handling the ones you're thinking about."

"Did it get very cold up there in Wisconsin?" Nicky Hill jumped in on the conversation.

"Yeah. You guys think it's cold up at twenty-five thousand feet, and it is. But I've felt it before. A Wisconsin blizzard in February is every bit as cold. Most days we had to use an axe to chop holes in the lake ice so the cattle could get a drink."

"*Brrr*," Hill responded. "I come from Northern California. We have some cold nights, but nothing like that. My Dad's vineyard wouldn't last one Wisconsin winter, I bet."

Stapleton went up to officers' country for a few minutes, then came back. "Cap'n says man your posts and test fire your weapons," he said.

A few minutes later, a flight of P-47s joined the bombers.

"There are our little friends," Kyle Waits joked over the interphone.

Hilton had noticed that Waits looked a little better today, and his joke lifted the waist gunner's spirits. The extra day's rest had been good for him.

"Yeah, and here come our little enemies," Stapleton remarked from the top turret. "Bandits at eleven o'clock high."

Hilton watched the P-47s peel away to intercept. The B-17s remained in tight formation. One of the defensive strengths of the B-17 was its ability to protect and be protected by the other bombers in its formation. It was critical that they stay together. Eventually, Mike knew, some of those German fighters would filter through the P-47 screen and attack the *Reba Jean* and the other bombers.

"Here comes one. Ten o'clock level," Stapleton sang out. Mike could hear the tension in his voice.

Hilton cursed. From his left waist gunner position, the German's approach would be shielded by the number two propeller, and he had no shot.

Stapleton's gun chattered, along with the gun in the *Reba Jean*'s nose, the one manned by the bombardier, Doug Cannon. A blur flashed by over the top of the bomber.

"No joy," Stapleton muttered, Air Corps jargon for a miss.

The next fifteen minutes felt like fifteen hours as the dogfight continued. One of the advantages of a short mission was that more of the trip was protected by fighter cover. Eventually, though, both the P-47s and the German fighters ran low on fuel and had to peel away.

Despite the drone of the engines, the airship seemed silent in the absence of machine gun fire.

"Okay, guys," Bishop said, "eyeball your areas. See any damage?"

Mike looked around while his pounding heart slowed. He grabbed a Baby Ruth candy bar from his stash. Getting shot at sure made him hungry. One of the things he tried not to think about during the dogfight was that he was standing right next to six thousand pounds of bombs while hot lead flew all around him *and* the explosives.

"Just a few bullet holes, Cap'n," Hilton said into the interphone. His fellow crewmen said much the same. Getting a hole in the skin of the aircraft was no big deal.

"No leaking fluid?" Bishop pressed.

"No, sir," Hilton responded.

"So far, so good."

The gunners stayed at their posts, in case another wave of Luftwaffe planes took up the chase, but everybody knew the bomb group was in the middle of a transition from fighter attack to anti-aircraft fire. The dirty gray puff clouds that suddenly appeared in their midst confirmed the fact.

It was called by many names: anti-aircraft fire, ack-ack, flak. Eighty-eight-millimeter guns on the ground launched their shells into the path of the bombers. When those shells reached their pre-set altitude, they exploded, sending deadly shrapnel flying in all directions.

"The Fuhrer's farts," said Cyrus Lisenbe over the interphone.

"Huh?" Hilton asked.

"The flak. That's what it is. Fuhrer's farts."

"Well," Gary Davis interposed, "Der Fuhrer should switch to food with less iron content."

"You got that right," Hilton said.

The aluminum skin of the *Reba Jean* rang from time to time as shards of flak struck its sides, but their luck still held. No serious damage.

The gunners followed the interphone conversations between the officers as the formation approached the initial point, referred to in Air Corps lingo as the IP, the spot in mid-air that designated the start of the bomb run.

"Lead bombardier reports Romily-Sur-Seine is socked in," Doug Cannon said. "We're changing targets."

The entire crew, except the pilot, took turns expressing its opinion of that piece of news, using four-letter words. When the grumbling subsided a bit, Cannon continued, "New target is Amiens."

"At least we're not likely to get more fighter attacks, but we get to enjoy another dose of flak," Nicky Hill observed.

"Think we'll have enough oxygen?" Kyle Waits asked.

"Just don't breathe," Donnie Stapleton advised. "That'll leave more for us."

"Kiss my bum," Waits responded, using the British term for backside.

"No need to worry, Sergeant Waits," Warren Lowery said. "We'll be okay as long as the oxy system doesn't take a piece of shrapnel." He didn't add what the crew already knew: oxygen was flammable, and hot metal could ignite it, turning the aircraft into a flying fireball.

Clouds continued to cover the space below the bomber formation, and the crew began to doubt if Amiens would be a viable target. When they reached the IP, however, the clouds had begun to thin, and patches of green were visible below.

The bomb run began. Captain Bishop switched flight control over to Lieutenant Cannon. The planes flew into a bank of high-level clouds.

"We're not gonna be able to see the target," Donnie Stapleton complained. "Lieutenant Cannon, why don't you just drop anyway?"

"Shut up and be patient," Doug Cannon advised. "It may clear before we reach the drop point."

Mike pictured the bombardier as he sat behind the bomb sight, alternating between looking through the Norden device's viewfinder and looking up to track the bomber ahead of him, assuming the lead plane was visible.

The cloud bank thinned a bit. "Approaching drop point," Cannon intoned. "Opening bomb bay doors."

The double doors beneath the rack of bombs just off Hilton's right shoulder whined open, and the gunner was hit by an increased blast of frigid air.

The formation burst through the clouds into dazzlingly bright air.

"Oh, God! Bank right! Bank right!" Stapleton wailed.

Hilton peeked out the gun port in the side of the plane and saw the enormous bulk of another B-17, with bomb bay doors open, flying right above them. His gut clenched. The flight that should have been trailing them had put on too much speed in the clouds and had overtaken their aircraft.

The *Reba Jean's* left wing tilted up and the plane began to slide out from underneath the other aircraft. Hilton knew Captain Bishop had retrieved flight control from the bombardier, and had undertaken an evasive maneuver. Almost simultaneously, the bomb rack to Hilton's right began rattling, as the twelve, five-hundred pound bombs dropped through the open doors. The last one clipped the edge of the right-most bomb bay door as it fell through.

A series of shadows passed the left waist gunner port, and Mike realized the bomber flying above them had dropped its load, too. He held his breath, waiting for the crash that would signal the *Reba Jean's* collision with one of the bombs. The device wouldn't have had time to arm yet, but five-hundred pounds of metal could do a lot of damage to a wing or a fuselage, or a gunner.

Nothing happened, and Hilton resumed breathing.

When Cannon tried to close the bomb bay doors, the right one wouldn't move.

"The door is sprung," Hilton reported. "One of the bombs hit it."

"Mr. Stapleton," Captain Bishop said to the engineer. "See if you can get that door closed. The increased drag will slow us down."

The bomber flight passed out of the flak field.

"Bandits at nine o'clock low," Kyle Waits sang.

Hilton looked out his window and down. Sun glinted off a trio of FW 190s closing fast. A B-17 could cruise at about three hundred miles per hour, maybe two hundred and seventy with the bomb bay doors open, but the '190 could make just over four hundred MPH.

The lead fighter opened fire, and the blazing twenty-millimeter guns on each wing looked like headlights. A drumroll of bullet strikes sounded along the hull of the *Reba Jean*. Hilton aimed his gun and returned fire, but his line of tracers indicated that he couldn't quite catch up to the enemy aircraft.

Behind him Stapleton climbed into a harness and clipped a webbed belt, leash-like, to it and the airframe.

"You should be on the top turret," Hilton yelled to him.

"Nicky's got it," Stapleton answered, referring to Nicky Hill, the radio operator.

Hilton resumed firing, now at the second '190.

Another rumble of bullet strikes hit the plane.

"Shit," Stapleton said. "That was close."

Hilton lined up and pulled the trigger, aiming at the third German fighter. His row of tracers disappeared into the engine cowling of the enemy plane, then trailed along its cockpit canopy and fuselage. The '190 began smoking and rolled over, losing flight stability.

"Booyah!" Hilton yelled. "I got one."

A squadron of P-38s arrived not long after, and chased the remaining German planes away.

Mike was about to turn and help Donnie with the bomb bay door when he noticed a fluid trail behind the left wing. He thumbed his throat mike to activate the interphone connection. "Uh, Cap'n, we've got a leak from the left wing. Looks like fuel from the wing tank."

"Roger," Bishop's voice was calm. "Lieutenant Lowery is going to pump fuel out and over to the right wing tank."

Stapleton was still struggling with the bomb bay door. He cranked the hand winch, which was supposed to allow manual closure, but it had no effect.

Mike looked around the cabin for something with which to help. "If we don't get that door up, it'll drag the ground when we land," he said over the interphone.

"Tell me something I don't know," growled Stapleton.

Hilton spotted a pole with a hook on the end. "I think the bomb stripped the door loose from the gear mechanism," he said. "Maybe we can pull it up with this hook."

He lifted the pole, and leaned over the open hatch. When he saw the ground, his stomach did a somersault. *That must be what Kyle feels when he's in that ball turret*, he thought. He extended the pole and slid the hook under the door's edge. Donnie grabbed the pole to help, and the two of them succeeded in pulling the door up and securing it by using a length of rope to tie it to a strut on the airframe.

"Okay, skipper. Door's up," Stapleton reported. "Don't bounce too much when you land, though. It might come loose."

"Thanks, Stapleton," Bishop responded. "Good work."

"Thank Mike," Stapleton said. "He did it."

"Thanks, Hilton," Bishop said. "By the way, the *Suzy Q* confirmed your kill of that '190. Congratulations."

Hilton exhaled, looked out his gun port, and was surprised to see that they were already over the English Channel. *Milk run, my ass*, he thought.

The Navigator's Tale

September 6, 1943
Stuttgart, Germany

While Cannon and Lowery participated in the sing-along at the O Club, in the short time remaining before lights out, Aaron Hoffman decided to stretch his legs with a walk around the base. He went by his quarters to pick up a jacket, and found Bishop sitting in a rocking chair, reading a dog-eared copy of Faulkner's *As I Lay Dying,* and smoking a pipe.

"Nice chair," observed Hoffman. "Where did you find it?"

Bishop took the pipe from his mouth and smiled. "I found it at a furniture store in Molesworth. When I asked the price, the proprietor gave it to me. There's nothing as relaxing as sitting in a rocking chair. Now, all I need is a front porch, a couple of magnolia trees, and a warm summer evening."

"You make it sound appealing." Hoffman picked up the jacket from his bunk. The four officer crew members shared quarters. "Are you a Faulkner fan?"

"I'm obligated. I teach English in Mississippi, or at least I did."

"Ah, a foreign language teacher."

Bishop pointed the stem of his pipe at Hoffman and smiled. "Watch it, Bub." Hoffman smiled in return. "You'll be back there someday, teaching again."

"Yeah."

"What do you think are our chances?"

"Of what?" Bishop placed a marker in his book and closed it. "Winning the war?"

"Yes." Hoffman pulled up a chair and sat.

Bishop leaned his head against the high back of the rocker. "We southerners spend an inordinate amount of time studying the Civil War, or as we call it, the "War of Northern Aggression." He smiled to let Hoffman know he was being humorous. "Without getting into the merits of the causes of the war, I mention this to point out that the North won the war because it had a superior ability to produce war materials: guns, bullets, cannons—not to mention manpower. About all the South could produce was cotton, which makes terrible bullets."

Hoffman laughed.

"From an aerial warfare point of view," Bishop continued, "this war will be won by the forces that can destroy the opposition's planes faster than they can be replaced. The same holds true for tanks and guns—and people."

"Then we'll win," Hoffman observed.

"I think so, too. The question in my mind is whether you and I will survive it." Bishop paused to puff on his pipe. "The way we're losing planes, the odds seem to be against our making twenty-five missions."

"That's a sobering thought."

"Indeed."

"The *Memphis Belle* crew did it. So there's hope."

They sat silently for a moment.

Bishop rocked in his chair. "I should tell you that one of the enlisted men doesn't care much for Jews."

"That doesn't surprise me. Who is it?"

"Don't know. Blevins told me about it. How he found out, I have no idea. I asked a couple of the non-coms, but they're keeping mum."

Hoffman shrugged. "When I attended Princeton, there was a quota on the number of Jews they admitted, but most of the guys acted okay toward me. My family wasn't observant, so I didn't worry about Saturday classes or dietary laws. But there were some dances I couldn't go to, and some clubs I couldn't join. And, most importantly, some girls I couldn't become friends with. When I was a freshman, the dormitory hazing got particularly nasty a time or two. Whoever the anti-Semite is, I can live with him, as long as he doesn't try to sabotage a mission just to get at me."

Bishop shook his head. "I don't like to let an un-lanced boil fester. If there's a problem, and it seems there is, I plan to resolve it."

Hoffman leaned back in his chair. "That in itself could cause a problem, or make it worse. I assure you, our crew mate isn't the only one on base who dislikes Jews." He paused, gathering his thoughts. "You familiar with how Hitler and his Brown Shirts treated the Jews in Germany before the war started?"

"Yes."

"And you've heard the rumors about how the Nazis are imprisoning Jews in ghettos in Poland now? Plus sending Jews from all over Europe to concentration camps in Poland? And the rumors of death camps?"

Bishop nodded. "In light of what we know about *Kristallnacht*, I have to believe those rumors are true."

"So do I. Yet if Lindbergh had his way, we'd be allies of Germany right now. And even with what we know about how the Jews have been treated, no country in the world, including America, is willing to allow Jewish refugees into their country."

Bishop rubbed his eyes. "Shit . . . So, what do you suggest?"

"Don't stir up trouble. If a problem arises, we'll deal with it then." Hoffman smiled. "It is comforting to know that you'll back me up if I need it."

"Good. I will."

Hoffman made to get up, then paused. "I'm curious. What *do* you think of the merits of the Civil War's cause?"

Bishop drew on his pipe. "Nobody deserves to be a slave. My ancestors put up a noble fight for an ignoble cause."

Hoffman smiled again. "I thought you'd say that." He rose and started for the door.

"Oh, one more thing," Bishop said. "The *Reba Jean*'s supercharger is still acting up. We're to take the *Bottle Rocket* out tomorrow."

The day before, the *Reba Jean* had aborted its mission before it reached the Channel, when the supercharger on the number three engine ran hot, threatening to destroy itself and to burn up the engine along with it. While the bomber was returning to base, the crew learned the rest of the mission had been scrubbed anyway due to general cloud cover in Europe.

Hoffman frowned. "That's not good news. Flying a mission is hard enough without having to do it in a strange plane."

"That's not all. Word among the ground crews is the *Bottle Rocket* is a jinx."

"Have you told the boys yet?"

"Yes."

"How'd they take it?"

"They were not happy."

"Well, Uncle Sam didn't send us here to make us happy," Hoffman said. "Is that all?"

"Yep."

"Okay, see you later."

Another 0330 reveille, which meant another flight deep into Europe. Breakfast. Walk in the pre-dawn darkness to the briefing.

Hoffman's conclusions were verified when the drape covering the map was removed to show a skein of red yarn stretching into Germany.

"Our target today is the SKF engine bearing plant in Stuttgart," Colonel Stephens, standing at the front of the room, said. "Take-off is 0600." He yielded the floor to his aides, who shared the details with the flight officers.

First they showed reconnaissance photographs of the target so the bombardiers could visually identify them using the Norden bombsight. Next, they gave the information needed for the bomb run.

Hoffman sat ready, notepad atop his knee. When the captain started giving the navigational data, he took notes. The formation would fly a heading of one-one-five degrees on their way to the target, and two-nine-five degrees on the return leg. Cloud cover nominal. Wind speed bearing two-one-zero degrees at twelve knots. He recorded the location of the IP, the initial point, where the bombing run would begin. Since the *Bottle Rocket* was not the lead aircraft, Hoffman's role would be merely to use these figures to double check the lead navigator. The entire formation would fly on the lead navigator's calculations.

Colonel Stephens reclaimed control of the briefing. "You've got a long flight. Fuel conservation will be critical. Be careful."

The non-coms were already at the *Bottle Rocket*'s hardstand when the officers' jeep arrived. Hoffman scanned faces, wondering who the anti-Semite was. Whoever it was, he'd done a good job of hiding his feelings. No hostile expressions were evident. The crew had gone through several weeks of preparatory training before crossing the big lake to England, and the crewman had been circumspect enough to avoid mentioning his prejudice to anyone who would consider it a problem. Probably, once at Molesworth, he'd made a comment to someone who'd passed his comments on to Major Blevins.

Hoffman climbed through the B-17's forward hatch and into the cramped navigator's station behind the bombardier's post in the Plexiglas nose. The plane had none of the "homey" feel of the *Reba Jean*. The smells of engine oil and cordite mixed with another sharp odor, made the whole scent seem foreign. Hoffman even thought he could smell another man's sweat in the leather and canvas upholstery. He clambered back out of the aircraft and huddled with the rest of the crew.

Bishop stared toward the southeastern horizon. Hoffman stood beside him.

"Wind's bringing in some low clouds," Bishop observed. "Might cause a problem when we form up, but otherwise shouldn't hamper us too much."

"Hey, Chief," Cyrus Lisenbe said. "You heard this rattletrap we're flying today is a jinx, right?"

"I've heard it, but I don't believe it."

"Sergeant Ashley said they voted to rename it after that bad luck guy in the 'Li'l Abner' funnies. You know, the guy who's always walking around with a cloud hanging over his head. Only nobody could spell his name. Joe Bftsplk, or something like that."

Bishop grinned. "With a name like that, no wonder he has bad luck."

"What say we develop engine trouble shortly after takeoff, and fly this baby back home?"

Bishop's smile faded. "I'm sure you're joking, Lisenbe. Because if I though you were serious, I'd be very upset."

Lisenbe ducked his head. "Of course I'm joking, Boss. You know that."

Someone atop the control tower fired a green flare.

"Okay, boys," Bishop called. "There's our signal. Let's load up."

Cannon and Hoffman crawled into the tight space in the aircraft's nose. "Something stinks," Cannon observed.

"Yeah," said Hoffman.

"Vomit. Somebody didn't clean up very well."

Hoffman snapped his fingers. "That's what it is. I couldn't place the smell."

They went wheels up at 0607. As Bishop predicted, they flew into a low cloud bank shortly after takeoff.

"I don't like this," Cannon said to Hoffman. He sat in the Plexiglas nose, staring out at a misty gray wall. "In this fog somebody might fly up our ass."

The captain seemed to have read his mind. "Gunners, man your posts and watch for other planes. Sing out if you see something that's not a cloud—or sky."

A few minutes later, Bishop came back on the interphone. "It looks like we're not going to fly out of this right away, Mr. Hoffman, and we haven't received an abort command. Better plot us a course for the IP. Maybe we'll get clear air soon."

"Roger, sir," Hoffman replied.

"Captain," Gary Davis spoke up, "do you mean we're going to fly this mission alone?"

"There are other planes up here," Bishop answered. "We just can't see 'em. If we don't make contact with the formation by the time we reach the coast of Belgium, we'll turn back."

"Captain, please make your course one-one-five degrees," Hoffman aid.

"One-one-five degrees it is. Thanks."

A half-hour later, having had no close calls with other aircraft, the *Bottle Rocket* flew into clear air.

"Ah, that helps with the claustrophobia," Kyle Waits said over the interphone.

"Liar," Cyrus Lisenbe said. "You can't sit in that little glass bubble if you have claustro-whatsit."

"Hey, Skipper," Donnie Stapleton said, "that looks like our formation at two o'clock level. Somebody drifted off course."

Hoffman looked over Cannon's right shoulder and out the *Bottle Rocket*'s nose window at the cluster of miniature bombers flying a parallel course. "Wasn't us."

"Of course not," Stapleton retorted.

The B-17 went into a shallow bank, as the aircraft moved to intercept the formation and join it. "Good eyes, Stapleton."

The Krauts hit before the P-47s left, and, for a while, the fight hovered around the perimeter of the formation. Eventually, a few German fighters fought through the screen and attacked the B-17s.

Cannon hunched over his nose gun, firing at enemy planes as they flew across the front of the *Bottle Rocket*. Hoffman crouched behind him. He had a flexible gun that could be fired out small ports on each side of the nose window. The gun was hung by a hook from a cable suspended from the compartment's ceiling. To switch his fire from one side of the plane to the other,

Hoffman had to unhook his gun, avoiding the hot barrel, and hook it to the cable on the other side. Hoffman's innards curdled each time he saw a stream of German tracers flying toward his aircraft. The *Bottle Rocket* was taking some hits. Had to be. But so far nobody reported major damage.

The P-47s reached their fuel limit and had to turn back, leaving the Me-109s and FW-190s to mount an unabated attack on the B-17s.

"How much fuel do they have?" Lisenbe muttered over the interphone. "They have to be running low."

A '109 came over the top of the *Suzie Q*, the *Bottle Rocket*'s flight leader, and made a beeline for Hoffman, or so it seemed, the twin thirteen millimeter guns on its wings lit up like a fireworks display. Hoffman pointed his gun at the aircraft and fired a burst to no effect. He heard a *pop, pop* sound, followed by a high-pitched whistle, and the German plane disappeared over the bomber. His heart hammered in his chest. That had to have been close. He scanned the interior of his and Cannon's compartment and found two bullet holes, one for entry and one for exit. He fought a wave of nausea. The bullet had pierced the B-17s aluminum skin on the right side behind the glass nose canopy, and exited the left side. It couldn't have missed Hoffman by more than six inches.

That assault must have been the Krauts' last hurrah, because they disengaged and returned to their bases to rearm and refuel. They would be waiting for the Americans on the return leg.

Hoffman bent over his workstation. "Ten minutes to IP," he reported to Bishop over the interphone.

"Roger," Bishop responded.

The anti-aircraft barrage began. The concussion of air bursts made the *Bottle Rocket* jounce like a jalopy on a bumpy road. Hoffman had learned that the best way to handle the flak was to ignore it. Shrapnel either got you or it didn't.

The formation reached the IP and began its bomb run. Cannon crouched over his bombsight and received control from the pilot. The planes flew over a spotty undercast, with clouds shaped like white pillows passing beneath the aircraft. Hoffman held his breath and stared over Cannon's shoulder at the lead plane. If one of the clouds blocked the lead bombardier's view of the target, he'd either have to drop blind or go around for another pass.

Bishop's voice came over the interphone. "We're going around again."

"Cripes!" Cannon shouted. "I can see the target!"

"Drop! Drop! Drop!" Lisenbe chanted.

"Shut up, Lisenbe," Bishop ordered. "We drop with the formation."

"What didn't the lead bombardier understand about conserving fuel?" Cannon asked aloud.

"Pipe down," Bishop said, his voice strident.

The flak barrage continued, as the formation made a slow, shallow turn to circle back to the IP. Hoffman knew the second pass would allow more time for the German artillery gunners to refine their aim, getting a better handle on the bombers' altitude, direction and speed.

The B-17s began their second bomb run. The Germans continued to pound at them. As the *Bottle Rocket* neared the drop point, again under Cannon's control using the Norden sight/automatic pilot interlink, an anti-aircraft shell burst just ahead of the right wing. A thin stream of liquid began trailing from the plane.

"We've got a gas leak in the right wing tank, Captain," Cyrus Lisenbe announced.

"Lowery, shift the fuel to the left tank," Bishop ordered.

The seconds ticked away. Hoffman heard the whine of the bomb bay doors opening.

"Target is visible," Cannon announced. Then a moment later, Cannon's "Bombs away!" was accompanied by the sudden extra lift as the aircraft dropped its ordnance. Cannon closed the bomb doors.

"Captain, the hydraulic fuel transfer pump is out. I'm going to move it manually," Lowery said.

"Okay," Bishop responded. "Stapleton, give him a hand."

"Yes, sir," Stapleton said.

"Captain, we've got a smoke trail from engine number three," Lisenbe reported.

Hoffman looked out the right side flexible gun port and saw a narrow black exhaust trail behind the engine nearest the fuselage.

"Cannon, help Stapleton pump fuel. Lowery, get up here and help me watch that hot engine. If it burns up before we get the prop feathered, we'll have a problem." Bishop's voice sounded strained.

Doug Cannon clambered past Hoffman, swaying in time to the jolts caused by flak bursts, and headed to help manually transfer the fuel.

Hoffman fidgeted. He wanted badly to get out of this glass bubble.

When the flak barrage tapered off, Bishop said, "Hill, take over the fuel pump. Cannon and Stapleton, man your guns. The Germans will hit us again soon."

"Are we saving any fuel?" Hoffman asked Cannon, as he returned to his nose gun.

"Some," Cannon answered. "Don't know if it'll be enough."

"If number three dies, maybe that'll save some fuel."

"Maybe, but we'll be flying lower and slower. We'll be a sitting duck."

"Bogeys. Seven o'clock low," Gary Davis shouted.

From behind and below. Coming straight from the German air base. Probably the same fighters that had attacked them going in.

"They see our smoke trail!" Davis' voice rose in pitch. "Skipper, they're keying on us!"

Everybody knew the Luftwaffe pilots focused their attacks on damaged ships, since they were more vulnerable. If they dropped out of place, they wouldn't have the protection of the formation's interlocking fire pattern.

"Acknowledged," Bishop tried to speak calmly, but the stress in his voice was evident. "We've got to keep number three going to hold our position in formation. Gunners, I'm relying on you to keep us alive."

"Damn jinx plane," Lisenbe grumbled. "I told you we should have aborted!"

"Shut up," Bishop ordered.

Hoffman tried to look backward out of his gun port. No luck. A silver flash shot by, and he snapped off a belated burst, knowing as he did so he was too slow.

The limited fuel available to the fighters meant that, after flying from their airbase and allowing enough fuel to return, they could only engage the enemy for a few minutes. To Hoffman, and to the other crew members, those few minutes seemed like hours.

"There goes number three!" Stapleton shouted over the interphone.

Hoffman looked to see engine number three shrouded in flames.

Bishop and Lowery exchanged frantic words as they struggled to shut down the engine, and extinguish the fire. After a moment, the flames died out, but the propeller continued to spin. They'd failed to feather the prop in time.

Hoffman knew, from tales he'd heard in the O Club, of the danger afforded by an uncontrolled spinning propeller. When feathered, the prop was locked in place, and wouldn't act like a windmill in a hurricane. Unfeathered, the prop would spin until the cap which secured the blades to the engine driveshaft broke, and the propeller flew away. In that unlucky circumstance, the prop blades could slice into the fuselage, damage the structural integrity of the aircraft and possibly kill a crewman inside. One sergeant had claimed he'd seen an entire nose compartment sheared off by a rampant propeller. Hoffman shuddered.

With only three engines, the *Bottle Rocket*'s speed slowed. She could no longer keep up with the rest of the formation, and began losing speed and altitude.

The German fighters increased their attacks on the wounded airship.

"Flap your wings, boys," Mike Hilton said from the left waist gunner's position. "We need more speed."

"Adjust your trim, Ray." Over the interphone, Warren Lowery's voice sounded shrill, tense. "With only one right side engine and no right wing tank fuel, we're out of balance."

"I'm workin' on it." Bishop's voice sounded equally tense.

A German plane was visible in every direction Hoffman looked.

"I'm almost out of ammo," Stapleton shouted.

"Hoffman," Bishop screamed.

"Right," Hoffman answered. He clambered back toward the rear of the aircraft, relieved to be out of that glass bubble and doing something. He crawled through the short passageway under the cockpit, past the empty bomb bay, and between the two waist gunners as they fired their guns. With the narrow fuselage, the waist gunners couldn't stand back to back. Their movements, timed to avoid crashing into each other, almost looked like a dance. They had to shift out of the way to allow Hoffman to pass.

"Hurry up," Lisenbe growled.

Hoffman scooted between them, keeping his head down to stay below the gun port openings, although the B-17's hull was too thin to stop a bullet.

The sound of bullets hitting the fuselage made an arrhythmic tattoo, like a spastic Thor raining hammer blows on the airship. When Hoffman looked, the aluminum skin of the aircraft looked like Swiss cheese.

The ammunition was stored along the sides of the bomber, as it narrowed from the waist gunners' positions back toward the tail gunner. Hoffman *schlepped* belts of ammo, first to Stapleton, who greeted him with, "What took you so long?" then to the other gunners, ending with a belt for Cannon that he carried as he returned to the nose compartment.

Finally, the Luftwaffe planes disengaged, heading back to their airbases, leaving the crew in the semi-silence of the drone of their own engines and wind noise.

"They stayed too long," Kyle Waits said. "They wanted us too bad. Bet they run out of gas before they get back to base."

"God, I hope so," Cannon answered.

"Here come our escorts," Stapleton reported.

Hoffman spotted the glint of sunlight reflecting off the windshields of a squadron of P-47s.

"What took you so long, you SOBs?" Nicky Hill shouted, unconsciously repeating Stapleton's snarling remark to Hoffman a short while ago.

"Hoffman, get out your whiz wheel. Tell us if we can make it home," Bishop ordered.

As Lowery fed him information on remaining fuel, airspeed, wind speed and wind direction, Hoffman dialed the data into his E6B navigational calculator, an aluminum slide rule/computational wheel used by all American navigators. He grimaced and thumbed his interphone throat mike. Then he changed his mind and climbed through the narrow opening behind and between the cockpit seats.

"Doesn't look good, Captain," Hoffman said to Bishop. "We'll only make it halfway across the Channel, by my calculations."

Bishop nodded at Hoffman, then switched his gaze to Lowery. "Think we ought to bail out? Take our chances with the Germans?"

Lowery reached under his oxygen mask and rubbed his chin. "The French resistance might get to us first."

"Hoffman?" Bishop asked.

"You know what I think of the Germans," he answered.

Bishop stared out the window. "Let's lighten our load. See if that won't get us to dry land—dry *British* land." He engaged his interphone mike. "Okay, guys. Dump some weight. Guns, ammo, everything that's not bolted down."

"What if the Krauts come back?" Kyle Waits asked.

"We'll rely on our fighter escort to help us," Bishop answered.

Hoffman ducked through the passageway, and crawled back to the nose compartment.

"Help me with this gun," Cannon said.

The two men disengaged the nose gun from its mount and, with Hoffman crawling backward and pulling while Cannon crawled forward and pushed, worked the gun through the narrow passageway under the cockpit and back to the waist gunners' stations, where the larger gun ports allowed them to jettison the weapon.

"What about the Norden bombsight?" Hoffman asked.

Cannon shook his head. "That's top secret. If we go down before we get to the Channel, or if we jump, I'm to destroy it. But we don't throw it out over enemy occupied territory."

They turned back toward the front of the plane in time to see Stapleton climb out of the passageway. Hoffman frowned, but said nothing.

The next minutes were filled with frantic activity, as the crewmen threw out ammo belts, tools, any equipment that wasn't vital.

If we bail out over Belgium, Hoffman thought, *I'm going to throw away my dog tags. They identify me as Jewish. Of course, all they have to do is make me drop my pants.*

"When we get down to ten angels, throw out the oxygen equipment, too," Bishop ordered. "Then check your chutes, in case we have to jump."

Eventually, with the *Bottle Rocket* scoured and free of all equipment except Nicky Hill's radio and Cannon's bombsight, Hoffman looked for his parachute. It wasn't stored where it should be.

He looked around. "Doug, have you seen my chute?"

Cannon, holding his own parachute, looked up. "No, why?"

"I can't find it."

Cannon cursed and looked around the cramped compartment. There weren't many places for something like that to be hiding.

Hoffman went back to the bulkhead behind the cockpit, where the non-coms had gathered. "Anybody seen my parachute?" he asked.

"No, sir," the six men answered in unison.

"Stapleton, you were in the nose earlier. What were you looking for?"

"Stuff to throw out, sir."

"Like my parachute?"

His brown eyes blinked. Hoffman thought he was fighting a smirk.

"No sir, I—" Stapleton began. "Wait a minute! You think I dumped your parachute?"

"You were the only person in the nose other than me and Cannon."

"Well, you'd better ask Cannon, then . . . Lieutenant Cannon, I mean. Or, maybe in all the excitement, you tossed your own chute . . . sir."

Hoffman stared at Stapleton, who stared back. He turned and climbed up into the cockpit.

"Captain, my parachute's missing. I think it got jettisoned," Hoffman said.

Bishop stared at Hoffman's expression for a long moment. "By accident?" he asked.

"I don't think so."

"What?" Lowery said.

"Later, Warren," Bishop said. He stared out the forward cockpit window. "Well, I guess that answers our question about whether to jump before we reach the Channel."

"That's not fair to the other guys. You should jump without me," Hoffman pleaded.

"Nope. You can use my chute. I might survive the crash." Bishop still stared out the window.

"No, sir. I won't do that."

"Then we go for a swim." Bishop turned to look Hoffman in the eye. "Try your whiz wheel again. Check your numbers. Maybe, with our lighter weight, we can make it.

Before Hoffman could move, a *whang!* sounded from below the cockpit, followed by a curse from Cannon and an increase in wind noise.

Lowery looked to his right. "Number three propeller!"

Hoffman descended the short ladder, and looked toward the aircraft's nose. Cannon lay curled up as far forward as he could get, and stared back at a gash in the plane's airframe on the right side of the fuselage. The unfeathered propeller had broken loose and chopped a hole in the nose compartment.

"Good thing you were up in the cockpit," Cannon said to Hoffman. "Otherwise, you'd be chopped liver."

Hoffman puffed out his cheeks and blew air between his lips. He waited for his heartbeat to slow before reporting the damage to Lieutenant Bishop.

After a moment's thought, Bishop said, "Have Stapleton take a look at it."

68

Hoffman called the engineer forward for an assessment.

After scanning the damage, Stapleton climbed up between the two pilots. Hoffman listened from behind the non-com.

"How does it look?" Bishop asked.

"Well, the nose isn't going to fall off, as long as another prop doesn't break loose," Stapleton answered.

"Okay. Steady as she goes, then."

Hoffman ran the numbers on his E6B navigational calculator again. In addition to the risk of drowning, dying of hypothermia, or getting eaten by sharks, ditching in the Channel meant the crew might get picked up by a German gunboat, before the British air-sea rescue boat could reach them.

Hoffman climbed back up into the cockpit. "Captain, if you steer a heading of three hundred degrees, we'll get close to Beachy Head, on the English coast."

"How close?"

"Six, eight miles."

"Okay, tell Hill. Have him broadcast that data. In code, of course. Maybe a British high-speed launch will meet us there."

"Yes, sir."

Except for Bishop and Lowery in the cockpit, Hill, who feverishly broadcast and re-broadcast their expected splashdown coordinates, and Hoffman, who constantly re-calculated his navigational data, hoping for a better outcome, the crew had nothing to do and gathered at the bulkhead behind the cockpit.

Bishop put the *Bottle Rocket* on a shallow descent path, trying to milk an extra mile out of the doomed aircraft's flight. A P-47 flew just off each wingtip, providing escort in case a German fighter happened to be cruising in the vicinity.

When the B-17 was about ten feet above the wave tops, Hill hit the ditch alarm buzzer. Hoffman left his post and joined the other crewmen. He wasn't surprised to find Hill already there.

"All hands, brace for impact," Bishop intoned over the interphone.

Hoffman sat, shoulder-to-shoulder with Hill and Hilton, with his back to the forward bulkhead. The other crewmen took up similar positions.

With Bishop at the controls, the *Bottle Rocket*'s flight was so near level and their descent was so gradual, their first contact with the water was just a kiss, as it crossed the top of a wave. Another, rougher, blow followed, and the B-17 began skipping across the sea like a thrown pebble skipping across a lake. Then the bomber plowed a flat path into the sea. Sometimes, a plane's wing would catch a wave first, and the aircraft would wind up in a cartwheel. Not so with the *Bottle Rocket*. The aircraft stayed horizontal, and she ended up floating straight and level, for the time being, at least.

Hoffman clambered to his feet and looked down the passageway toward the nose. Water geysered up through the gash made by the loose propeller. Under the best circumstances, a B-17 was not very seaworthy. With the damage to the *Bottle Rocket*'s nose, the plane would sink in minutes.

"Get a move on!" Hoffman shouted to the rest of the crew. "Use the emergency exit behind the top turret."

His words were unnecessary. The crew needed no encouragement.

"Don't inflate your Mae Wests until you get onto the wing!" If a crewman inflated his life vest too soon, it might get cut as he crawled out of the hatch.

While everybody else climbed out, Hoffman stuck his head up into the cockpit. "Don't dawdle, skippers. The nose is flooding fast."

Bishop and Lowery had already disengaged their seatbelts and were heading for the opening occupied by Hoffman.

"Get out of the way, then," Lowery growled.

A life raft was stowed in an exterior compartment above each wing. The crew was divided into left wing and right wing groups for evacuation purposes, with two officers and three non-coms in each group.

Hoffman was assigned to the left wing crew, since his station in the nose was slightly left of the imaginary center line which bisected the aircraft. Ray Bishop, who occupied the left cockpit seat, led the group. Mike Hilton, the left waist gunner, was included, as was Donnie Stapleton, although his station straddled the center line. Maybe it was because he was left-handed. Kyle Waits completed the group.

As each crew member cleared the exit hatch, he hopped down onto the left or right wing, depending on which evacuation group he belonged to. When Cannon came out of the hatch, he held his precious Norden bombsight cradled in his arms, like a baby.

By the time Hoffman jumped onto the left wing, he stood ankle deep in water. He pulled the tab which inflated his Mae West, and felt the pressure hug his rib cage as the vest filled with air. "Hurry up, we don't have all day."

Hilton opened the life raft compartment and extracted the neoprene bundle. He also retrieved a flare gun package, which he handed to Waits. Hilton pulled the tab that opened the compressed air canister. Air *whooshed*, and the raft unfolded, but it did not grow taut.

Hilton cursed. "A bullet or shrapnel or something punctured the raft. It's got a hole in it."

At the same time, Hoffman heard a second *phsssh* sound, and he felt the pressure around his chest ease. He put his hands on his Mae West and felt it relax. He spun around. Stapleton was in the process of turning away. Hoffman thought he held something in his hand.

The water was knee deep. Waves, gentle though they were, threatened to wash the five men off their feet.

Hilton climbed atop the *Bottle Rocket*'s fuselage. "Our raft's no good," he yelled to the right wing crew. "We need help." He turned back to Bishop. "They've already boarded. They're rowing around the nose."

The water reached Hoffman's crotch, and its coldness made him gasp. He grasped Stapleton's elbow. "What did you do? Did you cut my vest?"

Stapleton gave him an innocent look. "I don't know what you're talking about."

"Show me your hands."

Stapleton held out his hands, palms up. They were empty.

"You cut my vest. Where's your knife?"

"Lost it. I'll bet you cut your vest when you climbed out the hatch. What did you do, inflate it too soon?"

Hoffman felt bile rise in his throat. "We'll discuss this later."

Stapleton held Hoffman's gaze, but his face grew pale.

"Okay, swim toward the nose," Bishop yelled. "The other guys will pick us up."

Before beginning his swim, Doug Cannon threw the Norden bombsight as far away from the sinking aircraft as he could.

The right wing's orange raft bobbed around the nose of the aircraft.

The problem was, Hoffman couldn't swim. Water rose above his navel, and he staggered around, trying to keep his balance against the force of the waves. His heart pounded in his chest.

Kyle Waits was about to launch himself toward the raft when he glanced at Hoffman and stopped. "Hey, Loot," he said. "You're vest's not inflated."

"It's got a hole in it."

Stapleton, halfway to the raft, looked back and offered Hoffman a smirk.

"Can't you swim?" Waits asked.

Hoffman shook his head.

"C'mon. I'll help you."

Hoffman canted his head to one side. "I outweigh you by thirty pounds."

"C'mon, Lieutenant. You gonna argue with me now?"

Hoffman's foot slipped, and he bobbed underwater. He came up coughing.

Waits took advantage of his slip. He grabbed Hoffman by the shoulders, and spun him around so he faced the airplane's tail. Then Waits slid an arm around Hoffman's chest under his armpits.

"Just relax, now," Waits spoke soothingly. "I've got you."

The other three of the left wing group had already reached the raft. When Waits and Hoffman got there, Bishop said, "Row away from the plane. When it goes down, it may try to suck us down with it."

The gash in its forward compartment caused the front end of the plane to sink by the nose. By the time the tail disappeared, the raft was a safe distance away.

Nicky Hill had possession of the right wing crew's flare gun. He fired another flare skyward.

"The raft won't hold all ten of us. It's not buoyant enough. The left wing group will have to hang onto the sides." Bishop said.

"What if a German gunboat sees that flare?" Gary Davis asked no one in particular. "What if a shark sees our legs hanging in the water?" prompting Stapleton to try to clamber into the raft.

"Hold your position," Hoffman ordered. "I don't see any fins circling around." He was pretty sure the absence of fins did not guarantee the absence of sharks, but he needed to reassure the guys in the water.

"Lieutenant Hoffman's Mae West is punctured," Waits said. "How about one of you guys in the raft swapping places with him?"

"What about the rest of us?" Stapleton said in an indignant tone of voice.

"Your hot air will keep you afloat, Stapleton, Mae West or no Mae West," Waits retorted.

"I'll swap," Cannon said, and swung his leg over the side.

"Stay put, Doug," Hoffman said. "I'll be okay."

Cannon hesitated, then said, "Well, wear my vest anyway."

While they were exchanging vests, Cyrus Lisenbe swept the horizon, looking through binoculars. "There's a boat."

"German or British?" Davis asked. "Do you see a swastika on the side?"

"Can't tell," Lisenbe answered.

"Fire another flare, Hill," Bishop ordered.

"Wait. What if it's German?" Davis' voice held a note of panic.

"Then we won't die of hypothermia," Bishop answered. "Now shut up."

The boat drew closer.

"What does its silhouette look like?" Davis asked, with a guilty glance at Bishop.

"I study plane silhouettes. I don't study boat silhouettes," Lisenbe said. "I still don't see any insignia. It has HSL 189 painted on its prow. That's a Limey designation, isn't it?"

"Who the hell knows?" Warren Lowery said.

The boat drew nearer. A seaman leaned over the side with a bullhorn. "Need a lift, mates?"

"Thank God!" Davis said. "Brits!"

Hoffman let out a sigh of relief, too.

One of the boat crew threw a line, which Hill tied to a grommet on the raft's side. The raft was pulled alongside the rescue ship, and a ladder lowered. One by one, beginning with the men in the water, the *Bottle Rocket* crew climbed aboard.

"Welcome aboard the High Speed Launch number 189, gents. I'm Leftenant Mayweather, ship's captain."

"Thank you, Captain Mayweather," Bishop responded. "You guys are Johnny-on-the-spot."

"Righto," Mayweather said. "Your radio reports were dead on. We came right to you." He gestured toward a hatch which led belowdecks. "Let's get you below and into some dry clothes."

A half-hour later, the *Reba Jean/Bottle Rocket* crew sat at the tables in the ship's galley, wearing a mismatched conglomeration of dungarees, canvas trousers, chambray shirts, sweaters, with wool blankets draped over their shoulders.

They were tended by a seaman.

"Care for a spot o' grog, gents?" the sailor asked.

"What's that?" Lowery asked.

"Why, rum o' course. Mother's milk for the swabbie."

"Yeah, I'll take some." Lowery watched as the seaman poured a dollop into a glass for each bomber crew member. "You guys get to drink on duty?"

"You blokes have made a merry holiday for His Lordship and the rest of us. When a launch brings in a bunch of pilots what got dunked in the sea, we get treated like bloody heroes, for a day, at least." He raised his glass. "So here's to a saltwater bath."

The airmen dutifully raised their glasses.

"You said His Lordship," Lowery asked. "Who's that?"

"Lord Mayweather, the Earl of Arundel. Not every launch in the Royal Navy has a noble as its skipper."

Captain Mayweather entered the room with a bashful smile. "Captain Bishop, I've a favor to ask of you. Will you and your crewmates line up on the ship's rail as we enter port? Let the other boat crews see our catch of the day, wot?"

Bishop smiled in return. "It's the least we can do."

After the HSL 189 docked, and as the bomber crew prepared to disembark, Mayweather spoke to Bishop again. "A bus will take you to Ford, an RAF base not far from here. It's a collection point for rescued airmen such as yourselves."

Bishop held out his hand. "Captain, my thanks to you and your crew. You saved our lives today."

Mayweather grasped the extended hand. His eyes glistened. "You blokes have saved us many times over. Godspeed."

* * * * *

The crew filed onto a rattletrap bus along with nine members of another B-17 crew and three fighter pilots. When the Americans were aboard and seated, the bus took off with a smoky roar.

Hoffman looked out the back window at the billow of smoke in the bus's trail. "The Limeys could use this bus to conceal their targets. All they'd have to do is put the vehicle upwind and the Krauts would never be able to see anything."

Nobody responded. They were just too tired.

One of the officers from the other bomber sat across the aisle. "Who'd you lose?" Hoffman asked him.

The Lieutenant looked at him with red eyes. "We were coming apart. The pilot kept us in the air long enough for everybody to bail out. Except him."

Hoffman could think of nothing to say. He looked over at Bishop, who sat, slump-shouldered, staring out through the front window.

As the bus continued its journey, Hoffman thought of the events before and after the *Bottle Rocket* ditched. He couldn't prove it, but he was sure Stapleton had jettisoned his—Hoffman's—parachute while they were lightening their load. He just didn't know if he acted deliberately or if he was caught up in the frenzy of the moment, tossing everything he could put his hands on.

Stapleton had also been near him when his Mae West had mysteriously deflated, and Hoffman thought he'd seen something in Stapleton's hand. A knife? Maybe. Maybe not.

The rescued Americans were young, and their youth, along with the vigor of realization that they'd survived a life-threatening event, restored their energy. By the time they reached Ford RAF Base, they were all singing a spirited rendition of "It's a Long Way to Tipperary."

They disembarked and filed into a barracks where they showered. This was followed by a hearty meal in the mess hall, along with another hundred or so airmen. Afterward, they were led into a stifling hangar that had been converted into a dance hall. A swing band was already in action, providing a rhythmic tempo for a houseful of British lasses there to help the men forget their ordeal. The ale flowed, and in no time the men's and women's sweaty bodies gyrated in synchronous motion — *most* of them.

Bishop sat on a stool at the bar, a pint of lager near his hand, as he quietly watched the proceedings. He seemed to wince every few breaths. Hoffman walked up and stood next to him.

"That blond over there is giving you the eye," Hoffman said to Bishop. He had to put his mouth near Bishop's ear to be heard above the din.

Sure enough, a curvy, blue-eyed blond in a Royal Navy uniform stood ten feet away, giving him a look that required no interpretation.

Bishop met her gaze and gave a slight shake of his head. A disappointed expression crossed her face, and she turned away.

"Now she'll think you're . . . *funny*." Hoffman held up his hand, palm down, and waggled it from side to side.

Bishop turned and gave Hoffman a hard stare. "Her problem. My fiancée back home knows different."

Hoffman motioned to a bartender, who brought a mug filled with dark beer.

They silently drank and watched the goings on for a time.

After a while, Bishop turned to Hoffman. "Want to get out of here?"

They walked through the darkness to a nearby barracks, and seated themselves on the outside steps.

Bishop took a pipe and tobacco pouch from his pocket.

"I see you saved your pipe," Hoffman observed.

Bishop shook his head. "I got thrown forward when we hit that first wave as we ditched. My chest slammed against the steering yoke. Bruised some ribs, I think. My pipe was in my jacket pocket, and the stem broke. Then my tobacco got wet." He held up the pipe in his hand. "Some British major gave me this, and a pouch of tobacco."

Hoffman fished a cigarette from his pocket and lit it. "I think I might know who wants me off the flight crew."

"Oh, yeah? Who?"

Hoffman told him about Stapleton's suspected actions.

Bishop listened as smoke swirled about his head, his eyes on Hoffman's. His fist squeezed the pipe bowl.

"I'll talk to him when we get back to Molesworth," Bishop growled. "I'll have him court-martialed."

"How are you going to prove it?" Hoffman countered.

"How am I going to prove it?" Bishop seemed taken aback by the question. "With your testimony, of course."

"But I'm not going to testify."

"What? Why not?"

"It'll just be my word against his. He says he didn't throw my parachute out. If I say he did, where's the proof? He says my Mae West must've been torn when I exited the hatch. If I say otherwise, where's the proof? It'll divide the crew, and maybe the entire base, between officers and enlisted men."

Bishop tapped his pipe stem against his teeth. "What do you propose?"

"Do nothing, but be aware," Hoffman answered. "I don't want him to kill me, but more importantly, I don't want him to cause the death of any of our crewmates." He reached down and plucked a blade of grass, and twirled it between his fingers. "Sooner or later, he'll do something to give himself away."

"I think I should give him a dressing down, at least,' Bishop said.

"Playing this thing with a heavy hand will only cause morale problems among the crew," Hoffman counseled. "Trust me."

"Okay." Bishop didn't sound convinced.

They sat for a few minutes, listening to the beat of the band.

Hoffman dusted his hands. "Well, I've had an exciting day. I think I'll hit the sack."

"Now there's good advice," Bishop said. They rose and made their way to their assigned barracks.

Next morning, they rode with a bus full of other bomber crewmen who'd been plucked from the sea the day before. Their vehicle ran a route from one air base to another. Hoffman realized the Brits probably did this every day. Tomorrow a bus would run this same route, delivering the airmen who would be rescued today.

It was mid-afternoon when the bus dropped off Hoffman and his crewmates at Molesworth. They were met by a grinning clerk-sergeant. "Air Boss wants you and your men to join him in the officer's briefing room," he said to Lieutenant Bishop.

The ten men exchanged quizzical glances before Bishop led the bedraggled parade to the building.

Hoffman stepped up to walk between Bishop and Lowery. "Are we in some kind of trouble?"

"I don't think so," Lowery answered. "The clerk seemed in too good a mood to be summoning us to our execution."

They entered the door to the briefing room, and were met by a crowd of cheering, foot-stomping airmen. A smiling Major Blevins, standing on the raised platform at the head of the room, motioned the crew forward. Once on the platform, the clerk who'd met them at the bus distributed shot glasses of Scotch whisky.

Blevins waved for silence, and the audience quieted and sat down.

"The men of Molesworth Air Base, upon hearing of your adventure yesterday," the major said, speaking in a formal tone, "wanted to commend you, unofficially, of course, for two accomplishments." His eyes twinkled as he spoke.

"As you probably know, the *Bottle Rocket* had a reputation as a jinx. We of Molesworth want to thank you for depositing that wretched piece of junk on the bottom of the English Channel, where nobody will ever have to fly her again."

The audience members leapt to their feet and cheered lustily.

When the din had quieted a bit, the major continued, "Secondly, we want to congratulate you for accomplishing that feat with no casualties!" He lifted his glass.

"Hip, hip, hooray!" The crowd roared. Everybody drank their toast, then gathered around Bishop and his crew for a round of handshakes and backslaps.

After a few minutes, Blevins said, "Well, Lieutenant Bishop, do you feel up to debriefing me on your mission?" The two walked away toward the major's office.

Later, as Hoffman, Lowery, and Cannon made their way to the officer's quarters, Lowery commented, "We're probably the only crew to be praised for ditching their airplane in the ocean!"

Tom Hooker

INTERLUDE A

The Pilot's Tale Continued

Bishop figured the Molesworth air base had been built sometime during World War I. It must have been used as a training facility, or perhaps as a staging point for British Sopwith Camels waiting to be ferried across the Channel to France. It was too far from the previous war's battle zone to allow planes of that era to fly over, fight, and return home.

Major Blevins' office reflected the heavy use of the rest of the base. The wooden walls were darkened by age and tobacco smoke. The oiled floor showed a track worn by the thousands of boots that had marched from the door to the desk and back.

Blevins sat behind his desk, as Bishop, sitting in front, gave the air boss his account of the Stuttgart mission, up to the ditching of the *Bottle Rocket* off Beachy Head.

The Lieutenant paused to take a deep breath, then explained about Hoffman's missing parachute, and his mysteriously punctured life vest.

"Do you remember warning me after our first mission about a crew member of mine who was rumored to hate Jews?" Bishop asked.

Blevins leaned back in his chair, holding a lit cigarette between the middle and index finger of his right hand. "Yes."

"Well, Lieutenant Hoffman thinks Sergeant Stapleton jettisoned his parachute on purpose, and that Stapleton cut Hoffman's Mae West.

Blevins sat quietly for a moment. "So you think Stapleton is your Jew hater?"

"It looks that way."

"What do you propose?"

"Court-martial him for jeopardizing a crew member's life."

Blevins leaned forward and put his elbows on the desk. "Do you have any proof?"

"Only Lieutenant Hoffman's word," Bishop said.

"Have you talked to Stapleton, to get his side of the story?"

"Not yet."

"Do you think he will go along with Hoffman's charges?"

"Of course not."

"What about the rest of the crew? Did they see anything?"

Bishop steepled his fingers and tried not to frown. This wasn't going the way he'd planned. "I haven't talked to any of the non-coms about this incident. I made some inquiries earlier, but nobody wanted to rat on a fellow crew member."

The major stood and walked to the window. Bishop wanted to stand and pace, but he didn't think Blevins would approve.

"So, barring some corroborating testimony from another crewman, you're going to have a court-martial with only an officer's word against an enlisted man's word." Blevins spoke with his back to Bishop. "With no tangible proof, it will be almost impossible to get a conviction. And that kind of trial would only divide the officers and enlisted men."

Bishop blanched. "That's what Lieutenant Hoffman said."

"Sounds like Hoffman has a better perspective on the situation than you do."

"May I stand, sir?" Bishop asked. "I need to stretch my legs." Bishop had expected more support.

Blevins nodded and turned to extinguish his cigarette in an ash tray on his desk.

Bishop stood, clasped his hands behind his back, and slowly paced the width of the office. "Maybe we can transfer Stapleton to another crew."

Blevins looked sharply at Bishop, who straightened his back. The major obviously had no compunction about frowning. "You want to foist your problem off on somebody else? Hoffman isn't the only Jew at Molesworth, you know, and Stapleton isn't the only Jew-hater."

Bishop stood still, unable to come up with any words.

"We're losing aircraft, Lieutenant, every day. We're losing them to German fighters and anti-aircraft fire.

Every time we lose a plane, we lose ten men. I'm not going to take a gunner off a crew because another crewman doesn't like him."

"What do you suggest, sir?" Bishop struggled to keep his voice steady.

"When we talked about this after Schweinfurt, you said you'd take care of it. That's what I suggest you do."

Bishop swallowed the lump in his throat. "Yes, sir. May I be excused, sir?"

"You may." Blevins turned back to stare out the window.

Outside, Bishop stopped and took a shaky breath, trying to slow his runaway heartbeat. He'd wanted to ask Blevins just how he was supposed to "take care of it," but he knew that would just piss Blevins off more.

The lieutenant adjusted his cap and started a slow walk in no specific direction. He needed to think.

Aaron Hoffman and Major Blevins were right. Without proof that Stapleton had done something, formal discipline was impossible. Bishop realized that he'd over-reached by suggesting a court-martial.

But he couldn't let Stapleton think he'd gotten away scot-free. Of course, he only had Hoffman's word that anything at all had happened. How well did he know Hoffman? Could he trust him?

Better than he could trust Stapleton.

Or was that one officer's prejudice in favor of another officer? Bishop began to see the problem Blevins had tried to describe.

Bishop stepped into the lee of a building to fill and light his pipe. Once he had done that, he leaned back against the weathered wood, and allowed the exhaled smoke to envelope his head.

After some time, he pushed away from the building and strode toward the wing headquarters. Once there, he corralled an unoccupied orderly. "Find Sergeant Donald Stapleton," he told the corporal. "Have him meet me in Conference Room A."

"Yes, sir," the orderly said, and departed.

A half-hour later, Stapleton arrived at the specified location. Bishop sat at the table in the center of the room. Its finish had been worn by years of buffing by shirt sleeves. A hefty book lay near his right hand, along with a legal pad containing a half-page of scribbled notes.

"Come in, Sergeant, and close the door."

Stapleton complied and stepped forward to stand at attention before the officer, with the table separating the two. Stapleton wore a scowl, clearly uncertain about what Bishop was up to.

"At ease. Have a seat."

Again, Stapleton complied. The sergeant had dark hair with thick eyebrows. His hands were calloused, his knuckles swollen from thousands of bumps while working on machinery, and, perhaps, from contact with a few jaws and noses inside and out of the boxing ring.

"I've been trying to go over the events of our mission, so I can prepare the after-action report. I have a few questions," Bishop said.

"Okay, sir," Stapleton said.

"During the period when we jettisoned gear, trying to lose weight and increase our range, Lieutenant

Hoffman's parachute disappeared. Do you know anything about that?"

Stapleton leaned back in his chair. "What did Hoffman say?"

"Who?"

"Lieutenant Hoffman." Stapleton caught his error. "Did he say something about me and the parachute?"

Bishop sat silently and studied Stapleton, whose scowl had deepened.

After a moment, Bishop said, "Lieutenant Hoffman said he saw you coming out of the *Bottle Rocket's* nose section. What were you doing up there?"

Stapleton fidgeted. "Lookin' for stuff to throw away. Sir."

"Like parachutes? A specific parachute, perhaps?"

"I don't care what that Ki—*man* says. I didn't throw out no parachutes, and you—*he*—can't prove that I did."

Bishop picked up the legal pad and looked at his notes. "What about after we ditched, while we were abandoning the aircraft. What happened then?"

"Is Hoff—Lieutenant Hoffman saying I had something to do with the life raft?" Stapleton's voice rose. "It came out of its storage compartment like that. Ask Mike Hilton. He'll tell you."

"Yes. The raft was punctured by enemy fire. I know that. But you were standing beside Lieutenant Hoffman when his Mae West mysteriously deflated. What do you know about *that*?"

"Not a damn thing. Sir." Beads of sweat popped out on Stapleton's brow. "Maybe he cut it climbing out the escape hatch."

Bishop stared at Stapleton and said nothing.

"What're you askin' *me* for? Is he accusin' me? You can't prove nothin'!"

Bishop remained silent.

"That Hoffman. Maybe he's got shell shock, or somethin'."

"When you speak of an officer, Sergeant Stapleton, you will use his rank," Bishop said coolly.

"Lieutenant Hoffman, then. He's tryin' to make trouble for me for no good reason."

"I'm not here at Lieutenant Hoffman's behest. I'm trying to ensure the safety of my crew, *all* of them. And to ensure the proper conduct of that crew, as well." Bishop paused to take a deep breath. "We have enough trouble fighting the Germans. We can't afford to fight among ourselves, too. I'm not sure you understand the relationship between enlisted men and officers, and how they function together." He placed his hand on the large book beside him. "You may not know that I was a teacher before this war started." He didn't mention that he had taught for less than a year. "So I'm experienced at giving study assignments and tests."

Stapleton looked at the book with an expression of alarm.

"This is the Uniform Code of Military Justice," Bishop continued. "Now I'm not going to make you read the whole thing . . ." He pushed the volume toward the sergeant, ". . . but there are two sections I want you to study and be prepared to answer questions about.

"Article eighty-eight addresses the subject of contempt toward officers, and article ninety discusses assaulting or willfully disobeying a commissioned officer. You are to familiarize yourself with those sections."

"But, sir," Stapleton whined, "how am I going to understand that legal stuff?"

"I'll bet you've got someone in your barracks who's had some legal training. Or someone from the Judge Advocate General's office can explain it to you."

Stapleton stared at the book as if it was a rattlesnake waiting to strike.

"Oh, and one more thing," Bishop said.

Stapleton's gaze shifted from the book to the lieutenant.

"I've asked the senior non-com in your barracks," Bishop checked his notes, "Master Sergeant Lang, to assign you to cleanup detail, on the days we don't have a mission, for the remainder of the month. That will also involve cleaning the latrine, of course."

"Is that all? Sir?" Stapleton asked in a voice that trembled with anger.

"Yes, Sergeant. Dismissed."

The sergeant stood, turned, and stalked out the door, book in hand.

Bishop leaned back in his chair and puffed out his cheeks as he exhaled a gust of air.

He'd told the truth when he'd said he was a teacher, but that had been for only a few months before Pearl Harbor. Most of Taliposa High's students had been cooperative when faced with the authority inherent in the teaching position. The one or two bullies had been careful not to push too hard against Bishop's rules. Most of his experiences in dealing with hard cases had been his observation of his teachers during his student years, and of his flight instructors during his first years in the air corps. So his confrontation with Stapleton had been difficult. Handling the Bumblebee, the old Stearman biplane in basic flight training, had been a piece of cake compared to this — on the nerves, at least.

But the job of dealing with troublemakers came with the silver bar on his collar. He hadn't decided yet if he would actually test Stapleton on the contents of the UCMJ articles. He only wanted the engineer to know that he was under suspicion and observation. And, maybe he had given Stapleton somebody else to be mad at instead of Hoffman.

Bishop wiped his brow, picked up his notes, and left the room.

Tom Hooker

The Right Waist Gunner's Tale

September 16, 1943
Nantes, France

It felt good to get back to the *Reba Jean* after the nightmare of ditching in the *Bottle Rocket.* Maybe there was some truth to the rumor that the *Bottle Rocket* was a jinx. Anyway, the *Reba Jean* did seem to provide a sense of security. Nobody on the crew had been seriously injured so far, and their most dangerous encounter with death had come when they flew another bomber. Maybe the *Reba Jean* had been jealous, and had flung her jealousy at the *Bottle Rocket.*

The next two missions were "milk runs" over French targets. Scuttlebutt had it that the Eighth Air Force brass was shaken after Schweinfurt and Stuttgart, and, helped by criticism from the "limey" prime minister, Churchill, and they were re-thinking their entire air war strategy. Word was Churchill favored safer night missions, while the American brass complained that the night-time runs were less accurate.

While Cyrus Lisenbe knew their decisions would affect his chances of coming out of this war alive, he also knew there was nothing he could do about it, so he decided to take advantage of his few hours of liberty and hit a pub or two in Molesworth.

Because the air base was so large, and jeeps were so few, the quartermaster had obtained a fleet of bicycles. They allowed airmen to travel to and from the far corners of the field, but occasionally a guard at the gate could be temporarily blinded by the sight of folding money, allowing an airman to ride through and into town while the guard admired Washington's portrait on a dollar bill.

Lisenbe unearthed his stash of hospitality rations — chocolate bars and packs of American cigarettes — and filled a musette bag. The hospitality rations were given to the Americans for distribution to the locals, as a little goodwill bribery. It worked, too. The chicks, deprived of such luxuries, were often persuaded to shower a "Yank" with all sorts of good will in return for some chocolate or smokes. God bless you, Mr. Hershey! And if the guy could wrangle a pair of silk stockings, oh, boy. No Adonis, and not in possession of anything silk, Lisenbe counted on sheer volume of chocolate to get him through Heaven's portals.

He sauntered up to a bike rack and selected a sturdy-looking model. He rode, first toward the control tower, then around it and toward the hangars on the far side of the runway. It was too light to make a run for the gate. Besides, making a beeline would only telegraph his intentions. By heading for one legitimate destination, then another, he could place himself near the gate at sunset. Then he could cycle the road between the base and the town while drawing less attention. All he had to do was be alert for vehicular traffic, and hide when he heard an approaching jeep engine.

The gloom of dusk had begun to settle. The corporal at the gate gave him a skeptical look. "I hope you're not planning to take that bike off base."

"I've got a pass," Lisenbe said, handing him his liberty papers. "And one for the bike, too." He added a dollar.

The guard grunted and handed Lisenbe's papers back to him, keeping the money.

"Hey, I need to see a pass, too." A second guard stepped from the gatehouse.

"Aw, man," Lisenbe complained. "Can't you guys split the dough?"

The second guard said nothing. He reached inside the gatehouse and lifted the Bakelite handset of the telephone.

"All right, all right," Lisenbe grumbled. He fished another bill from his pocket and handed it over.

The second guard grinned. "Enjoy your evening, sergeant."

Lisenbe pedaled through the gate and pointed his bike down the narrow road toward Molesworth.

Although he'd spent the last six weeks in eastern England and before that, some time in Idaho, Lisenbe still hadn't gotten used to the vast open spaces that existed outside his hometown, The Bronx, and, in England at least, the green of everything. The cool climate and the moist, foggy air made for a vivid landscape. Sure, there were several parks near his home: Crotona Park, Bronx Park, and others, but nothing like the open country around him.

Lisenbe continued to pedal down the narrow road. The fact that limeys drove on the wrong side of the street had no effect on a non-driver like Lisenbe, except that as a pedestrian he tended to look in the wrong direction for oncoming traffic. More than once he'd turned to his left and almost got clobbered by a car coming from the right. Only the whiny *meep, meep* from the wimpy car horns had saved his skin.

Of course, these country roads were so narrow they were, effectively, one lane thoroughfares.

The sun was well below the horizon, and the indigo sky had begun to show off its blanket of stars. The starlight was broken by the uneven foliage alongside, leaving the road a black ribbon for Lisenbe to follow. When the whine of an engine sounded from beyond the hilltop ahead of him, Lisenbe dismounted his bike and stepped off the road, hiding himself and his cycle in the prickly roadside gorse. A moment later, a jeep rumbled by on its way toward the airbase. Because of the blackout conditions, the vehicles headlights were taped over, leaving a tiny slit which allowed a sliver of light to shine through.

Lisenbe returned to the road and pedaled the remaining distance to Molesworth without further incident. In town, he found a pub, stashed his bike, and lit a cigarette before entering the building.

The pub was long, narrow, and poorly lit. A pall of smoke surrounded everything. A couple of soldiers sat at a table along the left wall, and three sour-faced local men sat on stools at the bar. Two young women sat at another table making eyes at the soldiers, who were making eyes back, which accounted for the sour expressions on the faces of the locals. They didn't like having interlopers rustle their flock of birds. It was hard to compete with free chocolate and cigarettes—*and* Yankee accents.

Lisenbe assessed the battleground. If he interrupted the semaphore session going on between the girls and the soldiers, he might have two groups of enemies: the soldiers and the locals.

Ah, what the heck.

He walked up to the women. "Buy you a drink, ladies?"

They looked at him uncertainly. Lisenbe figured they were trying to compare their chances: one of him, two of the other yanks. He was about to lose. He pulled a bar of chocolate from his musette bag.

The two women smiled, and one of them indicated an empty chair at their table.

Lisenbe turned to the bartender. "Three pints, Jeeves, if you please." He laughed. "Look at that. I'm a poet and don't know it." Once the bartender pulled the beers, Lisenbe paid, took them to the table, and sat.

He sized up the two ladies as he fished another chocolate bar from his stash, giving them the opportunity to see that he had more. If he played his cards right, he'd have his pick of these two chicks.

The girl on the left's auburn hair was cut in the Betty Grable style, short with a mass of curls sitting on the foretop of her head, like a hat. She had a lipstick source, because her lips were as red as a cardinal's feather. She was plump, but not too plump.

The second girl wore her blonde hair like Veronica Lake: shoulder length and straight, hanging along the side of her face. She may have resorted to eating berries to give her lips a purplish color. They were considerably more muted.

"Wot's your name, Ducks?" The blonde asked. Her accent made the word sound like "nime."

"Cyrus. What's yours?"

"Ilsa."

Lisenbe's mouth moved before his brain had a chance to stop it. "Ilsa? That's German, ain't it?"

The next thing he knew his left ear was ringing from the slap she gave him.

"It's Swedish, you idiot!" she said, before she and her lady friend gathered the beers and chocolate he'd provided and moved over to join the other soldiers.

He resolved to say nothing about the next girl's name, even if it was Brunhilde.

The soldiers at the other table laughed uproariously at his blunder, and Lisenbe had to wait for another dame to come in.

As the evening progressed, traffic in the pub increased. Eventually he spotted a dark-haired beauty. She had a naughty girl curl—a spit curl, they called it— at each temple, obviously modeled after Betty Boop.

Lisenbe waited for her to find a seat, so he could make an approach, but she spotted him alone at his table and shot him a questioning look. In answer, he rose and grabbed the back of the vacant chair, a gentlemanly invitation to join him.

Once seated, she accepted Lisenbe's offer of a cigarette and a light. "Flying solo tonight, Yank?"

He didn't know if she was a lady of the evening, or not. Some of the women in England, and at home for that matter, saw their contribution to the war effort as helping to "improve the morale" of their fighting men.

"Not anymore," Lisenbe responded.

"What's your name?" she asked, exhaling a cloud of smoke into the tobacco fog already blanketing the room.

"Cyrus."

She made a face, and Lisenbe amended his answer. "Call me Cy if you want."

She smiled. "I want. I'm Agnes."

Lisenbe breathed s sigh of relief at his lack of urge to make some stupid remark at her name.

"So tell me," she continued, "killed any Jerries?"

"Of course."

"How many?"

Cy touched his fingertips to his thumb, one after another, in a counting gesture. The true number was a respectable one, but there was no way he was going to quote anything fewer than double digits. "Twelve."

Agnes' eyes widened. "Wow. What airplane do you fly on?"

"C'mon Agnes. You know I can't talk about stuff like that."

"Oops." She put her fingers to her lips. "I didn't mean to ask about classified information."

"That's okay," Cyrus responded.

They spent the next hour drinking beer and making small talk. Agnes made it clear that her time was for sale, and Cyrus relaxed, confident that the two of them would end up in bed before the night was done.

And that was the case.

Lisenbe forked over to Agnes most of his chocolates and smokes, plus a hefty wad of his cash. She took him to a nearby inn.

"'lo, Harry," she said to the innkeeper, an anemic-looking man with a black bowtie. "Got a room?"

"Saved one for ya special, Aggie, for you and your beau," Harry answered. And Cyrus had to ante up a few more pounds for his night's lodging, a small, poorly furnished room with a rickety bed — and a loo at the end of the hall. That was all they needed.

They kissed. Lisenbe inhaled the aroma of Agnes' scent, blended with rosewater. He fought his way out of his shirt.

"Take your time, luv," Agnes crooned. "We've got all night."

While Cyrus kissed her lips, Agnes unbuttoned her blouse.

Lisenbe's hands roamed over her torso. She wore a stretchy camisole that felt like silk, but wasn't, over a brassiere with an elastic band.

"Do they still make this stuff?" Lisenbe asked. He was going to have a doozy of a time getting it off.

"This is pre-war, Yank," Agnes breathed. "Don't tear it."

Lisenbe cupped one buoyant breast, encased in fabric, then slid his hand down the side, feeling the camisole's flexible tautness over her skin.

It felt like the inflated Mae West, and the life raft.

In the next second, he was back in the cold water of the Channel, heart pounding, wondering if these were the last moments of his life.

His body began to shake uncontrollably.

"Are you all right?" Agnes asked.

A series of scenes flashed through his head: In the *Bottle Rocket* with a Me-109 bearing down, bullets smashing through the aluminum skin all around him; flak bursts causing the bomber to buck as if it were in the midst of an earthquake; back to the Channel, with him and his crewmates being shaken like a bunch of rag dolls as the *Bottle Rocket* skipped across the ocean's surface.

"What's the matter, Luv?" Agnes seemed worried. "Are you a virgin?"

Cyrus would have snorted, if he could have drawn a breath.

Agnes wrapped a hand around the back of Cyrus' neck and drew his head into the curve formed by her neck and shoulder. "Now, now, dear," she crooned.

"I . . . I'm sorry," Cyrus sobbed.

"Hush, now," Agnes soothed. "Don't talk like that. Sometimes a good cry is the best medicine."

So Sergeant Cyrus Lisenbe, United States Army Air Corps gunner, with a kill to his credit, lay in a strange woman's arms and cried until there were no more tears left. Then he fell into a deep and restful sleep — the best he'd had since he crossed the Atlantic Ocean.

When Cyrus awoke the next morning, Agnes had her blouse back on and was sitting on the edge of the bed.

"What time is it?" he asked around a yawn.

She glanced at her watch. "Five o'clock."

"I've got to get back to base." He sat up and rubbed his eyes. "Look, I'm sorry about last night."

The skin around Agnes' dark eyes crinkled. "Don't be. I think it made you feel better. Can't say that's ever happened before, though."

Lisenbe cringed. "Look, you won't tell anyone, will you?"

"Of course not." She grew serious. "I can't imagine what you fly-boys go through. I shan't say a word."

"Okay."

On the bike ride back to the airbase, Lisenbe tried to understand what had happened to him. He'd gone through eight missions, so far, and while he'd experienced the adrenaline rush of fear during the heat of battle, it hadn't paralyzed him. Last night, when he should have been feeling an altogether different set of emotions, he'd crumbled like a mud wall.

Now, he felt uncertain. What would happen the next time he faced a charging German fighter? Would he stand and fight, or would he collapse into a blubbering puddle of tears? He drew a deep breath.

Lisenbe came back through the gate without having to pay another bribe. Simonsen, a buddy, had guard duty. Lisenbe returned the bicycle to storage and made his way to the barracks, stopping for a drink of water. He caught a flicker of motion out of the corner of his eye. Somebody was behind the coal storage shed. It wasn't likely a German spy or saboteur could get on base, and if he did, this area probably wouldn't be the focus of his attention. Nevertheless, Lisenbe altered course to investigate.

Donnie Stapleton and Mike Hilton were standing toe-to-toe. Lisenbe rounded the corner in time to see Stapleton swing and clip Hilton a glancing blow to the chin. He rushed forward.

"Hey! Stop!" Lisenbe stepped between the two. "What's going on?"

Stapleton took a step back, his fists balled.

Lisenbe swung his gaze back and forth between the two men, waiting for somebody to speak, or throw another punch.

"Aw, Hilton's just imagining things," Stapleton snarled. He spun on his heel and walked away.

Cyrus turned to Hilton, a quizzical look on his face.

Hilton stood with his hand to his chin. He sawed his jaw from side to side, checking to see if Stapleton's punch had done any damage.

"Stapleton's trying to get us all killed," Hilton said.

Mike Hilton was the left waist gunner. During a dogfight, he and Cyrus worked together, back-to-back, facing in opposite directions. There was nobody on the crew that Lisenbe trusted more than Hilton. "How's he plan to do that?" he asked.

Hilton sat down on an overturned bucket. "Stapleton's got it in for Lieutenant Hoffman. Because he's a Jew."

"Wow," Lisenbe breathed.

"I've seen him sniffing around Hoffman's compartment on the last couple of missions, like he's looking for a chance to do something. That's bad enough, but I'm afraid he may go overboard—and do something to bring the *Reba Jean* down. Kill everybody."

"Well, that's dumb. Then he'd kill himself, too."

"I don't think he'd do it on purpose. I just think he'd try something on Hoffman that would kick back on all of us."

"Like what?"

"I don't know." Hilton scratched his nose. "Something."

Lisenbe paused to think. "Does Captain Bishop know? About Stapleton, I mean."

"I think so. He was real upset after the Stuttgart mission."

"No shit. He had to ditch in the sea," Lisenbe responded. "That would shake up anybody."

"I guess so," Hilton said, "but he talked to Stapleton, and now Stapleton's walking around like an overheated boiler. I was just trying to cool him off."

"By hitting his fist with your chin?"

Hilton looked embarrassed. "My plan didn't work very well."

"Are you gonna tell him—Bishop, I mean—about Stapleton's sniffing around Hoffman's compartment on the *Reba Jean*?"

Hilton shook his head. "I don't know. He's asked me who the Jew hater on the crew was once already, and I wouldn't say anything."

Lisenbe sat on the ground beside Hilton's bucket. "Y'know, I've noticed that Stapleton has no love for Hoffman. I just didn't know how much he hated him."

"Help me keep an eye on him, will ya?" Hilton asked. "I don't want to rat him out. But I don't want him to commit murder, either, especially if I'm one of the victims."

"Will do."

Non-coms weren't considered important enough to receive an official briefing before each mission. Their job was to shoot the guns, and they didn't have to know where they were going to do that.

Most of the time, the grapevine had enough information to allow the crew members to learn their mission, but not always. Even without such information, they often had clues. F or example, a late takeoff meant they would spend less time in the air, and that usually meant France or Belgium.

On 16 September, Lisenbe guessed France because they'd been allowed to sleep later than usual. Most French targets lay northeast of Paris.

Once the *Reba Jean* left the ground and had formed up with the rest of the squadron, Lieutenant Bishop spoke over the interphone.

"Listen up, guys. Our target is Nantes. That's a port on the Loire River about thirty miles inland from the west coast of France."

"West coast? That's odd," Gary Davis said.

The non-coms were bunched in their customary huddle spot behind the forward bulkhead.

"The brass changed our orders at the last minute," Bishop continued. "French resistance fighters discovered that the *Kertosono*, a German freighter carrying U-boat parts, has had engine trouble and had to put in at Nantes for repairs. We're going to try to knock her out."

"You said she's in port, right?" Cyrus Lisenbe's voice sounded a bit stressed. "We're not going to have to hit a moving target, are we?"

"Who died and made you bombardier, Lisenbe?" Doug Cannon's voice was light. "You don't think I can hit a moving target?"

"Sure, Lieutenant. I trust you. But we're not the lead plane, so you're not the lead bombardier. Am I right?"

"You're right."

"Like I said. If you ain't the lead bombardier, I don't trust him."

Cannon had no comeback for that comment.

Bishop's voice came back over the interphone. "We're at ten angels and climbing. Begin oxygen protocol and man your posts. And make sure your flak jackets are on."

"Hey, Cap'n?" Kyle Waits spoke over the interphone. He'd gotten settled into his ball turret mechanism.

"Yeah, Waits?" Bishop responded.

"How come we have to fly so high? I mean, it's so cold, and we have to wear these freakin' oxygen masks. And it can't help with the bombing accuracy.

"When they first started making these daylight bombing runs, they ran a mission at eighteen thousand feet, thinking it would make it easier for the bombardiers to hit their targets. Problem was, it also made it easier for the German anti-aircraft gunners to hit *their* targets. Now we run at twenty-five thousand feet."

"Oh. Forget I asked."

Their P-47 escort joined them. Not long after, a squadron of German fighters swept in.

"Look at that," Mike Hilton said. "Those '109s have got yellow noses."

The crew took a few seconds to process that information. That meant JAG 51, the most feared German pilots in the sky. If the plane flying at you had a yellow nose, it was time to start praying.

Despite the P-47 fighter screen's best efforts, some of the Jerrys got through, and the *Reba Jean* gunners had to start work early.

The P-47s ran low on fuel much too soon, and when they peeled away and flew for home, the gunners of the B-17 squadron were left to fend for themselves.

Any thoughts about freezing up when the shooting started soon disappeared. Lisenbe thought the *Reba Jean* was caught in a meteor shower; the red pathways of the tracer bullets were so thick. He danced left, right, up, and down, trying to keep first one Messerschmitt then another in his sights. Then he stood, hypnotized, as he watched a German pilot put his plane in a flat skid, flying sideways, as he approached the *Reba Jean*, so that his guns kept the bomber in their trajectory longer. Bullets walked down the length of the aircraft, their impact on the hull sounding like hail on a tin roof. Once the plane was past, Lisenbe had to pat his hands over his body. He didn't see how he'd missed getting hit. "Stapleton, Waits, Davis, did you see that?" he shouted over the interphone. "Are you okay?"

"Shut up and shoot some Germans," Kyle Waits shouted back.

When the Luftwaffe fighters broke off, the Americans knew the flak was yet to come.

The American squadron pressed on through the artificial thunder of the anti-aircraft batteries. The gunners, with nothing to shoot, spread out along the fuselage and tried to make themselves small, something difficult for shrapnel to find and hit.

Things moved quickly. The squadron formed up on the lead bomber. Lisenbe peeked out through his gun window. Very little undercast. The lead bombardier should have a clear view of his target.

The bomb bay doors opened, and the noise and buffeting from the wind increased, along with the cold. Then came the deafening metallic clatter as the released bombs slid through the brackets designed to ensure even spacing as they fell. Didn't want those five hundred pound behemoths bumping into each other and setting themselves off in mid-air.

The bomb bay doors closed, and the relative quiet sounded like silence—except for Doug Cannon's cursing. His voice came over the interphone, Lisenbe knew, but Cannon's voice would've been audible above the *ack-ack* and engine noise even without help.

"He dropped too soon!" Cannon wailed. "The SOB dropped too soon!"

Lisenbe felt a sick, queasy feeling in his gut. It was bad enough to endure the frigid air, low oxygen, and attacks by German fighters and flak, but to know that it was done for naught was enough to make him want to puke.

"He dropped on the town," Cannon's voice continued over the interphone. "We killed civilians." He sounded like he wanted to puke, too.

Trouble was, this feeling was getting to be familiar. Everyone, the brass included, was getting more tired of failed missions because of inaccurate bomb drops.

Lisenbe leaned back against the curved side of the *Reba Jean*'s fuselage and closed his eyes.

He didn't want to be there.

The interphone chatter was almost non-existent during the squadron's return through the flak. This was usually when the gunners tried to psych each other up for the coming gun battle with the fighters, but nobody could muster any words of encouragement, it seemed. Lisenbe sighed and turned his attention to his gun. JAG 51s Messerschmitts and Focke-Wulffs would be back soon.

"Bogey at three o'clock," Donny Stapleton intoned. "Look lively, Lisenbe."

"I hear you," Cyrus answered, and pulled the handle that cocked his weapon. Wouldn't it be a bitch to get killed on a wasted mission?

The *Reba Jean* was on the squadron's right wing, the German's first target, and Lisenbe would be the first gunner to engage the Jerry.

A glint of sun off another plane told Lisenbe that another fighter was following along the first one's path.

Just before he pulled the trigger to fire at the lead aircraft, Lisenbe spotted the "headlights" on the wings of the trailing plane, which meant the Jerry was firing his own guns. Funny, Lisenbe thought, that guy's going to shoot his buddy in the ass.

When the tracers flew over the wings of the lead '109, that pilot broke off his attack, banking left and removing himself from the line of fire. But that trailing fighter sure had a bead on the *Reba Jean*. Lisenbe's gun had no sooner begun its chatter than a hammer hit him in his chest. He fell to the bomber floor.

At their twenty-five-thousand foot altitude, the air temperature was forty below, and Lisenbe thought he couldn't feel any colder. But through the encroaching dark of borderline unconsciousness, he felt his arms and legs turn to ice.

"Where're you hit?"

Lisenbe couldn't have been out more than a couple of seconds. Hilton crouched over him, running his hands over Cyrus' body, looking for a bullet hole. "Am I alive?" Lisenbe asked his buddy.

"So far," Hilton replied. "I don't see any blood. How do you feel?"

"Can't get my breath. Feel like a mule kicked me in the chest."

Hilton focused his search on Lisenbe's torso. "Here's a hole in your flak jacket. Still no blood."

Aaron Hoffman arrived, having left his post to investigate Lisenbe's condition. The navigator had also had some first aid training, and served as the crew's medic.

Hilton hooted with joy and held up a shiny rectangle. "You lucky son of a bitch! That bullet hit a deck of cards in your pocket!"

"What?" Lisenbe, energized, sat up. "Let me see."

Hilton handed him the deck. The crushed remains of a bullet were lodged in the center of the stack of cards.

Hoffman looked over Hilton's shoulder. "That was a thirteen millimeter shell. No way could a bunch of cards stop a bullet that big."

Lisenbe thought a bit. Hoffman was right. Except for one thing. "That fighter was way out. He was firing from long range. The bullet was almost spent when it hit me. Then the cards and my flak jacket did the rest."

Hilton was still jazzed over his buddy's close call. "You are one lucky bastard. You'll need to write that reporter, Andy Rooney. I'll bet he could write an article on it"

"Yeah." Lisenbe was beginning to realize just how lucky he was. He felt nauseated.

"Okay, guys," Hoffman broke in, "we've still got bad guys to shoot." He rose to give a report to Bishop, and to return to his post.

Hilton rose and turned toward his gun. "You gotta keep those cards. What a souvenir!"

"Yeah," Lisenbe said. He struggled to his feet.

Hilton gave him a closer look. "Let's switch guns, Cyrus. I don't think you're in any shape to guard the perimeter of this formation."

"Yeah," Lisenbe said. He paused. He barely had time to yank his oxygen mask off before he threw up.

"I don't care how shook up you are, Lisenbe," Hilton said, "you're cleaning this mess up when we get back to base."

"Yeah."

Hilton helped him get his oxygen mask back on, and Lisenbe spent the rest of the mission at the left waist gunner's post, firing in the general direction of the fighters as they harried the bombers. When the P-47s showed up, he stopped shooting altogether, not trusting himself to distinguish between good guys and bad guys.

Back at Molesworth, safely on the ground and waiting for debriefing, Lisenbe and his bullet-card deck hybrid were the focus of all the other crewmen's envy. Lisenbe allowed the souvenir to be passed around, keeping his eye on it all the while.

Major Blevins was equally impressed when he called the *Reba Jean* crew in for debriefing. "You lucky duck," he said, holding the object in his hand. "You'll be able to show these to your grandkids."

Lisenbe blushed. He noted Captain Bishop seemed uncomfortable in the major's presence.

"You debriefed the lead crew, didn't you, Major?" Doug Cannon asked. "Why'd he drop so early?"

Major Blevins pressed his lips together. "As you know," he said, looking at Cannon, "the Norden bombsight has a feature where a magnification lens can be dialed in to allow the bombardier to spot his target early."

"Yes," Cannon said.

"The lead bombardier turned this feature on to help in acquiring his target. Then he forgot to turn it off. He thought he was on top of his target when he dropped. Instead he was miles away."

Cannon put his head in his hands.

"The Norden bombsight has been proven to be a crackerjack piece of equipment," the major continued, "but we can't overcome the human error factor. The Eighth Air Corp's bombing record is an embarrassment to the Allied Forces."

Tom Hooker

116

The Bombardier's Tale

October 8, 1943
Bremen, Germany

After dinner Doug Cannon wandered into the officer's club. A month into the fall season, the weather in Southeastern England was not what he had expected. The atmosphere was gray, damp and chilly; much different from the biting, windy cold his fellow Chicagoans were already experiencing back home. He'd put his leather bomber jacket on over his waist-length uniform jacket more to keep him from getting soggy than for warmth.

Members of various other bomber crews, some B-17 guys and some B-24 guys, filled the O Club.

Two lieutenants sat across from each other, studying a chess board. Another table held a handful of men poring over poker hands. A lone man sat at a piano and picked out a tune on its ivory teeth.

The bar sported a line of men nursing a variety of non-alcoholic drinks, since tomorrow was a mission day for most. Ray Bishop was one of them, and he looked like he'd just bet his house on a hand with a pair of deuces. He'd lost weight he really couldn't afford to lose.

Cannon sidled up to him. "Evening, Cap'n. Use some company?"

Bishop studied his bombardier's face, then glanced around the room. "Let's take a walk."

"Okay," Cannon said, "but if you try to hold my hand, I'll slug you."

Bishop offered a weak smile in response.

Everybody had been disappointed about the poor outcome of the Nantes mission, but Lieutenant Bishop had taken the news hardest of all. Cannon thought he knew why. As crew captain, Bishop felt responsible for the welfare of his men. That was fine as long as Bishop focused on those things he had some measure of control over. But Cannon believed Bishop was beating himself up over the Eighth Air Force's heavy losses while delivering such shabby results.

They'd been damned lucky to have all survived the ditching of the *Bottle Rocket*. Some thought that meant they were charmed, and that nothing bad could befall them. Others believed that lucky break only increased the odds for a bad outcome in the future.

Cannon knew that Bishop could push himself over the edge if he took this too seriously. The infirmary was full of people who'd done just that.

Outside the O Club, the two men pulled their coats closer about their necks. Bishop had already gone to a woolen, calf-length overcoat. He also wore a silk scarf around his neck.

Cannon smiled. "Not like Mississippi in October, is it, Captain?" His breath misted in the crisp air.

Bishop smiled back. "In Mississippi, we'd still be in the cotton patch, wiping sweat off our brows." He glanced around. "Why don't you call me Ray when we're alone, or just with Warren and Aaron, for that matter. Just don't call me late for dinner . . . or supper, as we call it in the south."

Molesworth's northern latitude rendered more dramatic sunsets than either Yank was accustomed to. The sun plummeted toward the horizon, and the darkness pounced like a panther, rather than creeping like a sloth, particularly since they were past the autumnal equinox and the nights were growing longer. As the two walked along a gravel path near the runway, sounds of metal clanging against metal drifted from the rows of planes being serviced by the night crews.

Bishop adjusted the scarf around his neck. "Do you know why silk scarves became a popular item for pilots?"

Cannon wanted his crewmate to get to the nut of the conversation, but he understood that Bishop wasn't ready yet. "No, why?"

"In the previous world war, when airplanes were first used, pilots wore jackets with wool collars, like the one you're wearing now, because it was cold in those open cockpits. While flying a mission, the pilot had to always be on the alert, looking over first one shoulder, then the other, trying to spot any enemy aircraft flying behind him.

"The skin just below the jawline," Bishop rubbed the spot on his neck, "got rubbed raw by the rough texture of the wool. The pilots began wearing silk scarves to serve as a barrier between the wool collars and the skin. The silk caused much less friction."

"Hmmm. That's interesting."

"Besides, it's dashing, don't you think?"

Cannon raised an eyebrow. "On some people, I suppose."

Bishop smiled, accepting the jab. He took his pipe from his coat pocket and put the cold stem between his teeth, but didn't put tobacco in the bowl or try to light it. He stared into the dark night. "I'm sick of seeing us lose so many men on futile bombing raids because our lead bombardier couldn't beat a blind man."

"I don't see general's stars on your shoulders, Ray. You're trying to be responsible for stuff way above your pay grade."

Bishop stood silently staring at nothing.

"You just have to work at keeping yourself alive," Cannon continued.

"And my crew."

"Up to a point. Unless you've figured out how to shield *Reba Jean* against flak and German bullets, there's only so much you can do."

Bishop spun around and looked Cannon in the eye. "If you were lead bombardier, do you think you could hit the target?"

Doug didn't hesitate. "Damn straight! I'd love the chance."

"I'm going to the air boss and request that we be given the lead position."

"Think he'll do it?"

"I don't know. I hope so." Bishop looked at his watch. "It's too late to ask for tomorrow's mission. They'll have already set the formations and designated the lead bomb group. But I'll talk to him as soon as we get back."

They walked quietly for a few minutes, while the bombardier absorbed this piece of news.

"There's another thing," Bishop said after a short while. "It seems one of our crew hates Jews."

"Why is that . . . oh, so he's not a fan of Lieutenant Hoffman."

"Right."

"Who?"

"Stapleton, I think," Bishop answered.

"Didn't he get that sprung bomb bay door closed on the Amiens mission? Saved us from falling out of formation, and maybe a case of frostbite or two?"

"Yes, with Hilton's help." Bishop pulled the scarf tighter around his neck. "He's a good gunner, and an even better mechanic. But Aaron thinks Stapleton jettisoned his—Hoffman's—parachute on the Stuttgart mission, and that he punctured his Mae West when we ditched."

Cannon stopped, his mouth agape. "Good God! What did you do?"

"I had no proof. I talked with Major Blevins about it. He read me the riot act and told me to clean up my own mess."

No wonder Bishop is so depressed, Cannon thought.

"I had a talk with Stapleton, to try to get a read on him."

"And?"

"He denied it, of course, but he acted like a fox who'd been caught raiding the hen house. I tried to put the fear of God in him, to get him mad at me instead of Aaron. Don't know how that worked."

"How can I help?"

"Keep an eye out. Let me know if he tries something dangerous—again. Better yet, stop him and then tell me."

"Will do."

Walking back to his quarters, Cannon knew he wouldn't get much sleep that night.

The next day's mission was a return to Nantes, and a second try at the *Kertosono*. Anticipating this, the Krauts had moved the ship further upriver, and no doubt had warned their ack-ack batteries and Luftwaffe squadrons to be ready. The result was another busted mission, along with a gauntlet run of hairy resistance.

Everyone was tired. Cannon hung around the O Club, waiting for Bishop to show and give him some news. Scuttlebutt, confirmed by the air boss's aide, was that his squadron would make a run for a second consecutive day. Unusual. Evidence in Cannon's mind that the brass was pressing, trying to get results. But Cannon knew that tired crews didn't perform better.

Eventually he returned to the *Reba Jean*'s officers' barracks and learned Bishop had already gone to bed. He expected to have trouble sleeping again, but the trying day after a restless previous night rendered him unconscious almost immediately.

Cannon grabbed a seat beside Bishop at breakfast the next morning, and shot him a questioning look.

Bishop glanced around at the other officers close by. "We'll talk on the flight line," he said. He didn't look like he had any good news.

The mission briefing confirmed Cannon's intuition. They were to hit Emben, site of a ball-bearing assembly plant, and the *Sugar Daddy* was to lead the flight. The *Reba Jean* was to fly in the lower squadron, in the middle.

The crew assembled at the *Reba Jean* as she sat on her hard stand. Bishop waited until the NCOs were busy loading their gear, and Hoffman and Lowery were occupied with tasks in the B-17 cockpit and nose.

"I talked with Colonel Stephens," Bishop said to Cannon. Kermit Stephens was the wing commander, also called the Air Boss. He was responsible for the 303rd Bomb Group's flight operations.

"What did he say?"

Bishop made a face. "He gave me a song and dance about seniority and shit like that." Bishop paused, seemingly shocked that he'd said, "Shit."

"He said we weren't even lead of our own squadron," Bishop said.

Cannon waited for the pilot to continue.

"Then I asked him to put you in the lead bomber, even if it wasn't the *Reba Jean*."

A chill ran down Cannon's spine. He wanted to be lead bombardier, but leaving his crewmates would be hard. "What did he say to that?"

"He didn't want to break up an established crew."

"Did he chew you out for being so uppity?"

Bishop smiled. "No. He seemed pleased that we were going after a bigger job. I think his usual requests are for sick call."

"So, it's business as usual," Cannon observed.

"Looks that way," Bishop sighed.

The run to Emben was indeed business as usual. The outcome was deemed "Unsatisfactory."

* * * * *

"Your target this morning is Bremen," Colonel Stephens told the officers the day of the *Reba Jean's* next mission. He stood in front of a map in the briefing room, and a red string of yarn extended from Molesworth to the specified city, on the North Sea coast. "There's a sub base three miles northwest of the city center."

Stephens continued talking as aides brought in flipcharts with enlarged reconnaissance photographs of the base. "Lieutenant Blaylock's group will lead the attack."

Goose bumps popped up on Cannon's skin. The *Reba Jean* flew third position in his group. He might not be lead bombardier, but he would be near the front.

"Pilots, warn your gunners," Stephens continued, "the Luftwaffe has bolstered its fighter defense forces by pulling some Me-110s and '210s from the Russian front. Those are twin-engine fighters, so your gunners should have no trouble identifying them." He paused to take a sip of water. "Nevertheless, Captain Robbins will give you pages with silhouettes of those aircraft as you leave the briefing room. Make sure your crewmen review them before you reach the European coastline."

The morning routine ran smoothly for a change, even the balky English weather cooperated, giving them a sky filled with nothing more than a few fluffy cotton-ball clouds.

"I'd love to have weather like this over the target," Cannon said to the other officers as they loaded their gear through the nose hatch of the *Reba Jean*. "But meteorology predicts a moderate undercast."

"I won't object if they cancel," Warren Lowery said. "I just hope they wait until after we've crossed the European coastline."

If the aircraft went "feet dry" over the European mainland, they'd get credit for a mission.

"Let's not count chickens," Ray Bishop observed. "If we get our hopes up, they'll just have farther to fall. Besides, if the past is an indication, moderate undercast won't do the trick."

Things stayed routine while the aircraft took off and formed up over eastern England. They hadn't gone halfway across the Channel before Bishop came on the interphone. "*Rack'em Up* has a hot turbocharger. They're turning back. That makes us second in our group."

Doug's heart did a double-thump. He took off his earphones and clambered up through the hatch that opened between and behind the two pilots.

He looked Ray Bishop in the eye. "Is this kismet?"

"Now, don't you go wishing something bad on *Suzie Q*," he said, and paused.

"But be ready?" Cannon spoke into the pause.

"But be ready," Bishop confirmed.

The bombardier looked out the cockpit window and into the blue sky before looking back at the pilot. "Request permission to arm the bombs, sir."

"Granted."

For this run, the *Reba Jean* and her squadron mates carried a dozen, five-hundred-pound bombs each. They sat in a rack mounted above the bomb bay doors. Stacked in two columns, each column six bombs high.

The front end of each bomb looked a bit like a round-nosed bullet. Four fin blades, set at ninety degree angles to each other so they formed a cross, were mounted at the back end of the bombs. A cutout had been positioned at the intersection of the fins so that a propeller, the shaft of which extended into the bomb, could be mounted inside the protected cavity of the fins.

This was the arming device. Safety precautions, and common sense, prescribed that the bombs not be armed while being loaded into the bomb racks. You could hit the bomb's nose with a sledge hammer and nothing would happen, although nobody had volunteered to test that theory.

When the bombs were dropped, the air flowing over the casing caused the propeller to spin. After a certain number of revolutions, the arming mechanism inside the bomb would engage. After that, hit the nose, and *BOOM*!

To keep the bomb from arming too early, the propeller was held stationary by a cotter pin threaded through a small hole in the propeller shaft. Airmen and artillery men had an advantage over the infantry, in Cannon's opinion. They didn't have to see up close the carnage their work caused. But Cannon had a good imagination. He could visualize what happened when those bombs detonated at ground level. He could see the shower of shrapnel that cut through the equipment and buildings—and people—thousands of feet below.

Cannon worked his way around the bomb rack. "Morning, boys. Ready for some action?" This to Cyrus Lisenbe and Mike Hilton, the waist gunners, who had taken up their positions behind their guns.

"Ready to smoke 'em, Lieutenant. How about you?" Sergeant Hilton answered.

Cannon patted the rump end of one of the bombs. "My bullets are a little bigger than yours, but I plan to put them to good use. Just call them suppositories for Mein Fuhrer."

The boys laughed.

Cannon pulled the cotter pins on the bombs. As he was leaving to return to the bombardier compartment, he turned to the gunners. "Good luck. I'd love to see you add another swastika or two to that row under Captain Bishop's cockpit window."

Each German plane downed by a *Reba Jean* gunner got a swastika painted on the spot Cannon had indicated. Each completed mission got a silhouette of a bomb.

"Will do, sir," Lisenbe said.

Back in position inside the Plexiglas nose of the bomber, Cannon reviewed the recon photos of the target until he heard Kyle Waits sing out, "Bogeys at eight o'clock low."

He swiveled his head and tried to look back down and through the left side of his bubble canopy. What were the Germans doing hitting from behind and below?

While they were under fighter attack, Cannon functioned as the aircraft's nose gunner, so for the next while, he was busy trying to add a swastika of his own.

Cannon happened to be looking to his right, trying to get a bead on an Me-210 as it flew across the nose of the *Suzie Q*, when the lead B-17 flashed into a ball of fire. Tendrils of smoke and flames enveloped the *Reba Jean* and Cannon felt the heat of the explosion through the Plexiglas bubble.

"Good God!" Warren Lowery's voice came over the interphone. "Did you see that?"

"Scott Blaylock was piloting that plane." Bishop's voice was little more than a whisper. "He couldn't survive that. None of them could."

Hoffman leaned over Cannon's shoulder to try to get a better look. The ball of fire that was the *Suzie Q* nosed over and began an ever-steepening descent toward the Earth, twenty-seven thousand feet below.

Interphone chatter ceased as those who could see forward and to the right watched the death of ten of their squadron mates.

"What? What?" asked Gary Davis from the tail gunner's position, until the fiery *Suzie Q* passed into his field of vision. Then he said, "Oh."

"A hot tracer round must have cut a fuel line," Ray Bishop said into the otherwise quiet interphone.

A thudding began in Cannon's chest. He wondered if his "kismet" remark had somehow tipped the balance of luck against Captain Blaylock's plane and crew.

As if reading his mind, Bishop said over the interphone, "Don't get superstitious on me, Cannon. This is not your fault. I'm the one who went to Colonel Stephens. If anybody jinxed them, it was me."

Cannon couldn't trust himself to speak. He pressed his interphone mike button twice, the double-click sound it made was the non-verbal signal for acknowledgement.

Bishop continued to speak. "Okay. That makes us lead aircraft. Lieutenant Cannon, you will be the lead bombardier. Lieutenant Hoffman, let me know when we reach the IP."

"Right, Captain," Hoffman replied. "We'll reach the initial point in," he paused checking his watch and his chart, "twelve minutes."

Cannon could no longer hear Bishop's voice over the interphone, and he knew he was on the radio, advising the rest of the squadron of the *Reba Jean*'s new status. He positioned himself behind the Norden bombsight and peered through the viewfinder. The clear skies they'd encountered over the Channel had given way to a light undercast. The bright sun allowed Cannon to view a sea of white, fluffy clouds, with occasional gaps allowing a view of brown/green vegetation.

Aaron Hoffman's voice came over the interphone. "Approaching initial point. We'll reach the IP on my mark."

"Acknowledged," Bishop's voice responded. "We'll begin our bombing run on your mark."

Silence for seconds that seemed much longer.

"Mark!" Hoffman barked.

"Commencing bombing run." Bishop's tone seemed business as usual.

Cannon entered the data Hoffman, Lowery, and radio operator Nicky Hill had given him on heading: airspeed; wind speed and direction; and altitude, into the bombsight mechanism. Taking a deep breath, he leaned over and nestled his face into the sculpted eye sockets of the device. All he could see was white.

In the rough air, *Reba Jean,* jounced as if she were a Jeep traveling over a rutted road. Doug knew the skin on his brow and cheekbones would be sore, as they were after every mission, from bouncing against the eyecups of the bombsight.

He reached for the knob to switch on the magnification device for long range target acquisition. He paused, chewing his lower lip. "Hey, Aaron."

"Yeah?"

"Remind me to switch my bombsight back to normal view before we reach the drop zone."

Hoffman chuckled. "Will do."

Under magnification, Cannon discovered the undercast was not solid. He could make out some shapes. It was as if he were trying to see through a lace window curtain. It wasn't good enough.

"Standing by, Lieutenant Cannon," Bishop said.

"Don't forget to switch your view mode," Hoffman reminded him.

"Okay, thanks, Aaron." Cannon switched the bombsight view to normal. His heart pounded like a steam locomotive. This was a lot harder when everybody was relying on him. "Ready, Captain."

"Switching flight control to bombardier . . . now."

Cannon felt the slack disappear from the small joystick between the fingers of his right hand. "Bombardier has control of the aircraft."

"Acknowledged," Bishop intoned.

Cannon wondered if Bishop was really that calm, or if he was putting on a show for his crew. Then he remembered their conversation of three days ago and knew it was a show.

While peering through the viewfinder, Cannon felt for the switch to open the bomb bay doors. "Opening bomb bay." He flipped the switch. The hum of a motor carried through the *Reba Jean's* airframe, and the already frigid temperature dropped perceptibly as more air circulated inside the cabin. The wind noise and the *crump* of anti-aircraft shell explosions also increased.

Doug lifted his head long enough to visually identify the toggle switch he'd use to initiate the drop. It was still encased in the red guard that prevented it from being accidentally thrown. At the proper time, Cannon would flip the guard back and throw the switch. For now, he rested his fingers on the guard. That's where they'd stay until show time.

He returned his eyes to the viewfinder. The cross hairs had almost reached the point where the target was supposed to be, but he still couldn't see anything but white.

"Target is obscured, Captain," Cannon said.

A moment passed before Bishop's voice came back on the interphone. "Are you recommending we abort?"

"Yes, and make another pass. These clouds are spotty. We may get a clearer shot on another try."

"Very well," Bishop replied. "I'm retrieving flight control, and switching to radio, to advise the other pilots."

"Are you trying to get us killed, Lieutenant Cannon?" This came from Cyrus Lisenbe. "Another pass means two times as much flak, and twice as long for the German fighters to refuel."

"No, Sergeant," Cannon replied, "I'm trying to kill some Germans, and I have to see my target to do that with any confidence."

Bishop came back on the interphone. "No more bitchin', now. We've got a job to do, so we might as well do it right."

It took a while for the squadron to make its slow circle back to the IP. All the while, the German ack-ack batteries banged away at them. Two more B-17s faltered in flight, damaged by shrapnel, and turned for home. Everybody knew they probably wouldn't make it. Cannon wondered what living in a German POW camp would be like.

They reached the IP, and lined up for another run. Cannon re-entered the target data, and retrieved flight control from the pilot again. He re-opened the bomb bay doors, which he'd closed while the *Reba Jean* circled above Bremen.

Again his viewfinder showed only white clouds.

"Target is still obscured, Captain," Cannon said. He felt sick.

Everyone was quiet for a moment. Cannon knew Bishop was pondering the possibility of another run.

Cannon noticed the white wasn't so white anymore. "Wait! I think I'm getting a clear spot."

The gauzy white undercast thinned a bit more, and cannon saw the stubby shape of a sub tender, and surrounding it, a scattering of submarines, like goslings around a mother goose.

His viewfinder crosshairs hit the sub tender, and in one motion, Cannon pushed the red guard aside and toggled the bomb release switch. "Bombs away!" he shouted.

The *Reba Jean* lifted, relieved of her six-thousand-pound payload.

Behind him, he knew three hundred forty-four other B-17s were dropping their loads, too. Well, there'd been three hundred forty-four when the mission started. There were fewer than that number now.

Almost immediately, the cloud cover closed in. Cannon had no chance to see if his bombs hit. "Captain, you may retrieve flight control."

"Roger. Retrieving flight control. Let's go home."

Cannon leaned back, aware of sweat on his brow even as it froze in the frigid air.

"Closing bomb bay doors," he announced. He felt as if he had run a thousand miles. He still didn't know if his drop was any good, although it had felt good. And he still had to man the nose gun when the fighters came back.

Bishop spoke over the interphone, "*Cat 'o 9 Tails*, flying at the rear of our formation, had a gap in the cloud cover. Their bombardier reports a clean hit."

Cannon felt as if a weight the size of the *Reba Jean* had just been lifted from his shoulders. He'd have cried, but he didn't want Hoffman to see it.

As Cannon busied himself stowing the bombsight and getting his nose gun ready, the other crewmen came one by one, led by Ray Bishop, to clap him on the back and congratulate him. His soul felt as light as a feather.

Maybe it was his euphoria, but the German fighter resistance seemed half-hearted, and they made it to the North Sea with a minimum of further damage to the formation.

Colonel Stephens met them at their hardstands, greeting them as they lowered themselves from their nose hatch. He pulled Bishop and Cannon aside, walking between them with an arm over each one's shoulder.

"We won't know for sure until we get our recon photos processed, but the recon pilots had enough clear air to visually report significant damage. Our rating should be 'satisfactory' or better. Well done, Cannon, Ray," Stephens said, looking at Bishop. "I should've listened to you to start with. From now on, the *Reba Jean* will lead our formations."

The Tail Gunner's Tale

October 14, 1943
Schweinfurt, Again

The brass was not very talkative when it came to sharing information with the officers, and the officers were just as tight-lipped when it came to passing news along to the enlisted men. So one would think the NCO crewmen, gunners, engineers, and radio operators would have to wait a while to get the word on how things were going.

Not so.

Scuttlebutt worked faster than most telephone lines. File clerks eavesdropped on conversations between generals and colonels, even if it was only one end of a telephone conversation. Then they passed the news along to the cooks in the mess, who passed it to the ground crews and then to the bomber crews—all in a matter of minutes, it seemed.

"Aren't you on the *Reba Jean*? I heard you guys kicked some German ass at Bremen," a corporal said to Gary Davis over breakfast a few days after the Bremen raid. "Good for you."

"Thanks," Davis said. The tail gunner worried a bit about the danger of swapping grapevine garbage so freely. Who knew where a German spy might be found. Loose lips, and all that jazz. But he had to trust in the Army's security, so he didn't worry too much about saying something to someone on base. Off base was an entirely different matter, however.

"Word is, we're making progress," the corporal continued. "They say the Luftwaffe can't replace fighters as fast as we're shooting 'em down."

"I haven't noticed any difference," Davis said through a frown. This guy was clearly an office clerk. How many Messerschmitts had *he* shot down?

The corporal was on a roll. "That's what this war's been about, y'know? Our job is to replace our aircraft—and men—faster than the Krauts can shoot 'em down, while we kill German planes faster than Hitler can replace them.

"And in the Pacific? Those amphibious assaults? Same thing. The Marines' job is to put grunts on the beach faster than the Japs can kill 'em."

Davis felt bile rise in his throat.

"Nobody wearin' egg salad would admit such a thing, o'course." The corporal twirled his fork in the air as he spoke.

Davis rose and left the table, leaving his breakfast tray behind.

"Hey, What'd I say?" the corporal called after him.

The corporal was right about one thing, Davis thought, morale was up since they'd finally had a successful mission. He was sure the analysts would rate

Bremen as "satisfactory." But the scuttlebutt rated it as a number one, bulls eye.

Their next mission had been a run at the rail yards at Munster. The flak was atrocious and losses were heavy, but the *Reba Jean* had led the formation and Lieutenant Cannon had put them in the pickle barrel, yet again.

Weather moved in and the next mission was canceled. For the first time in a long time everybody griped. Now that they were on a roll, nobody wanted to give the enemy a chance to catch its breath.

Word on the scrub came early, so the crew knew they had a day off. Lisenbe tried to get up a crowd to sneak off base and into town. Sure, it was daytime, but he was sure he could get somebody to open a pub. Others started making plans for a pick-up football game—American football, that is, not the Limey game where you had to use your feet all the time, couldn't use your hands at all.

Davis was in the mood for neither of those activities. He decided to stroll around the base and enjoy a day free of oxygen masks and sub-zero temperatures.

Without planning it, he found himself out by the rows of heavy bombers, where the ground crews had forfeited some daytime sleep to apply a little more than first aid to their charges.

Davis approached the *Reba Jean* and heard Sergeant Butler, the ground crew chief, cursing a blue streak from inside the belly of the B-17.

Davis stuck his head through the crew hatch. "What's up, chief?"

Butler seemed unaware fresh ears had been there to hear his tirade. The other ground crew members continued their work, oblivious to their boss's language.

"Aah, just bitching. I need some struts welded, but Elliot, our best welder, had to go on sick call."

"Maybe I can help."

Butler seemed skeptical. "You're going to be flying in this bucket soon. Can you trust your own work?"

"Sergeant, I grew up in Coal Bluff, Indiana, a steel town. My father is a shift supervisor at a mill there. I worked as a welder, summers and after school. Molten steel is like mother's milk to me."

Butler gave him an appraising look before tapping a loose support strut with the screwdriver he held in his hand. "Re-attach that," he said. "Let me inspect it after you're done and before you do anything else." He started to turn away, then paused. "Wear goggles. You'll want to be able to see those German fighters when you shoot at them tomorrow."

"Will do." Davis clambered into the B-17's fuselage and took a closer look at the strut. He uttered a low whistle. The *Reba Jean* had to have undergone some powerful torsion stress to pop that piece of steel loose. The front half of the plane must have been trying to bank left, while the rear half had twisted to the right, like what happens when a wet towel is wrung out.

He tapped the aircraft's frame. "You are some kind of tough baby, baby," he whispered. "Aren't you?"

After donning goggles, Davis grabbed the welding wand and twisted the valve wheel to feed acetylene gas through the nozzle, sparking it into flame. He adjusted the blue-white flame until it was a small, sharp point. He fitted the loose strut back into its spot, leaving a fraction of an inch gap, and applied a tack weld to hold it in place. Taking a deep breath, he began his weld at the bottom, watching through the tinted lenses as the two metals, from the strut and from the airframe, liquefied under the torch's heat and blended together.

His father had taught him this, along with all sorts of metal-working skills. His father was as comfortable with steel as a carpenter was with wood.

"Don't be afraid, son," he'd said, "but respect the heat and what it does to the metal."

Under his father's tutelage, he'd learned to cut steel, to heal it with a weld, or to make it soft enough to bend. He could take this strut and bend it like a pretzel.

When he finished the weld, Davis extinguished the torch and inspected the joint while it cooled. The weld looked a bit like a healed scar. Using a wire brush, he scraped away loose pieces of metal chaff. "Sergeant Butler!" he called.

The ground crew chief came back and studied Davis's work before grunting with satisfaction. "Not bad." He looked down the hollow tube of the fuselage. "Make a visual inspection of all the joints in here, repair as necessary."

Davis sketched an informal salute. "Will do, Sarge."

By late afternoon, the *Reba Jean*'s skeleton was as strong, in Davis's opinion, as it had been when the bomber came out of the factory. He felt muscle-tired, but mentally refreshed. The tail gunner made his way back to the barracks for a shower.

He'd just gotten soaped up good when Donnie Stapleton came in with a towel wrapped around his narrow hips. The engineer's face was cut and bloody. That he'd been fighting was a conclusion a half-blind man could make. While Davis watched, Stapleton spat something out of his mouth.

Davis inspected the small piece of ivory lying on the floor. "Lose a tooth, did you?"

Stapleton's jaw worked as he performed a tactile inspection with his tongue. After a moment, he said, "Not my tooth." Then he removed the towel and began his shower.

Davis shook his head and returned to his own shower. Stapleton was a show-off, and Davis was sure the tooth thing had been performed for his benefit. Stapleton had definitely been in a fight, whether here on base or in town, Davis didn't know. But either that tooth really was Stapleton's, or he'd found one and put it in his mouth so he could spit it out in front of Davis. In either case, Davis didn't plan to encourage him.

He quickly rinsed off, dried off, and dressed, leaving Stapleton to keep his own company.

Having grown up in a steel town, Davis had seen guys like Stapleton all his life, guys who carried a load of anger around, looking for opportunities to unleash it on some undeserving bystander.

He remembered one boy who'd attended his school when Davis was about thirteen. The boy had tried to bully everybody and had succeeded until he put the screws on Davis. The two fought to a bloody draw. After that, the boy left Davis alone.

He'd explained his injuries to Pop, and avoided Pop's wrath by convincing him that he'd only acted in self-defense. Not long after, Pop stayed out late one night and came home with his own bloody cuts. Turned out, the boy's father had been using him for a punching bag, and Pop had given him a dose of his own medicine.

Stapleton was like that boy, and Davis wondered if he'd been worked over by his own father as a child. That seemed to be the pattern. Anger begets anger. Abuse begets abuse. Davis knew Stapleton was a Jew-baiter. And if any colored soldiers had been on base, Davis was sure Stapleton would be giving them grief, too.

They had one more day of cloudy weather, which Davis filled by helping Sergeant Butler again. Then, finally, a reasonably clear morning, and a mission. They had an early reveille, which meant a long trip, confirmed when the enlisted men got to the aircraft. Davis stuck his head up through the crew hatch. "What's this?"

One side of the bomb rack held only three half-ton bombs. The other side held a large supplemental fuel tank. The ground crew boys had been busy last night after Davis went to bed. "I don't think I'm going to like this mission," he said to himself.

Two days ago, everybody had been eager to go on another mission. Now all that enthusiasm had changed into a fearful anxiety.

Davis withdrew from the hatch to find Mike Hilton standing beside him. "I don't know about you," Hilton said, "but I'm gonna load some extra ammo and gun barrels."

"Where are we going?" Davis asked. "What about weight? If we load this baby down too much, we'll never get off the ground."

"Schweinfurt, again, and what Bishop don't know won't hurt him."

Davis's heart did a double-bump. *Schweinfurt.* "Yes it could . . . hurt him, that is—and us, too."

"Look, everybody else is doin' it."

Davis hesitated only a moment longer before getting a couple of extra ammunition boxes.

"Schweinfurt," Bishop confirmed when he and the officers arrived from the briefing. The crew had gathered under the *Reba Jean*'s nose to greet him. "Chin up, boys," Bishop continued. "We're on a roll. Let's make this our last trip to the swine fort."

Davis supposed that, for a pilot, the takeoff on a bombing run never became overly routine. But for the crew, with sixteen missions behind them, events up to reaching the European mainland were boring, at least compared to everything else.

Davis heard Bishop cursing before the wheels left the ground, and realized the pilot knew that the *Reba*

Jean was overweight. Getting airborne must have been close. Bishop didn't usually curse.

"Next time you boys add extra weight," Bishop's voice over the interphone seethed with anger, "at least let me know. Do you know what would have happened if we'd crashed while carrying all that extra fuel?"

For Davis, the mission didn't really start until he connected to his portable oxygen bottle and began his journey to the tail-gunner position. The B-17's fuselage tapered toward the tail, and Davis thought, not for the first time, that he felt like a turd making its way toward an asshole, one hanging thousands of feet above the toilet bowl of the North Sea.

His gunner's position was a bicycle seat, mounted behind twin, fifty caliber machine guns. When he was in firing position, he knelt on a couple of leather pads on the fuselage floor, with his backside on the seat, which provided some support for his spine during the hours-long, round trip to hell and back.

Davis disconnected the portable oxygen bottle and reconnected it to the aircraft's main system. He checked to make sure that both guns had full belts of ammo threaded into the firing chambers, and that the guns could swivel through their full range of motion.

He thumbed his throat mike. "Tail gunner in position."

"Roger that, Sergeant Davis," co-pilot Lowery responded.

Davis looked through the Plexiglas bubble in front of his face at a swarm of B-17s: three groups, each flying at a different altitude, yet interlocked in a tight formation that allowed the gunners of one airship to protect other planes as well as their own. As tail gunner for the lead aircraft, Davis would have to be doubly careful about his field of fire. He could hit a "friendly" just as easily as a "bogey."

He scanned the sky above and below the formation, looking for approaching enemy fighters whose first indication of presence might be the glinted reflection of sunlight off a canopy. The *Reba Jean*'s other gunners were doing the same, he knew.

While the guys in the other gunnery positions would never admit it, Gary believed the tail gunner's position was reserved for the best shooter. This was because an attack from the rear was the most damaging. When an enemy aircraft approached from behind, the relative closing speed was slowest and the enemy pilot could keep his guns bearing on his target for an incredibly long time, unless he had somebody to dissuade him from doing so.

The early B-17 models hadn't had a tail gunner position. The Germans had discovered that a Luftwaffe fighter could throttle back and hang in behind the bomber, matching the target B-17's speed, and chew the plane to pieces. By flying just above the bomber's centerline, he could place himself too high for the ball turret gunner to reach, and the top turret gunner couldn't shoot for fear of hitting the vertical stabilizer or the rear elevators. If a neighboring B-17 couldn't dislodge the German fighter, the target B-17 was dead meat. So the designers had cut a hole in the back of the plane, just under the vertical stabilizer, and stuck a bicycle seat and a pair of "fifty cals," and covered them with a canvas tarpaulin.

Davis still had a problem, though. With the design of the position, his sighting mechanism was located about a foot above his guns, which didn't seem like much, but at a couple of hundred yards, the parallax difference could cause his shot to be way off. So, when he aimed, he had to allow for that discrepancy, which was why he was the best gunner on the *Reba Jean*. It wasn't easy to aim at Point A to hit Point B. And since the *Reba Jean* was the best bomber in the 303rd Bomb Group, that made him . . . guess what? Yep. The best damn gunner on the planet.

The formation broke out of the lower overcast at about sixty-five hundred feet, but only for a moment, before plunging into an upper bank of clouds. They finally entered open air at sixteen thousand feet. Cannon opened the bomb bay doors, Stapleton detached the supplemental fuel pod from the ordnance rack, and they dropped their extra fuel tank, now depleted, at the Dutch coast.

"Here come the friendlies, nine o'clock." Mike Hilton reported over the interphone.

Since Davis was facing backwards, and six o'clock was straight ahead for him, he had to look to his right to see anything at the nine o'clock position. There they were, a couple of flights of P-38s. They fanned out on the perimeter of the formation. That was another thing that helped: The Allied fighter support wouldn't fly into the middle of the bombers. If a fighter was inside the B-17 group, it had to be German.

When the Krauts joined the party, they came in force. Either that desk jockey corporal had been misinformed or the Luftwaffe was throwing everything they had in a last ditch attempt to stop the air bombardment.

Davis busied himself with firing at just about every variety of German fighter known to him: Me-109s, '110s, '210s, FW-190s, Junkers Ju-88s, you name it. Many of them had yellow noses.

Most of his targets flew diagonally through the formation. In his position in the tail of the lead aircraft, not many came straight on from behind. Davis was sure the "tail end Charlie," the last B-17 in the formation, was not so fortunate. That plane's tail gunner was being harassed by German dogs snapping at his heels, for sure.

"Davis, over the top!" Donnie Stapleton's voice sang out.

Gary snapped his guns as straight up as possible, and pressed the triggers. As he did so, a blur flashed over the *Reba Jean's* vertical stabilizer. An ME-109. Davis smiled as debris flew from one wing.

"Winged 'im," Davis reported. "Good call, Donnie."

Some of the Jerries reeled away from the fight. *Almost out of fuel*, Davis thought. His grim relief faded when he spotted another flight of yellow-nosed planes headed in.

"Here comes more bad guys," he reported over the interphone. "The Germans are cycling their fighters. Bringing in fresh ones as the first run low on fuel."

"Tit for tat," Lisenbe added. "Here come some P-47s to relieve our P-38s."

"God bless 'em," Davis said.

"Man, I'm glad I loaded extra ammo," Hilton added.

"I knew it!" This from Bishop.

"Trust me, Cap'n," Hilton responded, "you're gonna be glad we did."

Davis continued firing at German planes as they strafed the formation, using short bursts to keep his gun barrels from overheating. While the other gunner, except for Kyle Waits, the ball turret gunner, could switch out barrels if they overheated and jammed, the awkward mounting of Davis's guns made that process slow, leaving the *Reba Jean*'s tail exposed and vulnerable while he did it.

A Ju-88 took up position above the *Hot Foot*, the B-17 flying directly behind the *Reba Jean*. "Why doesn't that top turret gunner fry that bastard?" Davis muttered aloud.

Davis sized up his own shot and realized the Ju-88 was out of range. *At least I'm out of range for him, too,* he thought.

A puff, accompanied by something that looked like a black softball appeared below the German's left wing. The softball rapidly grew larger.

"Shit! It's a rocket!" Before Davis got the words out, the missile had flown past. A miss. Thank God.

"Captain, you've got to juke around some. They're shooting rockets back here!" Davis shouted.

"Trying to make this plane juke is like trying to make an elephant dance," Bishop replied.

"Cha Cha, Lindy Hop, I don't care! Make this baby do something!"

The *Reba Jean* began a lumbering quarter-roll to the right, followed by a similar move to the left. Davis thought about the welds he'd made, and prayed they would hold.

The Junkers fired its second and last rocket— another miss. "Nicky, the *Hot Foot*'s top turret gunner must be hit. There's no firing coming from up there. Ask the other planes to try to keep the Germans from sitting on its head. Those Krauts are trying to give us a rocket enema."

"Will do," radioman Nicky Hill responded. He sounded like he was on a Sunday stroll.

The P-47s peeled away at Aachen, the German border, and the B-17s were left to go it alone.

The lead aircraft's tail gunner position gave Davis an excellent view of the air battle, as the complete formation spread out behind the *Reba Jean*. The B-17s looked like a herd of lumbering cows under attack by a flock of hawks. Many of them tried evasive maneuvers like those being performed by Captain Bishop, but Davis realized it was a crap shoot. The bombers weren't agile enough. The huge aircraft was as likely to turn into a rocket or stream of gunfire as it was to turn away from it.

Several of the bombers trailed smoke, which attracted Luftwaffe aircraft the same way blood in seawater attracted sharks.

Mesmerized by the sight before him, Davis didn't see the '109 angle in from above and take up position directly behind the *Reba Jean* until a 20mm cannon shell punched a neat hole through the Plexiglas canopy that shielded his face.

He found himself looking into the face of the German fighter pilot. Davis's fingers closed on the double triggers of his guns, and he fired without aiming. Luck was with him. Some bullets chopped away at the '109's spinning propeller; some, Davis didn't know how many, managed to pass between the propeller blades and through the pilot's windshield. It looked as if someone had splashed tomato sauce against the inside of the canopy and, just like that, the Messerschmitt rolled over and fell away.

Davis allowed himself a look over his shoulder and down the length of the fuselage. Lucky the bullet that had flown past his ear hadn't hit one of the bombs, or Hilton, or Lisenbe, or Hoffman, or — *my God* — Cannon.

"Lieutenant Cannon, are you okay?"

"Shut up. I'm plotting my bomb run," Cannon responded.

"Whew. Some Jerry bastard sent a bullet right past me and down the length of the plane."

"Hey, thanks for thinking about me," Lisenbe grumped.

"I can see you, and Hilton, too," Davis said. "Lieutenant Hoffman, you there?"

"Breathe easy, Davis. I'm okay."

Relieved, Davis turned his attention back to his field of fire.

The German fighters began to withdraw. That meant the formation was approaching the anti-aircraft batteries. Davis relaxed a bit, letting his gun barrels cool. When he was sure no German fighters would sneak in for a last strafing run, he'd change out his ammo boxes.

The flak barrage was every bit as rough as the fighter attack had been. Davis thought about going back to the bulkhead that separated the officers' stations from the non-coms in the rear, but he didn't like the idea of having that much flesh—his and his NCO crewmates'— gathered in one place. In his mind, that increased the odds of a shrapnel hit. He preferred to stay isolated and try to make himself as small as possible. Escaping injury or death from shrapnel was a question of luck, but he believed he could improve the odds if he tried.

"We've reached the IP. Beginning bomb run," Bishop's voice intoned over the interphone. Davis listened in an abstract fashion as Bishop turned the plane over to Cannon. He hugged himself a little more tightly when the opening bomb bay doors exposed his body to more of the frigid wind.

The bombs dropped, the doors closed. Cannon turned the flight controls back over to Bishop.

"Looked like a good drop, Captain," Cannon reported. Davis joined the other gunners in a ragged cheer. He imagined Waits, still locked in his ball turret, was cheering, too.

The formation turned and forged back through what Hilton called "Hitler's fart blossoms." When the flak diminished, Davis psyched himself up for another Luftwaffe assault.

"C'mon, you German dogs. I've got some lead kibble for ya."

It took a while for the Krauts to work their way past the formation perimeter. Davis watched a '110 overtake the B-17 flying in formation behind him. The fighter attacked from below, obviously unaware that the top turret was still unmanned. Ordinarily the radio operator or the co-pilot would take over the gun. The bomber must have more problems than just an injured — or dead — top turret gunner.

The bomber's ball turret gunner took a bead, and he and the German pilot fired at the same time. Smoke billowed from the B-17's number-two engine.

The '110 did a little dipsy-doodle in an effort to avoid taking a hit, but the belly gunner was good, too. Smoke poured from the Messerschmitt's engine cowling, and the fighter entered a slip turn that quickly evolved into a steep dive.

Davis thumbed his throat mic. "Confirmed kill for the *Hot Foot*'s belly gunner."

"Acknowledged." Nicky Hill, the radio operator, kept a tally of reported kills.

Davis looked back in time to see the wounded B-17's left wing fold up. The right side kept trying to fly, but with no left wing support, the *Hot Foot* quickly rolled into its own steep dive.

"One, two . . ." Davis counted aloud. No more. He thumbed his throat mic again. "The *Hot Foot* just went down. I counted two parachutes."

Now there was a gap directly behind the *Reba Jean*, and Davis knew the Krauts would try to take advantage of it before the formation could close up.

Sure enough, a Focke-Wulff 190 slid into the slot left by the *Hot Foot*. Davis didn't wait for the pilot to line up. The tail gunner cut loose with both barrels. He thought he got a piece of the Jerry, which banked and flew away.

Davis's left gun stopped firing. "Shit!" he said. He'd forgotten to change out his ammo belts.

He'd been trained to never let his ammo belt run dry, to never allow the last bullet on a belt to be fired until a new belt had been attached to the old one. Now there was no tail end of belt to which the new belt could be attached.

His right gun was okay. It was almost out, but he had a few bullets and a piece of belt still hanging from the gun. He quickly attached a new belt and fired off a burst to make sure the new belt was feeding properly.

"Kyle, watch our six. I've got to change my ammo belt," he yelled into the interphone.

"Okay," Kyle Waits responded.

This was why it was a mortal sin—emphasis on mortal—for a tail gunner to allow his ammo belt to run completely dry. Davis pulled out the now empty ammo can and shoved a full one into place. Then he released the bracket that held the bicycle seat in place and moved it out of the way. He lay on his back and slid in under the gun. Working by feel, he opened the lid on the gun's firing chamber, thankful for the leather gloves that protected his fingers from freezing to the forty-below-zero metal.

"Don't rush," he ordered himself. "Mess it up and you'll just have to do it all over again."

He pulled the ammo belt out of the canister, slotted the first bullet into the open firing chamber, and closed the lid.

"Davis, you've got company," Kyle Waits said, a thread of tension in his voice.

"Shit!" Davis slid out from under the gun and clambered to his feet. He looked out through his cracked canopy and saw a '190 lining up behind him. The pilot must have seen that the position was unmanned.

Davis squatted behind his gun, not taking time to re-attach the bicycle seat. He pulled the spring-loaded handle that cocked the newly loaded gun. Once the first bullet fired, its recoil would cock the trigger for the second bullet, and so on.

The pilot and gunner fired at the same time. Pieces of '190 flew around the fighter as Davis's guns found their mark. At the same moment, a hot poker seemed to impale his right thigh.

"Agh! I'm hit!" Davis held on to the gun, pressing both triggers, until the German fighter veered away.

He released the guns and fell back. A sticky warmth spread along his leg.

Hoffman, the *Reba Jean*'s designated medic, crawled back through the fuselage, followed by Warren Lowery.

"Where?" Hoffman asked, his brow furrowed, his brown eyes peering above his oxygen mask.

"Right leg," Davis gasped.

Hoffman grabbed Davis by the shoulders of his flak jacket and dragged him back into the wider area of fuselage just behind the waist gunners' positions. Lowery looked into Davis's eyes and clapped him on the shoulder before crawling around him to replace him as tail gunner.

After a quick look, Hoffman rolled Davis over onto his belly. He cut away a piece of flight suit to expose the back of Davis's thigh and buttock. Without further examination, Hoffman jabbed the tail gunner with an ampoule of morphine.

Within seconds, the jagged pain began to slide back. As Hoffman dusted Davis's exposed leg and buttock with sulfa powder, Davis faded into unconsciousness.

When Davis awoke, he found that Hoffman had wrapped his thigh and buttock in a thick gauze bandage. The pain was still there, throbbing, but dull. His oxygen mask was off. Lowery was gone—back to the cockpit, Davis assumed. Waits and Lisenbe knelt shoulder-to-shoulder near his head, all the room available in the narrow fuselage. Somebody else, he couldn't tell who, stood behind them. *We must be over the North Sea*, Davis thought. *The Germans have gone home.* He still lay on his belly. Hoffman knelt beside him.

"Am I gonna live?" Davis asked Hoffman.

The navigator/medic smiled. "Sure. The bullet flew past your knee, and entered the inside of your thigh. Traveled lengthwise, below your femur, and came out your right ass cheek. You're lucky it didn't cut your femoral artery."

"How do you know it didn't?"

"'Cause if it had, you'd be dead." Hoffman rubbed his nose. "If it had been a little to the left, you'd be singing soprano."

Davis swallowed hard. One of the fly-boys' greatest fears was of being castrated by a bullet or shrapnel.

"Hoo, boy! You've got a million dollar wound! You're going home!" Waits crowed. He was referring to an injury that was serious enough to warrant withdrawal from the war front, but which was not fatal.

"I'll bet General Eaker pins a Purple Heart on you," Lisenbe observed.

"No way," Mike Hilton said. He was the one standing behind Waits and Lisenbe. "I'll bet one of those pretty USO girls does it."

Davis offered a wan smile. Despite his groggy condition, he knew his buddies were trying to lift his spirits.

Lieutenant Bishop came back from the cockpit, and everybody, including Hoffman, went forward to give them some privacy.

"Every wound is serious," the pilot said, "but I'm happy yours isn't life-threatening." Bishop looked up, gazing out the tail gunner's window, Davis supposed, then back at Davis. "You did good work, Gary."

Davis felt a bit awkward having to look up from a belly-down prone position, but he knew the location of his injury prevented his lying on his back.

"I blew it, Captain," he said. "I let my gun run dry. If I hadn't that Kraut would've never got the drop on me."

Bishop shook his head a bit impatiently, "Don't beat yourself up." He gestured with his left hand, indicating his surroundings. "This is all just a crap shoot. We have very little control over our fate on these missions. All we can do is try to outlast the Germans."

Davis thought back to the words of the desk jockey. "Kill them faster than they can kill us, huh?"

"Something like that."

* * * * *

Sixty B-17s went down. Six hundred men lost: nineteen percent of those sent on the mission, plus those who died on the planes that returned, and those, like Davis, who were injured but survived. Davis was put on a stretcher balanced across the back of a Jeep. His buddies grabbed his hand, one-by-one, and wished him well, promising to visit him at the base hospital.

Davis knew how it would go. He'd get one visit from each, then they'd move on, with a new tail gunner, toward the goal of completing their twenty-five missions.

Davis would go home. I f he wasn't too gimpy after his recovery, he'd wind up as an instructor at gunnery school, with tales to tell the new recruits.

The Radio Operator's Tale

November 26, 1943
Bremen, Germany

Nicky Hill hadn't planned to eavesdrop on his pilot and copilot. It's just that he and everybody else on the crew had been so focused on helping the injured Gary Davis out of the plane and into the ambulance, offering encouragement all the while, that he'd abandoned his post without securing it.

Once the ambulance had gone, Hill returned to his compartment to get it squared away. He stored his codebook in the radio bay's safe, grabbed his logbook, which he would need during the crew's debriefing to report on the German kills that had been called in to him during the mission, and on the number of parachutes that had been spotted when a U.S. bomber had gone down. A lot of planes had gone down, and depressingly few parachutes had been recorded.

Then he sat in his chair and studied the bullet holes visible in the aircraft's hull. He tried to estimate the trajectories the bullets had taken, and how close they'd come while he'd been head down, busy sending and receiving messages and logging data. He ran his hand through his short brown hair, and, releasing a heavy sigh, descended into the *Reba Jean*'s fuselage.

Voices drifted down to him from the cockpit. Everybody else was gone except Bishop and Lowery. Hill paused, studiously quiet. Listening.

"I don't know why you're taking this so hard, Ray," Lowery's voice said. "Davis admitted that he let his ammo belt run out. Not deliberately, of course, but that's probably what led to his injury. It's not your fault."

"I know," Bishop's voice sounded tired, "but it sure feels that way."

"Did you see what happened? The Germans ate us up. We probably lost fifty planes or more. Blaylock thinks you're golden. A few weeks ago, you ditched a B-17 in the damn Channel, and we hardly suffered a scratch. Davis is the first, and only, Purple Heart casualty our crew has had. If you ask me, we're pretty damn lucky."

Bishop sighed. "That's it, I guess. I know you're right. But I keep having this heavy feeling in my chest, y'know? Like our luck is gonna run out. One day our number is gonna come up. Then what?"

Lowery was silent. He apparently had no response.

Hill heard a clicking sound that he interpreted as Bishop closing the snap on his flight satchel. The radio operator quietly snuck out the hatch in the plane's tail.

Gary Davis was the first *Reba Jean* crew member to suffer an injury serious enough to get sent home. In fact, he was the first crewman to miss a mission. Many of the guys had suffered bruises and cuts—contusions and lacerations, in medical speak—but the base infirmary just patched them up and they got back to business. The worst injury before this occurred while the *Reba Jean* had been cruising at twenty-five thousand feet. Mike Hilton had taken one of his gloves off when his gun had jammed. Touching metal at minus forty degrees is like the old stunt that kids pulled on freezing days at the school yard, daring the unsuspecting to touch their tongues to the flagpole. Mike realized his gaffe the moment his palm touched the steel. He didn't grab. When he pulled his hand away, only a small patch of skin stayed on the barrel. The guys had heard tales of others who'd done more serious damage to their hands that way.

But now, Gary was gone, and Personnel would have to assign a new tail gunner. Probably, most of the planes in the bomb group had mixed crews by now. Nicky was happy that Gary hadn't bought the farm. Davis was going home in one piece and with a beating heart.

As Lowery had said, the *Reba Jean*'s crew was lucky. He'd been off on his estimate. The Allies suffered sixty planes lost over Schweinfurt. Nobody yet knew how many of those few airmen who successfully bailed out had made it to Resistance safe houses.

In any case, things had gone so badly that, according to the grapevine, the brass decided to pull back on their missions and targets. Fewer sorties deep into Germany. Fewer missions overall—for the present.

Which meant the *Reba Jean*'s crew was due for a break. Somebody up the line decided a little R&R would fit the bill, so orders were cut for a trip to the rest home.

"Wouldn't you know it?" Donnie Stapleton whined. "The officers get sent to one place, probably a fancy resort, while us enlisted grunts get sent to another — probably a sheep farm."

The five enlisted men rode a bus, painted army green and driving on the wrong side of the road, by Nicky Hill's standards, toward their unknown "rest home" along with NCOs from several other B-17 crews.

"Stow it, Stapleton," Hill said. "I'm just happy to get a few days out of that flying cigar tube.

"Who do you think we'll get to replace Davis?" Cyrus Lisenbe asked. "Think we'll get a green recruit, fresh from the States, or a gunner who's had some missions?"

"Don't know, don't care," Stapleton responded, "just as long as he can shoot."

The guys fell silent as the bus jounced along the ancient road. Quiet little Eastern England had grown in population by thousands, and the roads and bridges showed evidence of the wear and tear they were being subjected to.

He took a deep breath. His job for the next week was to forget there was a war going on.

The bus turned into what appeared to be a narrow lane, and a few moments later stopped in front of a large, many-windowed building made of gray stone. Nicky grabbed his duffel and joined his buddies in scrambling off the bus.

A gray-haired man wearing a non-military uniform of navy blue with red piping stood at the front door.

"Welcome, one and all," he said in a stentorian voice. "This is the Braddock Manor Hotel, which you chaps have come to call 'The Rest Home.' The American Army Air Corps has leased it for the duration, and the lovely ladies of your American USO have graciously agreed to staff it."

At the mention of "ladies," the crewmen cut loose with whoops and wolf whistles.

The man gestured toward the door. "If you will follow me, we will enter the lobby, where the desk clerk will assign rooms."

As they lined up to enter the building, Hill leaned over and whispered in Stapleton's ear, "Not a sheep farm, after all."

Room assignments went as Hill expected. Lisenbe and Hilton, the waist gunners, shared a room. He and Stapleton, radioman and flight engineer, shared another. Kyle Waits would have roomed with Davis. Instead he wound up with the odd man from another crew.

Hill stayed in his room only long enough to drop his duffel and wash his face. Then he headed back to the lobby for a reconnaissance mission.

The hotel grounds were huge. He saw a bank of tennis courts, a baseball diamond, a football field— American football—and a golf course. That was on one side. The other held badminton and croquet courts, and stables for horses, along with open fields and meadows, for horseback riding or hiking, Hill presumed. *If the officers have it better than this, they must be in heaven,* he thought.

Nicky had never played golf. He stopped at the driving range, where a number of airmen, many of whom were obviously as inexperienced as Hill, practiced their swings.

One guy swung at a ball on a tee. He undercut it badly, and it flew almost straight up. All the would-be golfers paused to watch its flight. When it landed just a few feet in front of the guy who'd hit it, the backspin caused the ball to roll backwards until it stopped behind him. The red-faced sergeant smiled good-naturedly at the jibes thrown his way.

At dinner, Hill was relieved to see good old American food on the table—no bangers and mash, or shepherd's pie, no "shit on a shingle." Instead they had pot roast and fried chicken, cooked by somebody who knew his way around a kitchen.

"Nice to get away from barracks life, huh, Donnie?" Hill asked, once they were back in their room.

"Yeah."

Hill didn't care much for Stapleton, but he figured he could put up with him for a few days in the double-occupancy hotel room. Much better than the crowded barracks at Molesworth.

Stapleton left to find a card game, Hill supposed. He sat at the lone desk and wrote a short note to his girl.

My dear Charlotte,

Well, the team's getting a break this week. No games scheduled. We're getting a little change of scenery. Very nice. I think of you every day . . .

The censors wouldn't allow any details about where the airmen stayed, or what they did, just in case the letter fell into enemy hands. So he and Charlotte used a code: missions were games; activities were phrased in relation to sporting terminology. That way, she could decipher at least a little bit about what he was doing.

A German spy would certainly figure out that a game was a military action of some kind, but wouldn't know if it was an air mission, or an infantry recon patrol, or a naval engagement. Charlotte, on the other hand, who knew he was on a flight crew, could read between the lines.

Nicky paused in his writing and thought of Charlotte, seeing her walking through the rows of grapevines in her father's vineyard, her long thin dress plastered against her body by the light breeze, outlining her figure. If I survive this war, I'll marry that girl, he vowed. He left the unfinished letter on the desk, and crawled into bed to dream of California and Charlotte.

The next morning, while pretty USO girls wandered among the tables with pots of coffee and pitchers of orange juice, Nicky ate a breakfast of bacon and real eggs, as opposed to the powdered variety at Molesworth.

After breakfast, Nicky joined a few crewmates, and struck off walking across the meadows of the estate. It was strangely freeing to know you wouldn't be stopped by an airbase security fence, or MPs in a patrol jeep.

The group reached a narrow road about a mile behind the hotel, and followed along its edge. They'd just reached a stone gate when a Rolls Royce pulled up beside them. The driver looked straight ahead, not acknowledging them. The rear window rolled down.

"Are you chaps from the Braddock Hotel?" a matronly woman peered at them from the back seat. She flapped a hand at them before anyone could answer. "Of course, you are. I'm Lady Margaret Mayweather, the Dowager Countess Arundel" She gestured toward the gate. "This is Arundel Manor. Would you like a tour?"

The airmen glanced at each other for a moment before Nicky spoke. "Yes, Ma'am, that'd be nice."

"Right. Edwards will drive me up to the house. Then he will come back for you. Edwards!"

The driver vaulted from the car and opened the massive wrought iron gate. He drove the car through and stopped on the other side, while Nicky and the others stood looking confused.

Edwards climbed out of the car. "Step lively, lads," he said. "I must close the gate."

The airmen walked onto the grounds, and the driver closed the gate behind them. "Wait here. I'll be back in a trice." He jumped into the car and it disappeared down the narrow road.

"Well," said Lisenbe. "That was strange."

"Look, let's start walking," Hill said, gesturing in the direction in which the car had gone. "It'll beat standing around, waiting."

"Righto, old chap," Hilton affected a British accent. "Step lively there, lads!"

They ambled along for fifteen minutes, about a quarter of a mile, before the car re-appeared. Edwards, the driver, executed a three-point turn to get the vehicle pointed back in the direction from which it had come.

"Good thinking," Edwards commented when he stopped beside them. "Hop aboard."

The five of them piled into the car. Two had to get up front with the driver. He seemed much more relaxed, now that his employer wasn't present. "You've made M'lady's day," he said with a smile. "She just loves to show off the manor."

Hill estimated they rode another two miles before rounding a curve that revealed a massive stone building.

"It's a castle!" Kyle Waits exclaimed.

"That it is, lads. That it is," responded Edwards.

A doorman waited at the point where a walkway intersected with the driveway. He opened the Rolls' rear door. "This way gentlemen, if you please."

The airmen followed, gawking at the building and the manicured grounds. "It must take an army to maintain this place," Hill said, not realizing he'd spoken aloud.

"We don't discuss the size of Lady Margaret's staff," the doorman said. "Since all the young men are at the front, only women and elders are available. M'lady offered the use of the estate for the military. The Crown said the hotel where you chaps stay was a sufficient contribution." He paused and turned to face the men. "M'lady also has a son in the Royal Navy."

Hill scratched his chin. "Everybody has to sacrifice for this damned war."

The doorman lifted his eyebrows. "Indeed."

An intuition struck Hill. "Do you have a son in the war?"

"A grandson."

"I wish him well."

The doorman's eyes glistened. "Thank you."

Lady Margaret met them in the castle's main foyer.

Hill hadn't gotten a good look at the countess, or whatever she was, when she'd talked to them through the car window. He'd expected to see a gray-haired old woman. Instead she was middle-aged—she'd have to be to have a son in the navy—in surprisingly good shape. Her sandy brown hair stopped at her shoulders, and her face sported that pointy nose Hill had found characteristic of the Brits. Her cobalt blue eyes sparkled.

"Welcome, welcome," she said. "Simpson, take their coats, then show our guests to the library." She began to walk away.

"As you wish, madam," Simpson spoke to her retreating form.

The library lived up to its name. The large rectangular room held floor-to-ceiling bookshelves along all four walls, with an occasional bookcase that only extended about four feet high, leaving room for a few portraits, presumably of ancestors. Leather-bound books lined the shelves.

A large desk held position at what Hill took to be the head of the room. Over-stuffed leather chairs occupied the center, with a small table and reading lamp accompanying each chair.

Lady Margaret stood in the middle of the circle formed by the chairs. The airmen clustered around her.

"Please introduce yourselves," she said.

As each man stated his name, the lady questioned them briefly about where they were from and elicited a few personal details.

When his turn arrived, Hill said, "Sergeant Nicholas Hill, Sonoma, California."

About that time, Simpson arrived with a large tray that held mugs of a liquid the color of Coca-Cola.

"Ah," the lady said. "I'm told you Yanks like your alcohol, and that beer is your beverage of choice. Unfortunately, the closest we can come is lager."

Nicky thought about saying, since it was still morning, coffee might be more appropriate. Instead he grabbed one of the mugs and took a sip.

Lady Margaret was served a small cup which might have held tea, or her favorite alcoholic beverage. She turned back to Nicky. "Sergeant Hill, you're from Sonoma? Isn't that America's wine country?"

Nicky smiled and nodded. "My family owns a small vineyard there."

Lady Margaret's expression grew wistful. "With that ghastly Hitler running amok in Europe, and with the merchant shipping in the Atlantic being devoted to . . . higher priority materials, our reserves of quality wine are getting quite low."

"When the war is over, I'll send you a case of our label," said Hill.

The lady's eyes regained their sparkle. She placed a hand on Nicky's forearm. "How delightful! Did you know that in the thirteenth century," she made an all-encompassing gesture, "this region experienced a warming trend? England's climate became very similar to the wine country of France and Italy. We had vineyards here, on the estate. My husband's family did, of course. After about a century, the weather turned colder again, and our history as vintners came to an end."

Hill felt a warm glow.

Lady Margaret turned to the group. "Shall we tour the manor? You may bring your beverages with you."

For the remainder of the morning, Lady Arundel guided the Americans through the mansion, describing tapestries, regaling them, through the many portraits lining the walls, with the history of the earl's family. Hill's interest spiked briefly when the dowager countess showed them an original letter signed by Queen Elizabeth, complete with the scrawling signature at the bottom: *Elizabeth R.*

Nicky found things fascinating for about the first fifteen minutes, then he had to fight boredom. He hoped to get away at lunchtime, but Lady Arundel insisted they dine with her. Things picked up a bit as the dowager countess turned the conversation and asked the Americans to share some of their war stories. Nicky's initial nervousness eased when he realized his crewmates had the sense to be discreet about the details of their missions and the gory parts of their adventures.

"Your doorman told us you have a son in the navy," Nicky observed.

"Simpson is a footman, actually. Yes, my son commands a high speed launch in the Channel. His ship rescues airmen who've had to ditch at sea."

Hill's spine tingled. How could he ask this without violating security procedure? *Ah, what the heck.* "Does your son operate out of Beachy Head?"

"Why, yes. Yes, he does!" Lady Margaret sounded surprised.

"What is his name?"

"Nigel Mayweather."

Nicky looked at his crewmates, then back at Lady Margaret. "Our B-17 had to ditch in the Channel during our mission to . . . during one of our missions. Your son's launch rescued us. We owe him and his shipmates our lives."

Lady Margaret beamed as if she had just been crowned Queen of England. "It is such good news to meet some young men who've received aid from my son! You don't know how happy you've made me!"

After that, the event became less of a tour and more of a visit. Finally, the group ran out of things to see and things to talk about. Time to go back to the hotel.

"Edwards will drive you. I've so enjoyed our visit." Lady Margaret gushed. "If there is anything I can do for you, I'll do so happily."

"I noticed that the hotel has horses. I used to ride some back at home in Sonoma, and I haven't had a chance to go horseback riding since I joined up," Nicky said. "May I bring one of the horses over and ride on your grounds?"

"Wow!" Kyle Waits broke in, not realizing how rude he was being to the dowager countess. "You ride horses? I worked at Pimlico in Baltimore before the war. I was training to be a jockey!" (He pronounced the name of the city, "Balmer.")

"Ahem," Lady Margaret cleared her throat. It was obvious she wasn't used to being interrupted. "I'd be delighted to have you ride on our grounds—the both of you. We have our own stables, of course. Just ring the manor and Edwards will drive over and pick you up." She paused a moment, thinking. "I'll join you if my schedule permits." (She pronounced the word "schedule," without the "k" sound.)

On the way back to the hotel, Lisenbe slid back the divider between the rear seat and the driver's compartment, so they could talk. "I say, Edwards, old man," Lisenbe said to the driver, "is M'Lady married?"

"She's widowed, actually," Edwards said.

Lisenbe made a crowing sound. "Nicky, m'boy," he said. "You've got a live one on the line. Marry her and you could become the duke of . . . something."

Hill blushed. Romance was not their connection, he knew. He noticed Edwards scowling.

"Actually," the driver said, "her son holds the title, now. That's why she's known as the dowager countess."

When they arrived back at the hotel, Nicky lingered behind long enough to speak to Edwards. "I apologize for my buddy. He's just being a bit wild."

Edwards nodded curtly and drove off.

Hill smiled to himself. Hmm. Maybe Edwards had a thing for his boss.

* * * * *

Hill and Waits *did* get their horseback ride on the manor grounds, and Lady Margaret *did* accompany them. She was as effervescent as ever. There was a connection between the lady and Hill, but more parental than romantic. After all, Charlotte was at home in Sonoma, waiting, and Lady Margaret was old enough to be his mother.

The week passed much too quickly, but it was a tonic. Hill was amazed at how restful his nights were when he knew he didn't have to fly a mission the next day. The other crewmen also relaxed, pursuing other interests. Even Stapleton found his niche: The hotel had a gymnasium with boxing gloves, speed bag, heavy bag, and a sparring ring.

* * * * *

On the day of the next mission, when the bus dropped the NCOs off at the hardstand where the *Reba Jean* sat, no new tail-gunner had joined them.

"What's up?" Kyle Waits grumbled. "Are we gonna fly with our ass end exposed?"

"Who knows?" Lisenbe responded. "You know how the army works. The less us grunts know, the better."

"Well, I know they'd better give us a tail-gunner, or we won't have one when we get home — *tail* that is."

"Oh, yeah? What'ya gonna do?" Stapleton asked.

Waits, his bluff called, shut up. Everybody knew there was nothing he or any of the other crew could do, except what they were told.

The jeep carrying the *Reba Jean*'s officers pulled up, followed by an olive-green staff car flying flags from its front fenders. The flags bore a single star, signifying that it carried a brigadier general.

"Look sharp, boys," Mike Hilton spoke from the side of his mouth. "We're getting a visit from the egg salad squad."

The *Reba Jean*'s regular officer crew dismounted from the jeep, while a single officer clambered from the staff car. He wore a star on the epaulets of his leather bomber jacket. He put on his uniform hat, whose brim was adorned with the gold braid which had earned him the "egg salad squad" designation. The jeep and the staff car drove off.

"What the heck?" Hill muttered under his breath. "*Captain* Bishop?"

Hill did a double take. The double bars of a captain's insignia had replaced the single lieutenant's bar on Bishop's jacket. Doug Cannon also sported captain's bars. Hill smiled to himself. Uncle Sam had finally seen fit to reward good performance. On the other hand, Hill wondered what Lowery and Hoffman thought of the promotions.

Captain Bishop approached, and the NCOs came to attention.

"Gentlemen," Bishop said, "this is General Robert Travis." He indicated the egg salad guy. "He'll be sitting in the right-hand seat and serving as mission commander."

The sergeants saluted and the general saluted in return.

"Lieutenant Lowery," Bishop continued, "will man the tail-gunner's position today."

Reba Jean went wheels up at 0835, then orbited the airfield while the other bombers took off and formed up. Her next waypoint was the rendezvous with B-17s from other airfields.

The NCOs took up their usual position behind the bulkhead that separated "officer's country" from the rest of the plane. Lowery joined them.

"So, Lieutenant," Hill said. "How did you get the privilege of joining us grunts today?"

"General Travis saw that we'd lost our tail-gunner, and that a replacement hadn't been assigned." Lowery unwrapped a stick of gum and stuck it in his mouth. "Since the *Reba Jean* routinely leads missions now, the general decided to relegate me to fill the tail-gunner's spot and take the right seat for a ride-along." He blew a bubble and popped it.

The NCOs knew it was common for the co-pilot to man a vacant gunner's slot when a member of the brass wanted to see the war up close."

"Well," Lisenbe opined. "I guess that's okay. With all due respect, sir, just keep those Krauts off our ass."

Lowery sketched a two-finger salute. "Will do. General Travis will be relieved to know you approve, and I promise to pull my share of the load."

"Any idea where we're going?" Waits asked.

"Bremen. We're going to hit those U-boat pens again." Lowery zipped his bomber jacket up to his neck. "Uncle Sam has stepped up his shipments of troops and material to England, and he doesn't want any German subs to get in the way." He regarded his crewmates seriously. "Something big's coming down the pike, fellas."

That quieted everybody, for a few seconds, at least.

Hill slapped his hands together. "I'd better man my station. General Eaker might have issued a recall."

"You wish," Hilton called after him, as he clambered into the tiny radio room, "and so do I."

While the radio operator station was equipped with a flexible gun, allowing him to help out when his other duties permitted, gunnery was not his primary task. His job was to keep the bomber's radio operating and to monitor communications coming from Eighth Air Force Command, or from other bombers in the flight, and to keep Captain Bishop informed. While SOP—standard operating procedure—called for external radio silence, sometimes it was necessary to break that rule. When, or if, the Captain—or General Travis, in this case—wanted to broadcast a message to the other aircraft, Hill switched the Captain or General from the interphone system to the external radio. If a vacuum tube failed, Hill replaced it. If the radio suffered damage from shrapnel or a bullet, Hill repaired it, if he could.

175

"Mr. Hill," Aaron Hoffman's voice came over the interphone, "check the signal at 1430 kilohertz. I'm supposed to pick up a navigation beacon, but it doesn't seem to be coming from the prescribed vector."

"Will do, sir," Hill replied. Depending on where the mission was headed, European Resistance fighters were often asked to help by broadcasting a coded radio beacon. The navigator used this signal to triangulate the flight's position and keep the aircraft on track. In this case, the signal would be coming from a Dutch radio hidden somewhere in Holland.

Hill dialed in the requested frequency. The coded message embedded in the signal didn't match the one designated for use on today's mission, and the direction indicator showed the broadcast coming from a location which, if followed, would draw the formation off course. Hill thumbed his throat mic.

"Good catch, Mr. Hoffman. That's not our friends. Herr Kraut's trying to confuse us."

"Thanks."

Hoffman had already caught the deception, Hill knew. He just wanted confirmation.

He called Hoffman back. "The signal at 1380 kHz is drifting a bit."

"Yeah, we've got a bigger crosswind than meteorology predicted. Captain, you'd better change your heading five points farther south."

"Acknowledged," Bishop responded.

By then, the formation had reached its cruising altitude of twenty-five thousand feet. Condensation trails formed when the water vapor from the B-17's hot engine exhausts condensed in the frigid air. With six-hundred-plus bombers, the formation made its own cloud to trail behind it. *No way to conceal the flight's location*, Hill thought.

The gunners would have gone to their stations by now. As if in confirmation, Hill heard the guns chatter briefly as each crewman test-fired his weapon. Nicky wondered how Lowery was doing. "Hey, Lieutenant Lowery," he said over the interphone, "that thing in front of you? It's not a joystick. You pull the trigger, it goes rat-a-tat-tat."

Lowery chuckled. "Thanks for the heads-up."

Hill wasn't' trying to ridicule the lieutenant, it was just a subtle way of letting Lowery know he wasn't alone.

Static erupted from the external radio, then a voice, "*Yard Dog* identifies bogies at six o'clock. Look lively. They're trying to hide in our contrails."

Hill thumbed his mic to relay the message.

A new voice, gravelly, came over the interphone. Travis. "Radio, send this message over external com: Flight, you're too loose. Tighten up on the lead. No Krauts are to get in our formation."

"Roger that, General. I'll transmit right away." Hill grabbed his codebook and translated the language into code. Then he tapped the message on the Morse code key. He knew radio operators in each of the B-17s were listening, transcribing the data onto message pads, then decoding it before passing it along to their pilots. A cumbersome process, but it kept the Nazis from knowing what was being said. Certainly, Travis's message wasn't an earth-shattering piece of information, but the Krauts didn't know that.

"Okay, General. Message sent," Hill reported.

"Acknowledged," Travis replied.

Hill tried to picture the vast herd of B-17s as they inched in closer to each other, tight enough that no Messerschmitt or Focke-Wulff would be able to fly between the massive bombers. It wouldn't hold, of course. As the German onslaught progressed, the formation would drift some. A B-17 here or there would malfunction and have to drop out. But the longer the formation held, the fewer casualties the Americans would suffer at the hands of the Luftwaffe.

Even though the Germans approached from the tail, Doug Cannon got the first shot when a Me-109 completed a run over the right side of the formation, and turned around for a head-on assault. Soon, everybody manning a gun had a target.

Hill monitored the interphone, recording reports from the gunners. Lisenbe made the first one, "*Hot Potato*'s top turret got a '190," he said. "Confirmed."

"Roger that," Hill acknowledged. *Hot Potato*'s gunner wouldn't get credit for a kill unless another bomber also reported the kill. Two confirmations were required before the ground crew chief could paint a swastika under the pilot's window.

The flight transitioned from fighter attack to anti-aircraft bombardment. The heavy aircraft bounced as if on a bumpy road. Bishop turned the plane over to Cannon for the bomb run. Just after bombs away, the *Reba Jean* began to vibrate badly.

"We lost oil pressure on number two," Bishop reported. "Took a piece of shrapnel, I think."

The vibration continued. "Can't feather the prop," Bishop said. Hill could hear the tension in his voice.

Hill looked out the backward facing window of his "office." The *Reba Jean* was losing speed. He remembered what had happened when Captain Bishop had been unable to feather the prop on the *Bottle Rocket.*

"Radio," Travis' raspy voice came over the interphone, "send a message to the bomb wing, as follows: 'Lead aircraft hit. Dropping out of formation. Number two, take lead.'"

Nicky's fingers trembled as he encoded the command, then he struggled to keep the tremor under control as he rapidly pressed and released the Morse code key. It wouldn't do to garble the message, and have to repeat it. Even so, by the time it went out, everyone in the bomb wing would see that *Reba Jean* was no longer on point.

The interphone chatter died away. Everyone seemed to be calculating their odds. As before, when they flew the *Bottle Rocket* on a mission, they appeared to have the option of bailing out over Europe—Holland, in this case—or if they made it to open water, of ditching in the North Sea, or miracle of miracles, of making it to England.

Hill knew they'd been lucky to have had a rescue launch in their vicinity when they'd gone down in the *Bottle Rocket.* That had been in the Channel, near Beachy Head. This time, even if they made it out of Europe, they'd have one hundred fifty, maybe two hundred miles of open sea to cover. Ditching there would almost certainly be a death sentence. And recovery, if that occurred, would as likely come by way of the German Navy as from an Allied ship.

Hill peeked out his window again. The *Reba Jean* had lost altitude, now flying far below the formation as well as behind. She was still high enough to form a contrail exhaust. The vibration from number two continued, threatening to tear the engine loose from its wing, or the wing loose from the plane.

The Kraut fighters now focused their attacks on the *Reba Jean*, and Hill grabbed his gun and pounded away at every aeronautical blur that flew by. No Allied cover would have reached them yet. Hill forgot about his radio duties, and focused on firing his weapon, although the sounds and sensations of the gun battle seemed to come to him from a great distance. He would have loved to have visited Lady Margaret once more.

The B-17 was a big and slow aircraft. Captain Bishop had been unable to feather the number two's propeller. The vibration was bad, but the aircraft was still airworthy for the time being. If the crew chose to jump—and General Travis would make that call—they had a good chance of getting clear of the plane and under an open parachute in one piece. Once that happened, the issue of survival as a unit would evolve into the issue of survival as individuals.

Then they each ran the risk of being strafed by angry German fighter pilots. Hill had heard stories of helpless crewmen, hanging under their parachutes firing at approaching Luftwaffe planes with their .45 caliber pistols while the Germans fired back with twenty millimeter cannons.

If they managed to avoid or survive the strafing, they'd have to survive a landing in a lake, or a tree, or an open meadow. Broken legs were common. If they were still alive, they had to remember their escape and evasion training, hoping to encounter a Dutch resistance fighter who would hide them, rather than a Nazi patrol that would take them to a prisoner-of-war camp.

Hill couldn't imagine any kind of positive outcome to his situation.

A klaxon sounded. Apparently, General Travis had decided the *Reba Jean* wouldn't remain flyable much longer. The alarm was an instruction to prepare to abandon ship. Hill put on his parachute. He checked to make sure the straps were secure, then clambered through the hatch into the hollow tube of the fuselage.

Donnie Stapleton was already there. Waits's head poked through the ball turret hatch, and Hill reached down to give him a hand up. Lisenbe and Hilton detached their guns, and tossed them out the waist gun windows.

Lieutenant Lowery appeared from the tail. "Everybody check your bindings. When the Captain sounds the klaxon again, we'll jump."

"I ain't waitin'," Lisenbe said. He undogged the hatch in the aircraft's floor.

"Hold up, Cy," Hill said. "Let me check your 'chute."

Lisenbe already had his legs dangling out through the opening when the *Reba Jean* gave a sudden lurch.

The gunner was almost thrown out. Then she smoothed out, her flight as untroubled by vibration as she had been at the beginning of the mission.

"Something happened," Stapleton said, a bit of wonder in his voice.

Hill put his hand on Lisenbe's shoulder. The gunner shrugged it off.

"Wait, dammit," Hill barked. "Something happened."

Lisenbe ignored him, and leaned further.

Hill grabbed the shoulder straps of Lisenbe's parachute and hauled backward, pulling him bodily out of the hatch.

Lisenbe scrambled to his feet, looking ready to fight.

"Wait here," Lowery said to the group. "I'll go find out what happened."

The noncoms stood around looking perplexed, except for Lisenbe and Hill, who glared at each other. Hill had no plans to start a fight; he only planned to defend himself if necessary. He wasn't so sure about what Lisenbe planned to do.

Lowery came back. "Number two propeller sheared off. The one that was running wild."

"And we're still in one piece?" Waits asked. "The last time that happened, on the *Bottle Rocket*, the prop almost cut the plane in two."

"Yeah, we lucked out this time," Lowery observed. "You'd better get to your guns. Those Krauts won't like us being lucky."

"Oh, shit!" Lisenbe wailed. "We jettisoned ours!"

Lowery was already headed for the tail gun. "Well, pull out your short weapons and drown 'em in piss."

"Hey, look!" Hilton stared out the empty waist gunner's window.

Hill stepped up and looked over his shoulder. The *Chattanooga Choo Choo*, *Laredo Lasso*, and *Hoochie Koochie Mama* had dropped back and formed up on the *Reba Jean*.

While Stapleton, Waits, and Lowery headed for their posts, Hill climbed back into the radio room. When he put his headphones on, he heard General Travis yelling, "Radio! Radio! Where the hell are you?"

"Sorry, General, I'm back," Hill said.

"Give me an open channel," the General barked.

"Do you have your code book?"

"Hell, no. I'll broadcast in the clear."

"Roger," Hill flipped a switch. "Proceed."

"You three sonsabitches who've formed up on the *Reba Jean*," Travis snarled over the air, "break off and rejoin the main formation!"

Hill winced. One of the big "no-nos" was to state the name of a bomber in the clear.

"Sorry, Sir," an unidentified voice came back. Hill couldn't tell which of the three pilots had spoken. "You're breaking up. Last transmission garbled."

Hill smiled to himself. If they made it back to base, Travis wouldn't be able to identify the insubordinate pilot. He'd call them all on the carpet, of course, but this was war, and a general is not going to bust someone for trying to help a fellow soldier out of a tight spot.

Travis chose not to pursue the matter. "I'm wasting my breath," he growled. "Radio, return me to internal."

"Roger that, sir," Hill said, and complied.

Lisenbe climbed into the radio room, which was so small it was like two people trying to occupy a milk bottle.

"Give me that gun. Some Kraut's about to die of lead poisoning," Cyrus said, detaching Hill's flexible from its mount. He was gone as quickly as he'd appeared.

Hill couldn't believe the difference losing that propeller had made in the smoothness of the *Reba Jean*'s flight. *If our guardian angels can keep those Germans away, we might just make it home*, he thought.

He was right.

The Co-Pilot's Tale

December 20, 1943
Bremen, Germany

For ten days Europe had been socked in by bad weather, and the crew of the *Reba Jean* was growing antsy. Co-pilot Warren Lowery understood completely. They missed the sky. Lowery did, too. After all, he'd been born there.

Born and raised in Manitou Springs, Colorado, at the base of Pike's Peak, just west of Colorado Springs, he'd lived almost all his life a mile above sea level.

December 18th was partly sunny, although a slow-moving, low pressure system still had Europe under a cloudy, rainy ceiling, according to reports from resistance weather observers.

Lowery sat at his desk, writing a letter to his parents, trying to describe what Christmas in the ETO — European Theater of Operations — looked and felt like.

Ray Bishop stuck his head through the doorway. "Want to go up for a while? Shake off a bit of rust?"

Lowery left his swivel chair spinning in his wake.

At the hardstand, Bishop introduced a thin, hawk-faced man wearing captain's bars. "This is Dr. Paul Turpin," Bishop said. "If he spends four hours a month in the air, he gets flight pay. He wants to ride along with us."

After shaking Lowery's hand, Turpin turned back to Bishop. "You aren't going over the ocean, are you?"

Bishop smiled and shook his head, "Probably not."

They had more trouble getting the doctor settled than anticipated. Bishop tried to put him with Cannon and Hoffman in the nose, but he wouldn't go near the Plexiglas cone that encompassed their stations. The pilot then suggested that he stay back in NCO country with the gunners, but he couldn't abide sitting with enlisted men. He finally consented to sit in a jump seat in the cockpit, behind the pilots. He wouldn't need oxygen, since Bishop didn't plan to go above ten thousand feet, and he wouldn't have headphones, or an interphone connection.

After clearing a flight plan with the tower, Bishop took off, and put the *Reba Jean* in a race track loop around the airfield while the crew ran a few drills. After a while, Bishop put a hand to his headphones, as if listening to someone speak. Lowery knew that the usual interphone chatter was absent. Then Bishop turned and spoke to his passenger. "Doctor Turpin, will you take a look at Sergeant Lisenbe? He seems to be having some abdominal pain."

Turpin nodded, and crawled through the hatchway into the fuselage.

Bishop spoke into the interphone. "Okay, Lisenbe, he's coming to you first. Lieutenant Hoffman, when the doctor comes to see you in a few minutes, I want you to act very disoriented, like you don't know what you're doing, okay? Crew, play along with me on this, please."

He took off his headphones and interphone mic. Lowery followed suit.

"Lisenbe will string him along for a while," Bishop said. "Can you believe this? A guy who's afraid of flying wants to draw flight pay."

"What've you got planned?" Lowery asked.

"The grapevine says that 'Doctor Puckerbutt,' back there, who has no combat experience whatsoever, has been giving some of the crewmen on the other bombers a hard time. Claiming they're malingering when they're really struggling with combat fatigue. I promised a buddy that we'd show him what stress really feels like." He turned the steering yoke, angling the *Reba Jean* out toward the coast.

Lowery smiled. "You sneaky bastard. I didn't know you had it in you."

Bishop only smiled in response. They were quiet for a few minutes, before Lowery broke the silence. "Had a chance to talk to O'Hara yet?"

"The new tail-gunner? Yeah." Bishop scratched his nose. "He's not totally green. He came over a couple of months ago, and he's run a few missions pinch-hitting for guys on sick call. He's operated a waist gun and tail gun. Word is he can handle himself — in more ways than one. He's from South Boston."

"An Irishman from South Boston?" Lowery chuckled. "Lock up your beer."

Turpin's head came up through the hatchway between the two pilots. "Your waist gunner's okay, captain. Maybe he ate something that didn't . . ." The doctor stared out the cockpit window. "Are we over the ocean?"

Bishop looked out the window, and frowned. "I can never tell if I'm flying over the North Sea or the English Channel."

"You said we wouldn't fly over water!"

"I said we wouldn't fly over the ocean. We're not." He leaned forward, and tapped the directional compass with his fingernail. "I'm sure this is the heading my navigator gave me. Maybe you'd better go and check with him."

Turpin cast another fevered look out the window, before disappearing back down the passageway.

"Quick," Bishop hissed as he put his headphones and mic back on. "Kill the engines and feather the props."

"All of them?" Lowery said. "Captain, maybe this is going a bit too far."

"Just do it. When Turpin comes back, act catatonic. Don't respond to anything he says or does."

By the time Turpin's head reappeared, all four engine propellers sat motionless. Lowery had never been in a heavy bomber in glide mode. The only sound was the whoosh of the wind over the wings. Eerie. Bishop and Lowery sat and stared straight ahead, like statues.

"Captain, your navigator's acting wh—" Turpin's voice stopped with a squeaking sound. He stared at the right wing, then at the left, then uttered a girlish shriek. It was all Lowery could do to keep a straight face. Turpin grabbed Bishop's shoulder and shook it like a dog would shake a rabbit. "Captain! Captain!"

No response.

Turpin then shook Lowery, and added a slap, which drew a blink, but nothing else.

The doctor whimpered, and scuttled back down below.

Bishop moved. "I'm starting one and two. You start three and four."

"Roger that, and not a moment too soon," Lowery growled. "This is the stupidest act I've ever been a part of."

"Captain," Hoffman's whispered voice came over the interphone. "He's putting on a parachute."

"Over the water?" Bishop said. "Whatever you do, Hoffman, don't let him jump."

"Acknowledged, sir." Hoffman said.

While the two pilots worked to restart the engines, the sounds of Hoffman's and Cannon's struggle with Turpin rose through the passageway from below.

One by one, the engines coughed and caught, and the propellers re-engaged.

Bishop toggled his throat mic, "Tell Turpin the engines are running again."

No response.

"They're off the interphone," Lowery said.

Bishop turned and opened his mouth to shout down the passageway when the sounds of struggle abruptly ended.

Hoffman's face appeared. "He fainted, sir."

"Well, tie him up. In case he revives."

Bishop turned, and faced forward. A fine sheen of perspiration coated his face.

The two removed their headphones again.

Lowery cleared his throat. "With all due respect, Captain, that was a dumb stunt to pull. No matter what that doctor had coming."

Bishop wiped his face with his hand. "To misquote our British friend, this was not my finest hour."

The pilot turned the airship back toward base. The cockpit was quiet.

"I have to tell you, Ray," Lowery broke the silence, "some of the boys are worried about you."

"Yeah?"

"They think you're a little too intense."

Bishop didn't respond.

"We hoped that week of R&R would loosen you up a bit," Lowery continued. "But, I don't know."

Bishop exhaled a deep sigh. "I'm just worried about my boys."

"By taking them out over the North Sea on a practice exercise, and shutting off all four engines at seventy-five hundred feet?"

Bishop winced. "Like I said. Not my finest hour."

"I don't get it, Captain. Part of leadership responsibility includes concern for the welfare of your men. I get that. But you're not God. You can't shield them from everything. I grew up on my parent's cattle ranch about eighty miles south of Denver. The open range has been gone for about fifty years, now, but we still have round-ups, brandings, that kind of thing." Lowery spotted the Molesworth runway on the horizon.

Bishop adjusted the *Reba Jean's* flight path to put the airship in its race track loop around the airfield again.

"Our job was to take care of those beeves," Lowery continued, "and we took it seriously. I've been out on horseback in a blizzard, looking for a lost heifer."

"How many head of cattle did you have?" Bishop asked.

"Oh, ours was a small ranch. Only about seven hundred."

Bishop chuckled. "We — my pa and his family — had a dozen head. Milk cows. But I understand what you're saying."

Lowery's head bobbed. "Well, sometimes we lost one — to wolves, or to a wildcat, or to the cold. We understood that, too. It was just part of life."

"I remember when I was just a kid — ten, maybe . . ." Bishop looked out the cockpit window as if he was looking out at a Mississippi of fourteen years ago. ". . . We were pulling corn. I was too little to do much good, but I was out there trying, anyway. I don't know if you've harvested corn . . ."

Lowery nodded. He had.

". . . But the stalks and leaves are dry when the corn is ready for picking. They rustle when you pull the ear loose from the stalk. So I didn't hear the rattler when it went off.

"It was fat." Bishop held up his right arm. "About the thickness of my wrist, maybe four feet long."

The B-17 engines might as well have been silent again, so quiet was the cockpit.

"I saw it before I heard it. It was right under my feet." Bishop lifted his right hand, his thumb and first two fingers extended, depicting the open mouth of a rattlesnake. "When it struck, it seemed to do it real slow. I swear I could see a drop of venom hanging from one of its fangs.

"Then a blur jumped in from the side and knocked me out of the way. Pa. Screaming like an Indian. The snake latched onto his leg, just below his knee." The pilot didn't seem to realize his smooth grammar had slipped, and he sounded like that country boy he'd once been.

"Pa pulled the snake loose with his bare hand, holding it just behind the head, and he took his folding knife out of his pocket, opened it with his teeth, and cut off that snake's head."

Bishop's Adam's apple bobbed. His swallow was audible above the drone of the engines. Lowery realized his own heart was beating like a trip hammer.

"Pa near 'bout died. His leg swole up twice its size and turned black. He had a fever so hot you could have fried an egg on his forehead. Ma sent for the doctor, and then the preacher, and she began to sit a deathwatch."

Lowery leaned forward, "Captain—"

"But then he got better." Bishop ran his fingertips across his wet eyes. "He lived. His leg don't work too good anymore. But he's alive." Bishop looked Lowery in the eye. "I realized something then. He would have died for me. Pa would have died for me." He turned to look back out the cockpit window. "I realized something else, too. I realized he saw that was his job. His responsibility. If that's what it took. A history professor of mine at Ole Miss once quoted Robert E. Lee: 'Duty is the sublimest word in the English language' Pa would understand that."

"My God, Captain." Lowery breathed.

The moment was broken by movement in the hatch opening, as Nicky Hill's head poked up from below. "Are we just gonna fly laps until we run out of fuel? How come you guys don't have your headsets on?"

Colonel Kermit Stephens, the squadron's air boss, sat behind his desk and glared at Bishop and Lowery, who stood at attention before him. He held a sheaf of papers in his hand. "This is a request from one of the base doctors, a Captain Turpin, to have you certified as unfit for duty, Captain Bishop. Can you explain that?"

Bishop swallowed. "Well, sir, Captain Turpin wanted to ride along on our training flight. To get some time in for flight pay. He became—alarmed—at one of our crisis exercises, sir."

Stephens stood, and walked to the office window while Bishop spoke. Lowery wondered how many dressing downs he had conducted while staring out that window. The colonel turned back to Bishop. "Did you really shut down all four engines?"

"Well, sir, perhaps we—I—was a little too rigorous in enacting a crisis for our drill," Bishop said.

Stephens looked at Lowery. "And you let him, Lieutenant?"

It was Lowery's turn to swallow. "Yes, sir. It seemed a . . . plausible situation to reproduce."

"Did it?" Colonel Stephens didn't try to hide the skepticism in his voice.

"Yes, sir." Lowery assumed the question was for him.

"Lowery, do you think Captain Bishop is fit for duty?"

"Without question, sir."

The air boss walked back, and dropped the sheaf of papers on his desk. "If you weren't one of the best pilots in the squadron, I'd put you in the right seat for a while, or have you flying a desk."

Out of the corner of his eye, Lowery saw Bishop's shoulders relax just a bit.

"I convinced Turpin to withdraw his request before I called you in here. I still need you flying." The colonel rubbed his jaw with his fingertips. "Are the two of you familiar with Boeing's operating recommendations for the B-17 heavy bomber?"

Lowery winced. He was sure Bishop had, too. "Yes, sir," they said in unison.

"I should think so. They taught you this stuff in flight school. What are those recommendations, as they pertain to shutting down engines in flight?"

"If possible, the flight crew should never shut down more than one engine while in flight," Bishop said. Lowery said nothing. Bishop was the pilot, let him take the heat.

"But—" Bishop continued.

"Shut up!" Colonel Stephens snarled. Now his anger was showing through. The air boss looked at Lowery. "Is he right?"

"Yes, sir."

"Do each of you have a copy of your flight manual in your quarters?"

"Yes, sir." In unison again.

Stephens sighed. " All right. You want to act like air cadets, I'll treat you like air cadets. I want each of you to write an essay, separately. I don't want any of it to even smell like it has been copied. I want you to cite the section under discussion this afternoon, and I want you to explain, convincingly, why it is unwise to shut down all four engines at once. You will deliver the essay within forty-eight hours. Dismissed."

Outside the air boss's office, Lowery said, "Thanks a lot."

"How many more times do you want me to say I'm sorry?" Bishop grumped.

"I'll let you know."

Bishop went to bed early that night, complaining of a headache, while the *Reba Jean*'s remaining three officers gathered at the O club, word having come down that Europe would remain socked in for at least another day.

The three sat around a table in the back corner of the room, away from the other patrons. Up on the stage, a quartet, made up of officers from other crews, played a selection of swing music. Warren Lowery tried to relax into the music, without much success. He felt the thrum of the bass violin, as its strings were stroked by the fingers of a second lieutenant, backed by the *shoo-shoom* of brushes on a drum.

The pianist added melody to the rhythm of the other two instruments, and an alto sax delivered the notes that would have been sung by a vocalist, "Don't sit under the apple tree with anyone else but me . . ."

Lowery turned his attention back to Hoffman and Cannon, who'd just heard his account of Bishop's rattlesnake story in the *Reba Jean*'s cockpit earlier that day.

"He believes he's going to die," Lowery concluded.

Cannon snorted. "Hell, half the guys who go up every day believe that."

"That's a fact," Hoffman said. "Nobody will admit it, but some guys form clubs — what's the Chinese name? A ton-ton, or something like that. They pool their money. Last one alive gets the pot."

"Oh, really?" Lowery raised his eyebrows. "What happens if more than one guy survives?"

"They split it, I guess," Hoffman said.

"Y'know what bothers me?" Cannon asked. "If the Captain thinks he's going to buy the farm, what does that mean for us? After all, we'll be in that flying box with him."

"That's just it," Lowery said. "He thinks he's got to save us, somehow. That's my take on it, at least."

"Like a sacrificial lamb," Hoffman mused.

"Yeah," Lowery said, then took a deep breath. "Anyway, Turpin, that doctor who flew with us today, tried to certify him as unfit. That's what the meeting with the air boss was about."

"And?" Cannon asked.

"I told the Colonel I thought Captain Bishop was squared away," Lowery finished.

"Is he?" This from Hoffman.

"I don't know, but I think we have to back him."

The next day, the 19th, Molesworth's skies carried a low, dense overcast, threatening rain, but failing to deliver. The air was cool, but not cold. A group of non-coms had put together a pick-up game of baseball, ignoring the fact that December was basketball season. Lowery and Bishop walked beside the field, headed to the O club, but not to drink, as it was still morning. Plus, they didn't know yet if tomorrow would be a mission day. That's what they hoped to find out.

"I heard the USO is planning a wingding on Christmas Eve," Lowery said, to make conversation.

"I'm sure they'll do something," Bishop agreed. "But I'm betting if the brass has a viable target, some of us will be flying."

"I won't take that bet," Lowery said. The crack of a bat hitting a ball drifted from the ball diamond, followed a second later by a frantic shout.

"Heads up!"

Before Lowery could react, a baseball bounced off the crown of Bishop's head, sending his hat askew, and flew past the co-pilot's nose.

Bishop collapsed like a puppet whose strings had been cut.

"Ray?" Lowery knelt beside the captain. No response. The first of the baseball players arrived. Lowery looked at one of them. "Go get a jeep."

The guy took off at a run.

Bishop lay on his left side. He looked as if he were sleeping peacefully. Warren gently slapped his face. Still no response.

A lanky kid holding a baseball bat inched up beside Lowery. "Aw, Geez, Lieutenant. I didn't mean to hit him—the captain, I mean."

"I know, son," Lowery looked up at the green-faced kid. "If you'd been aiming at him, I'd recommend you for bombardier school."

That drew the laugh Lowery hoped for.

A jeep roared up, with the non-com Lowery had sent for it standing in the passenger seat, holding on to the windshield frame. He jumped down before the vehicle came to a stop. A half-dozen pairs of hands lifted Bishop, who'd begun to mumble a few nonsense words, into the rear seat. Lowery sat in the passenger's seat, and the jeep took off.

"Always in the right-hand seat," Lowery muttered to himself, and wondered, *Where did that thought come from?*

The captain's arrival on a non-mission day generated a moderate amount of pandemonium at the infirmary, and a pair of nurses quickly got him onto a gurney and into an examination room. The charge nurse began a perfunctory examination. By now, Bishop's eyes were open, but he was clearly out of it.

"Just sit tight," the junior nurse said briskly as she pulled a curtain around Bishop's bed. "Doctor Turpin will be with you shortly."

When Turpin saw his patient, Lowery was sure he spotted a glint in the doctor's eye.

Even though the curtain provided some privacy, the examination area's wooden floors and plaster walls seemed to magnify the sound.

"What happened?" The doctor put on a headband with a round shiny disk above and between his eyes, and picked up a small flashlight.

"He got beaned by a baseball," Lowery said.

"Hmmm." Turpin pulled one of Bishop's eyebrows up and shined the light into his eye. Lowery knew the shiny disk was to reflect more light onto the area under inspection. The nurse stood by expectantly.

"Patient is conscious. Pupils responsive." Turpin snapped his fingers, and Bishop blinked and frowned. "He does seem a bit dazed."

"What happened?" Bishop asked, seeming to confirm Turpin's assessment.

"Lie still," Turpin ordered. His fingers probed the pilot's scalp.

"Ow!" Bishop said, and winced. "Ow!" he repeated.

"Did Captain Bishop use his hands to block his fall?" Dr. Turpin asked Lowery, at the same time he grabbed Bishop's hands, and turned them palms up.

"Nope. He dropped like a rag doll."

"Thought so. Two knots. One from the baseball, and one from hitting his head on the ground."

Bishop tried to sit up, but Turpin put his hands on his shoulders, and pushed the pilot back down. He held three fingers in front of Bishop's face. "How many fingers am I holding up, Captain?"

"Uh, three?" Bishop said, with a note of uncertainty.

"He's moderately concussed," Turpin announced. He looked at Lowery. "Is he supposed to fly tomorrow?"

"We don't know yet," Lowery answered.

Turpin folded his arms across his chest. "Well, Captain Bishop won't be flying, in any case."

"Look, Captain—Doctor," Lowery stammered. "If this is about that joke we pulled yes—"

"Nurse, excuse us for a moment, please," Turpin interrupted.

She cast a disappointed look at the doctor, and stepped through the break in the curtain. Lowery was willing to bet she didn't go beyond earshot.

"Lieutenant," Turpin's stern look sent a chill down Lowery's spine, "I know you think it's funny that I'm an officer in the Air Corps, and that I'm afraid of flying. I also know you think it's unfair that I try to get some time in the air to qualify for my flight pay." He sighed. "I've got a family back home to take care of. I need that extra money. So I submit myself to your jibes and taunts and pranks. I'd love to have some retribution for that stunt yesterday. It would give me great pleasure to have been the man who hit Captain Bishop over the head, but . . ." He turned to look at Bishop, who, more alert now, looked back with a frown. ". . . Unlike some people, I'm a professional. I'm grounding Captain Bishop because he's in no condition to fly, and won't be for several days. Is that clear?"

"Yes, sir."

"I'm going to keep the captain for observation. For a day or two, at least. You may want to advise Colonel Stephens that he needs to find another pilot."

Stephens looked like a hungry man who'd just had a juicy steak taken away from him. "After I went to all that trouble to placate Turpin, Bishop managed to get himself hospitalized under Turpin's care?"

Lowery was back in the air boss's office, standing in his customary spot. "I don't think he planned it that way."

"And I suppose you want me to get him back on flight duty?"

Lowery pressed his lips together into a thin line for a moment before speaking. "That was my first thought, sir. But, he did take a hard blow to the head. Two, actually, according to the doctor. The second, when he hit the ground."

"Hmmm," Stephens walked to the window. Looking over the colonel's shoulder, Lowery saw a ray of sunlight peek through the clouds. Clearing.

Stephens turned back to Lowery, his eyebrows raised. "And you want the *Reba Jean*'s left seat."

Lowery stiffened. "Colonel, that's not —"

Stephens held his hands up, palms out and waved them as if erasing words in the air. "Scratch what I just said. I know you wouldn't misrepresent Bishop's condition. Not for any reason.

"In fact, and confidentially," Stephens paused and looked pointedly at Lowery, who nodded, "meteorology predicts clearing over the continent tomorrow, and I will need a pilot for the *Reba Jean*. You could use some left seat experience."

Lowery's heart rate ratcheted up a notch.

"I'll have to scrounge up a co-pilot for you."

"Yes, sir."

"Maybe this is a good thing for us," Doug Cannon said as he walked with Lowery and Hoffman toward the base hospital. "I mean, Captain Bishop will have some time with his feet on the ground to get over this sacrificial hero kick. And we've got Warren here to be our joystick jockey, right?"

"Right," Lowery responded. After Colonel Stephens had dismissed him, he'd gone looking for the *Reba Jean*'s other officers, to bring them up to speed on Bishop's plight, and to garner some moral support. He'd found Cannon and Hoffman poring over a chess board at Officer's Quarters. The three had then decided to go and try to cheer up their captain. They'd taken a wide detour around the baseball field, not at all sure lightning wouldn't strike twice.

Despite Colonel Stephens' assumption that Lowery wouldn't misrepresent Bishop's condition to get him grounded for a flight or two, and despite the co-pilot's sincere denial, he still wondered if he might have fallen prey to the temptation. After all, like every other co-pilot, he wanted the left-seat job.

The breeze threatened to blow Lowery's cap off his head. He had already noted that the base flag was waving like a mother who'd just spotted her long absent son. A steady wind like that would almost certainly bring clear skies by tomorrow morning.

The *Reba Jean*'s crew, except for O'Hara, had now flown twenty missions. Only five more to go. Lowery would almost certainly not get his own permanent command now, unless he agreed to extend his tour, and he didn't want to do that. He had enough experience over Germany to know just how close to the limits of endurance and survival each mission took him. Adding more missions would just shorten the odds of making it home.

". . . him yet? Warren? Are you listening?"

Lowery realized that while he'd been gathering wool, Aaron Hoffman had been speaking to him.

"Huh?"

"The new co-pilot. Have you met him?"

"No. I don't think Stephens has assigned anybody. After we talk to the captain, I'll check at ops to see what I can find out."

"Okay." Hoffman stuck his hands in his coat pockets. The weather front that brought the clearing skies also brought colder air. "I thought we could meet at the O Club tonight, and get to know each other."

"Good idea," Lowery said. "I'll see what I can do."

At the base hospital, Lowery obtained Bishop's location while Cannon enticed a couple of nurses to blush by making double entendres about his ability to put things where he aimed them.

Bishop lay in a hospital bed with enameled steel rails on each side. Since he was not afflicted with anything contagious, he was in a ward with several other officers. The room smelled of ammonia and alcohol. The captain had a cloth bandage wrapped around his head, making him look a bit like an Arab sheikh. Lowery didn't think he'd been injured badly enough to warrant a dressing like that.

Bishop waved his hand dismissively as the three approached. "I know. I know," he said. "I think the nurse was a trainee, and she got carried away. I kept lecturing her about conserving resources." He lifted his hand and gingerly touched the wrapping. "It looks worse than it is, really."

Despite Bishop's disclaimer, Lowery thought his eyelids looked a bit droopy.

"You know, Captain, in New Jersey, we generally catch our baseballs with a glove," Aaron Hoffman said with a smile.

Bishop smiled back, "I'll remember that next time."

"Did the doctor tell you about your flight status?" Lowery asked, deliberately avoiding the use of Turpin's name.

"Turpin? Yeah." Bishop frowned as he spoke. "I think he's just getting back at me for that practical joke. Warren, why don't you tell the air boss? When he learns about Turpin's grudge, I bet he'll override the order."

Lowery's shoulders sagged. "He already knows, Ray. He chewed us out about it yesterday, remember?"

"Oh . . . yeah."

Lowery, Hoffman and Cannon exchanged glances.

Bishop pushed his covers back, and made as if to get out of bed. "I'll go talk to him. He'll re-instate me. I'll let him see that I'm okay to fly."

Cannon put his hand on the captain's shoulder. "Tell me. How does your head feel right now?"

"To tell you the truth, it feels like somebody dumped a wheelbarrow full of mud into my brain."

"With all due respect, Captain," Cannon said in a firm tone, "I don't want to be in a plane being flown by somebody in your condition."

Bishop sighed and lay back. "I suppose you're right." He closed his eyes. The three officers stood silently, allowing the captain to grow accustomed to his plight.

After a moment, he opened his eyes, and looked at Lowery. "Did Colonel Stephens say what he planned to do while I'm grounded?"

"He knows this is temporary, Captain," Lowery said with a nod. "I'm to fly the *Reba Jean* in the meantime. He's going to find a co-pilot without a ride, and put him in the right seat."

Bishop nodded thoughtfully. "Good choice. Do we have a mission tomorrow?"

When Lowery hesitated, Bishop lifted his hand. "Forget I asked that."

Lowery noticed that Bishop's face looked drawn. "Look, we should get back to headquarters. See what else we can find out."

"Okay," Bishop said. "Make sure O'Hara is squared away."

"Don't worry, Captain." Lowery put a hand on Bishop's shoulder. "I'll take good care of your boys."

Things were hopping at ops as messengers rushed from Air Command to Meteorology to Intel to Logistics carrying memos and reports. The three *Reba Jean* officers dodged these couriers and made their way to the Air Command clerk.

"We got a co-pilot for the *Reba Jean* yet?" Lowery asked the master sergeant who manned the desk.

"And who are you?" The clerk was probably twice Lowery's age, with hash marks all the way down his left forearm. "Never mind, you were in here earlier. Lowery, right?" As he spoke he shuffled through a stack of papers on his desk.

Lowery considered calling him on his lack of respect for an officer. He knew the type, he was all kiss-ass and deferential to the senior officers, but had little regard for junior officers. He decided against it. As the air boss's chief clerk, he wielded a lot of power.

"Here it is." The sergeant held up a piece of paper. "Lieutenant John Manning."

"Where is he quartered? I'd like to meet him," Lowery said.

"That's him coming out of the colonel's office now."

The man indicated by the sergeant was short and squat. Bet he had to sweat—literally—to get under the maximum weight and pass the flight physical, Lowery thought.

"Lieutenant Manning?" Lowery asked as he approached.

"Yes?" The *Reba Jean*'s new co-pilot did have intelligent eyes, though.

"I'm Warren Lowery. This is Doug Cannon and Aaron Hoffman. I understand you'll be flying with us on the *Reba Jean*." He extended his hand as he spoke.

Manning's expression brightened. "Pleased to meet you." He shook hands all around.

"Want to come over to the O Club for a soda? Get to know each other?"

Manning checked his watch. "It's almost chow time. Why don't we go to the mess hall?'

"Fair enough," Lowery said.

"Chipped beef on toast," Manning said after they'd gone through the chow line. "Shit on a shingle. I thought officers were supposed to get better food."

Lowery restrained his urge to suggest that Manning should worry less about eating better and more about eating less. "Did you start out in the ranks?"

"Yeah. I joined before Pearl. I could see the writing on the wall. I had done some study in automotive engineering at Baylor, in Waco. That's where I'm from. So my drill sergeant suggested I apply for officer's training. And the rest, as they say, is history." He shoveled a fork full of food into his mouth.

Lowery perked up. "You from Texas? Ever do any ranching?"

"Ranching? Nah. I'm not much for horses. My old man has a used car lot. I love to tinker with cars. Anything with an internal combustion engine."

"With your seniority, I'd assume you'd be piloting one of these B-17s," Hoffman said.

"Took me a while to get through flight school," Manning said, oblivious to the alarmed glances his comment provoked among the other three men. "I wanted to fly single engine aircraft. Fighters. The faster the better. The brass thought I might have trouble fitting into the cockpit. Plus the aerobatics were a bitch."

"So, how did you wind up available for temporary assignment to our crew?" Cannon asked.

"I was on sick call when my aircraft, the *Buzz Saw*, got shot down. So, there I was, all by myself at the hoedown, with no dance partner, until your captain got beaned."

"You know about that?" Lowery asked.

Manning nodded. "Colonel Stephens told me."

Later, after Manning went back to his quarters and the remaining *Reba Jean* officers were walking back to Officer's Country together, Hoffman said, "I sure hope Captain Bishop recovers quickly."

At the officer's mess the next morning, Lowery didn't have to think long about why he had more than the usual number of butterflies banging around in his gut. He wondered if Captain Bishop dealt with the same anxiety on the morning of each mission. It wasn't the mission itself; Lowery had flown enough now to become acclimated to the mild case of nerves every fly-boy felt on mission day. It was the knowledge that, within the confines of the *Reba Jean*, at least, he was in command.

While the awareness of that power did give him a bit of an ego boost, it was the understanding that, also within his aircraft, his decision, whatever it might be, would be final. And for the first time, Lowery had a glimmer of comprehension about why Bishop behaved as he did.

If an engine began to smoke, Lowery would have to decide if it might ignite a leaking fuel line, and whether to shut down the engine, which might cause the *Reba Jean* to lag behind the formation, which . . . and so on.

He thought back to the day they had ditched the *Bottle Rocket*. While Bishop made the decision to ditch, everybody had a say. Lowery realized that, in all but those split-second crises, he'd be able to consult with his crew, and he trusted them.

The butterflies diminished a bit.

At briefing, Lowery sat with Manning, Cannon, and Hoffman. While the other three wondered aloud where today's orders would take them, Lowery, who knew, sat silently. But Lowery didn't know everything, as he soon discovered.

The steady murmur of voices subsided, and the officers stood when Colonel Stephens walked in and strode to the covered map at the head of the room. The aide removed the cover, and the murmur resumed as the group resumed their seats.

"Bremen, again." The phrase was repeated throughout the room.

"Hey, Colonel," one officer in the middle of the room shouted, "maybe we should establish an APO address to get our mail at Bremen. We spend so much time there."

The colonel smiled and said, "Soon." Then, he paused and surveyed the room. "Yes, Bremen again," he said. "But not the sub pens. This time, you'll each drop twenty-five hundred and twenty pounds. That's twelve bombs at two hundred ten pounds per . . ." The murmur increased over the news of the light load. ". . . Of incendiaries . . ." another pause to let another wave of muttering pass. ". . . On the city center."

Now he had an uproar.

The air boss folded his arms, and waited as the agitation worked its way through the crowd. Eventually a man Lowery recognized as the bombardier of the *Scourge of the Sky* stood, holding his hat in both hands in front of his chest. The room grew quiet. Everyone was curious about what he had to say.

"Beggin' your pardon, sir," the lieutenant said, a tremor in his voice. "I've not had a problem bombing military targets, and I knew some civilians would die, by accident, on those missions. But this sounds like we plan to burn the city, sounds like we plan to kill civilians . . . on purpose."

"Our purpose is to discourage the citizenry of the Third Reich from their support of this war. The Allies have already done some of this. We're now beginning to step up the frequency of these missions. Besides, this isn't a new idea. Just head about sixty miles that way," Stephens cocked his head southwest, "and take a look around. Ask the citizens of London how considerate Hitler was of their well-being, three years ago."

The lieutenant hesitated, as if planning to say something else. He apparently decided against it, and sat down.

Stephens unfolded his arms, clasped his hands behind his back, and began to pace across the front of the room. "I know this is a difficult task. This decision was not made lightly. The parameters of the mission come as an order—a direct order." He stopped, turned and faced the room. "You know the consequences of disobeying a direct order."

Lowery wondered if any bomb racks would mysteriously become fouled, preventing the release of the bombs from that aircraft. Personally, Lowery didn't want those oversized firecrackers in the belly of his bomber any longer than they had to be, especially with bullets and hot flak flying around. He leaned forward and glanced toward Doug.

Cannon caught his motion and returned Lowery's gaze. Cannon's face was solemn, but he winked.

A few more butterflies departed.

The officers joined the enlisted men at the hardstand under the upturned nose of the *Reba Jean*. The enlisted crew had already been informed of Captain Bishop's accident.

The six non-coms lined up and bowed, salaam-style to Lowery. "All hail, Captain Lowery," they said in unison, using the title for his command position instead of his rank.

Lowery blushed. "Shut up," he said.

"Speaking for the crew," Cyrus Lisenbe said, "we're happy you got picked to skipper the *Reba Jean* while Cap'n Bishop's on sick call."

"Thank you," Lowery acknowledged. He turned to business. "Now, this is Lieutenant Manning. He'll be our co-pilot."

Salutes all around.

While the other crew members attended to loading gear and preparing for the mission, Lowery approached the young freckle-faced noncom who seemed to have been accepted by the *Reba Jean*'s enlisted veterans. "Sergeant O'Hara, I presume," he said.

O'Hara saluted. "Cap'n."

"Let's see. Name O'Hara. From South Boston. Where's the red hair?"

O'Hara ran his hand through his sandy brown locks. When he spoke, his Rs sounded like Hs, and his O like a long A. " Like I haven't heard that before."

Lowery chuckled. "Word is you're okay with a fifty cal."

"Well," O'Hara shook a cigarette out of a cellophane pack, looked at it, and put it back. "If any Kraut comes sniffing around the *Reba Jean*'s ass, he'll discover she has quite a stinger."

Lowery nodded. "That's what I like to hear. Welcome aboard."

Manning stood near the nose hatch, struggling into an electric jumpsuit. The Air Corps had provided them as a means to help keep airmen warm at altitude, but many shunned them because the heating wires tended to break, thus defeating the suit's effectiveness. Plus, the airman had to stay plugged into the aircraft's electrical system.

Lowery was surprised to hear his co-pilot humming a Christmas carol.

Lowery grabbed the collar of Manning's jumpsuit and tugged upward to help the chubby man shrug into the tight fitting garment. "I'd almost forgotten Christmas is in five days. What's that song?"

"Hmm? Oh. 'Good King Wenceslas.' One of my favorites." Manning pulled the zipper up to his neck. "It helps to try to keep up the same routine we had back home—or close to, at least."

"Good idea." Lowery stood back to watch the co-pilot enter the *Reba Jean* through the nose hatch. An officer usually accomplished this by grabbing the sides of the hatch, and lifting his legs up through the opening. Essentially, he was upside down, or almost, when he went through.

Manning handled the job with surprising ease.

Lowery followed.

"Christmas a big deal with your family?" Warren picked up the thread of the conversation.

"Oh, yeah," Manning said. "We don't get as much snow in Waco as you do in Colorado, but we still manage."

* * * * *

Once Lowery had the *Reba Jean* airborne and in formation, he turned the controls over to Manning, and watched him for a while.

Colonel Stephens decided to move the *Reba Jean* back in the formation, since Ray Bishop wasn't the command pilot on this mission. Lowery assumed he didn't want a greenhorn to lead the bomb wing. Lowery was okay with that, although he considered making the argument that the *Reba Jean's* temporary demotion took Cannon out of the lead bombardier slot. Cannon had earned his reputation as the best in the 303rd Bomb Group. Lowery didn't raise the issue, because he was afraid Stephens might re-assign Cannon to the lead bomber, and the *Reba Jean* already had two unknowns aboard. She didn't need a third.

Manning seemed to know his stuff, so Lowery grabbed a portable O2 canister, and detached himself from the ship's oxygen and communications systems. He tapped Manning on the shoulder and said, "I'll be back."

He clambered down the narrow hatch that led from the cockpit, and went forward. Hoffman sat at his miniscule navigator's station, poring over a chart, while Cannon sat with his back curled against the arching side of the B-17s nose, reading a paperback.

Lowery pulled down his oxygen mask, and shouted, "Everything okay?'

Hoffman gave him a thumbs up.

He sat beside Cannon, "Watcha reading?"

"*Sister Carrie,*" Cannon answered.

"Dreiser?"

Cannon nodded.

"He's a Chicago boy, too, isn't he?"

Another nod.

"Look. I'm sorry you got bumped out of the lead bombardier spot. We went so long where we couldn't hit our targets. I don't want to waste this mission because you're sucking hind tit."

Cannon smiled, and shook his head. "Don't worry about it. We're dropping incendiaries on the middle of town. Accuracy won't be that big a deal."

"Good point."

They sat for a moment.

"That guy at briefing seemed upset about fire-bombing downtown Bremen," Cannon said. "Think anybody'll make problems?"

"I don't think so," Lowery said with a shake of his head. "Most everybody wants to end this war, and is willing to do what it takes to make that happen. Besides, Colonel Stephens made a good point. Just go look at downtown London."

"When Genghis Kahn was running things in Mongolia, he'd surround a town he wanted to capture. Then he'd send a message: 'You've got two days to surrender. If you don't, I'll kill every man, woman, and child.' Then he'd do it."

Lowery frowned. "I don't like being compared to Genghis Kahn."

"I'm just illustrating what you said, 'You do what you have to do.'"

"On that happy note," Lowery said, "I believe I'll go check on the kids." He struggled to his feet, and walked toward the back of the aircraft. As he approached the bulkhead that separated "Officer's Country" from the enlisted area, he saw Waits peek around the edge of the hatch. He didn't need to see the dice to know that they'd disappeared into somebody's pocket.

His question, "Who's winning?" was met with a half-dozen innocent stares. His gaze settled on O'Hara, who shook his head. "I'm not dumb," O'Hara said. "The new guy never wins on the first mission. Helps promote harmony that way."

Lowery laughed. "I'm not here to bust your chops. I just want to make sure everything's hunky-dory."

Still more innocent silence.

"Okay," Lowery sighed, "better man your stations."

The six sergeants scrambled to their feet, and headed to their various guns.

Lowery didn't really care about whether or not they gambled. It was their money, after all. But sometimes somebody lost a little too much, and then got jealous of the guy who won a little too much. Ah, well.

Manning surrendered the controls back to Lowery when the pilot returned to his seat. "Any problems?" Manning asked.

"No. Just taking the grand tour," Lowery replied.

They flew under a brilliant and clear sky, which surprised Lowery, since the weather had been so bad for the past week. The sun shone brightly, reflecting off the undulating surface of the North Sea, and making it seem like they flew over an expanse of diamonds. *The kind of sky,* Lowery thought, *where the Krauts can see the sun reflecting off our windshields from fifty miles away.*

The lead bomber made his course correction, turning from a northeasterly track to one that led due east.

Lowery thumbed his throat mic. "Won't be long now, boys. Stay ready." He didn't expect any responses, and he didn't get any. Nerves.

When the German fighters came, Manning almost broke his chair loose from its stanchion trying to follow the flights of the many FW-190s and Me-109s as they strafed the formation.

"Ease up, John," Lowery said, in a voice that sounded calmer than he felt. "The boys will keep us posted on the enemy planes' locations."

Sure enough, the gunners kept up an almost conversational chatter, punctuated by an occasional exclamation:

"'109 at four o'clock."

"Look up, Donnie. Comin' over the top."

"Shit! Give me a shave, why don't ya?"

Just about the time the formation transitioned from the fighter attacks to the anti-aircraft bombardment, O'Hara spoke from the tail gun position. "We've got one dropping back. He's trailing smoke. I don't know who it is."

"That's the *Omaha Zephyr*," Waits, the belly gunner, said.

"God, look at those Krauts go after him, the bastards," O'Hara continued.

Lowery could picture the scene. He'd encountered it before. When a sick or injured cow couldn't keep up with the herd, and fell back, wolves traveling in a pack would gang up on the unfortunate animal.

Now the *Omaha Zephyr* was surrounded by German fighters intent on bringing the B-17 down. The only upside was that the attacks on the other bombers in formation diminished while this took place.

"She just rolled over and started down," O'Hara said. "Rapid descent. I counted three parachutes."

"Only three?' Waits asked. "Damn. That means seven bought the farm."

"Now they're strafing the parachutes."

The entire aircraft went silent as they processed that piece of information, until Lisenbe said, "Maybe the guys who didn't get out are the lucky ones."

More silence.

Manning suddenly sat bolt upright for a second, uttering a surprised grunt, then began twitching in his seat.

"Settle down, Manning," Lowery complained. "My God."

Without responding, Manning jerked his oxygen mask off his face, stood as best he could in the cramped cockpit, and barged down the narrow hatch between the two seats.

"Hoffman," Lowery said over the interphone. "Manning's got a bug up his ass. Find out what his problem is,"

After a few seconds of silence, the sounds of a scuffle floated up the hatchway.

"He's trying to take off his jumpsuit, Captain," Hoffman shouted, not using the interphone. "I think he's oxygen deprived."

During training, the air cadets went through an exercise where they were taken to high altitude, then instructed to remove their oxygen masks. After a few moments, the cadets began to experience disorientation, hallucinations, and other signs of dementia. Only when the oxygen masks were restored did the cadets return to normal. Manning's behavior did sound like oxygen deprivation. Lowery grabbed Manning's mask. It looked okay. "Well, get a portable bottle on him."

"Wait," Hoffman said, then he laughed. "His jumpsuit's on fire. No wonder he wanted out of it."

Lowery cursed.

A few minutes later, a red-faced Manning returned to his seat, without his jumpsuit. "Sorry, Captain. A heating wire shorted out, and caught the fabric on fire." He uttered an embarrassed laugh. "Talk about a hot seat."

"It was all that fidgeting you were doing," Lowery grumbled.

Manning said nothing.

"Are you okay? Will you be warm enough? Without the jumpsuit?"

"Lieutenant Hoffman says I've got minor burns on my ass. The infirmary will see to that when we get back. As far as the cold, I've got long handles on under my uniform," Manning replied.

Plus all that fat, Lowery thought, but didn't say.

"Coming up on the IP." Cannon's voice came over the interphone. "Ready, Cap'n?"

"Stand by," Lowery answered, and set about readying the *Reba Jean* for her bomb run.

Lowery turned the B-17 over to Cannon, and began the longest span of seconds in any pilot's life: flying through a flak-filled minefield of air space, hands in his lap, unable to do anything but hold his breath.

"Bombs away!" Cannon sang.

The bomb load was so light, Lowery hardly felt it when the payload left the bay. He quickly retrieved control of the aircraft.

"How'd it look?" Lowery asked the bombardier.

"A-one," Cannon replied.

Lowery breathed a sigh of relief. "Looks like we may have a routine mission," he muttered to himself.

"Huh?" Manning asked.

"I just said, 'Looks like a routine mission,'" Lowery repeated.

"Don't jinx us."

They made the exit run through the flak barrage without incident, and turned onto their home leg over the North Sea. The formation had almost reached the point where the Luftwaffe attack would have to break off and return to Germany, or risk running out of fuel.

The westering sun flinted off a windshield in the distance. A diehard Kraut was going to make a last strafing run. Lowery reached for his throat mic, but Stapleton beat him to it. "Incoming bogey, one o'clock level."

An Me-109. Lowery focused on staying in formation, while watching the aircraft out of the corner of his eye. The *Reba Jean* flew just off the right wing of the lead B-17. The German pilot had a choice between the two. He chose the *Reba Jean*.

Lowery heard the yammer of the '109's 20 millimeter cannon, and the answering chatter of Cannon's and Stapleton's fifties.

A spider web spread across the *Reba Jean*'s right cockpit windscreen, and Lowery felt a fine mist cover his face above his oxygen mask.

"Wha—?" Lowery began, but stopped when he saw the red bib spreading down Manning's shirt front. "Dear God." He thumbed his throat mic. "Hoffman, Manning's been hit."

Hoffman, who served as the *Reba Jean*'s medic, since he'd had some medical training, was up in the cockpit in seconds. He took one look and said, "He's gone, Captain. Took a bullet right in his throat. Almost decapitated him."

Lowery couldn't bring himself to look. He fought to keep his stomach contents down. The *Reba Jean* had suffered her first fatality. He prayed to God it would be her last. "Okay, thanks." He spoke over the interphone. "Stapleton, Cannon, tell me you got that bastard."

"Sorry, Captain," Cannon said.

"No joy, Skipper," Stapleton replied.

"If Bishop hadn't gotten injured, that would've been me," Lowery whispered. He shivered as if his spine had turned into an icicle. He hoped Hoffman hadn't seen.

Hoffman still occupied the space between the seats. "You don't know that, Warren." He paused, thinking. "If Ray was pilot, we'd have been the lead aircraft. All sorts of things would have been different."

"I guess so." Lowery didn't sound convinced.

"Look," Hoffman pressed. "Guilt is one thing you don't need to deal with. You're not responsible for Manning's death. That Kraut is."

The '109 strafe turned out to be the German's last gasp for that mission. The Luftwaffe aircraft departed, leaving the Americans with an otherwise empty sky. Lowery flew the remainder of the mission in a daze, while Hoffman and Waits took Manning below, and put him in a body bag. Then Hoffman used a wet rag to wipe the blood spray — the mist Lowery had felt — from the acting pilot's face and uniform.

Afterwards, he left Lowery alone in the cockpit to think about what might have been.

The Flight Engineer's Tale

January 4, 1944
Kiel, Germany

"Ugh!" Donnie Stapleton woke with an involuntary grunt, and lay on his bunk in the dark, wondering what had occurred to jolt him awake.

Someone to his left snuffled and turned over, seeking a more comfortable position. Otherwise, the barracks was surprisingly quiet for a space filled with twenty-three other sleeping bodies.

The long room held a dozen double-decker bunks, six with the heads lined up against each wall, leaving an aisle down the middle of the room.

"There he is! Six o'clock!" a voice, muffled, came out of the dark from a couple of bunks down.

"I see 'im! Got 'im!" a second voice answered.

Damn stooges have got a dogfight going in their sleep, Stapleton thought. *Probably not even the same dream. Just responding to each other's words.*

"Shaddup!" a third voice snarled, followed by the whump of a thrown pillow. That seemed to draw the two sleep fighters out of their dream, and things settled down.

Only now Stapleton was awake. He lay on his back, hands behind his head, and stared up at nothing. He absently reached up to the windowsill beside his cot, and rubbed his fingers over the notches. Twenty-one. He'd flown his twenty-first mission on Christmas Eve. Only four more to go. He considered how he had gotten here.

It wasn't something he could admit to in this place, but like that Lindbergh fellow, Stapleton thought Hitler maybe had the right idea. Get rid of all the people whose skin was too dark, or whose nose and lips were too big, or whose hair was too kinky. He'd spent his childhood at his daddy's knee, learning all that was wrong with "that kind of people." Not that Daddy was all that tolerant of "his kind of people" either. Stapleton had spent his youth trying to figure out how to keep from getting a beating. Usually with no luck.

"You know why I'm doing this, boy?" Ronald Stapleton often asked his son. He'd stare at young Donnie with cold eyes, and rub the dark stubble on his chin. "You've got to learn how to stand up for yourself. I'm going to thrash you until you get big enough and mean enough to thrash me."

Then he would do it. Punching, slapping, kicking the boy until he was too tired to go on.

Donnie first tried to deal with his father's violence by the duck-and-cover strategy. He'd fall down and roll into a ball, hoping to outlast his Daddy's ire, but that only made the elder Stapleton angrier. "Stand up! Don't curl up like a baby, you coward!"

So Donnie stood up. Since he couldn't land punches with any power, he learned to slip those thrown by his father. Then to deflect most of them. But he was still too little to win, so he took out his own frustration on others who were too small and weak to fight back.

How could someone hate and love a person at the same time? All the while he suffered, he burned with a desire to please the old man. He watched, learned, and adopted his father's—and his community's—hatred of all people who were "not like us." All the while, Donnie knew the only way to gain his father's respect would be to beat him, and beat him bad.

Then the war and Donnie's eighteenth birthday came along, and he joined to get out from under his Daddy's thumb, and to be able to kill somebody. On the day he left for the induction center, he met Ronald Stapleton under an oak tree in the patch of back yard between the shack they called home and the tool shed, and he beat the older man senseless.

He'd planned to join the infantry. He'd have a gun, and be put on the front lines where he'd have his pick of targets. The Pacific seemed a good spot, where he could kill as many Japs as he had bullets. But if he drew Europe, that was okay, too—even if he *did* like the Nazis' philosophy.

While he was in boot camp, the drill sergeant's jeep broke down, and Stapleton had been dumb enough to fix it, thus revealing his knack for all things mechanical. The DS, impressed with his ability, changed his papers, sending him to the motor pool after his basic training was complete. Stapleton hadn't liked that, and began making trouble, winding up in the stockade on several occasions, and losing stripes as fast as he got them.

His sergeant called him into the motor pool office one day. It stank of oil and gasoline, but not as bad as the garage work area. "Sit down, Private Stapleton," he said.

Stapleton complied.

"I'm worried about you," the sergeant continued. "You're a good mechanic. The Army's gonna need men like you, but only if you can get a handle on that temper of yours. You're on the verge of getting yourself a dishonorable discharge. What's eating you?"

Stapleton sat silently for a few seconds, debating about whether to say anything. Finally, he decided he didn't have anything to lose. "I joined this Army to fight, not be a grease monkey."

The sergeant seemed surprised. "You want to go to the front, and get your ass shot off?"

"I want to shoot somebody else's ass off. Nips, maybe."

The non-com got up and poured two cups of coffee from the tin percolator that sat on the hot plate at the back of the office. He gave one of the cups to Stapleton, and sat back down. "You're too good a mechanic to be wasted in the infantry. That's for grunts who are too dumb to do anything else."

Stapleton had known a number of boots who had at least some college work, and were headed to the infantry. He knew better than to contradict the sarge, though. "All I know is I want to fight."

The sergeant stroked his chin. "Maybe you could go to the Air Corps."

"Will they let me shoot a gun?"

"There's a crew position called flight engineer. You go on the missions, and keep the equipment on the plane operating. According to what I've been told, you would also have a machine gun—a fifty caliber."

Stapleton sat up. "Tell me more."

The sergeant had conveniently neglected to tell him that the airplane would be flying so high that bare skin stuck to metal in a second. And shooting a machine gun at an airplane flying past at three hundred miles an hour wasn't near as satisfying as firing an M-1 rifle at a human being he could lay eyes on, but he'd made a go of it. He did have to admit that it was kind of fun.

He'd flown his twenty-first mission on Christmas Eve, a milk run just across the Channel to Vacquerette, France, Bishop's first mission back after getting beaned. The captain had looked pale and drawn. The crew, including Stapleton, had worried about going up with him.

"At least he's got Lieutenant Lowery to help him out if he needs it," Nicky Hill, the radio operator, had said. But that didn't make the creases on his brow go away.

Bishop made it okay, and Cannon made the drop in the pickle barrel. The target had been a buzz bomb missile site, and Cannon had put it on the nose, although half the bombardiers had not dropped because they couldn't see the target—not because of the weather, but because the missile site had been so well camouflaged. Stapleton had bet a few bombardiers got their asses chewed over that. After all, SOP was to drop when the lead bombardier—Cannon—dropped.

Some unlucky bastards in the 303rd had to fly a mission on Christmas, but the *Reba Jean*'s crew got the day off. The mess hall had an evergreen tree in the corner, festooned with garlands and tinsel. Crepe paper streamers stretched above the NCOs' heads. A band played holiday music, and the guys were fed a meal that was supposed to be turkey. The meat had been cut into slices, so you couldn't know for sure, except they also served drumsticks, which Stapleton thought looked suspiciously small.

Stapleton had discovered that the Army was filled with guys who loved to bash heads as much as he did, and the institution had come up with a way to let them blow off steam without causing too much collateral damage. On January third, Stapleton was scheduled to box against the best guy the ground crews could put up against him.

Stapleton would have fallen into the middleweight class. A heavier guy would never make it onto a flight crew unless he was an officer like that Manning guy, the temporary co-pilot who'd bought the farm a couple of weeks ago. The unwritten rule was that the ground crews were supposed to put up somebody of comparable weight, although Stapleton expected his opponent to be a little heavier. The ground guys would push any advantage they could get away with.

The bout was scheduled for 1400 hours, so Stapleton ate a big breakfast. He'd go light at lunch, so he wouldn't have a full gut when the match began. After lunch, he walked to the hangar where the boxing ring had been set up. He changed into his trunks in the hangar's latrine. The mat was elevated to about belt high. The corner stanchions and ropes added another three feet. There were no seats; everybody not in the ring would have to stand. A number of spectators had already arrived and were placing bets. There would be a lot more richer men, and just as many poorer in a few hours.

Charlie Williams, Stapleton's corner man and gunner on the *Hoosier Haymaker*, met him and began taping his hands. "How ya feelin', Champ?" he said. "Feelin' good? Yeah!"

"Yeah, Charlie, I'm feelin' good," Stapleton replied. He knew Williams was just blowing smoke, to psych him up, but he liked it just the same. "Who'm I up against today?"

"The ground crew guys call him Samson. I think his name's Cruz. Julio Cruz. He's supposed to be a tough guy, but I know you can handle him."

"Cruz? A wetback?" Stapleton smiled. "That's good."

Hands taped and gloves applied, Stapleton climbed into the ring and pranced around the springy surface, shadow-boxing without a shadow, loosening up his muscles. Cruz hadn't shown yet. Maybe he would default. Stapleton hoped not. That wouldn't help the odds, and Williams had put down a wad of Stapleton's own money.

By 1350, the hangar was filled with restless enlisted men, but no Samson. Stapleton looked questioningly at Williams, who shrugged. A flurry of activity cascaded forward from a side door, like a wave on a beach. A muscular man walked through the crowd. *Ah*, Stapleton thought, *he's just playing head games.*

Williams stepped up to stand beside Stapleton, and the two watched the man approach.

"He's got at least ten pounds on you," Williams said. "And maybe two extra inches in reach. Be careful."

Samson crawled through the ropes which bounded the ring. The crowd got a better look at him, and the hubbub increased. Stapleton knew the odds were swinging against him.

The combatants were introduced by a sergeant who'd been a radio announcer in his former life. The referee, who'd been in the business before the war, called the boxers together, accompanied by their corner men.

Stapleton looked into Samson's brown eyes. "I'm gonna break that big, fat face of yours." he said.

His opponent regarded him dispassionately for a second before turning to speak to his corner man. "Oh, look, the punching bag can talk," Williams' voice rumbled.

"Okay, men," the referee intervened. "We'll fight fifteen rounds of three minutes each . . ." The two boxers attempted to stare each other down while the official recited the rules. ". . . Now touch gloves, go to your corners, and, when the bell sounds, come out fighting."

Cruz extended his gloves. Stapleton brushed them, resisting the urge to strike them hard, a sure sign of insecurity. He was already berating himself for speaking first in the center ring meeting. He turned to his corner, and Williams met him and slathered his cheeks and brow with Vaseline before leaving the ring.

On one side of the ring, the timekeeper struck the bottom of an overturned bucket with a wrench, and round one began.

During the preliminaries, Stapleton had been studying his opponent, the way he held himself, the way he moved. If Stapleton had concluded that Cruz was inexperienced, he'd have jumped on him like a frog on a June bug, to use one of his Daddy's favorite phrases. But the "Spic" knew what he was doing, so Stapleton would have to spar with him for a while, and look for a weakness in his style.

Stapleton began slowly circling to his left, bouncing lightly on his toes, left glove up, ready to make a jab or to parry one. Samson did much the same, only he seemed a little more flat-footed. *Maybe I can out-maneuver him*, Stapleton thought.

He and Charlie Williams had crossed paths in gunnery school. Charlie loved boxing, but just didn't have the reflexes for it, so he'd settled for studying the sport and becoming an amateur manager. He'd spotted Stapleton killing time in the base gym, and had been amazed to discover that Stapleton had never received any instruction. He was a natural. Stapleton didn't bother to tell him that he'd learned a lot about slipping punches by avoiding those thrown by his father.

Samson threw a jab. He might move flat-footed, but his gloves were quick. Stapleton deflected the punch and adjusted his anticipation level.

Most people who were unschooled in the nuances of the "sweet science" would have found the first round boring. Probe. Feint. Advance and retreat. Neither did real damage to the other.

The off-key bucket thump that signified the end of the round sounded, and the two went to their corners and sat on stools.

"He's got slow feet," Williams said, as he mopped sweat from Stapleton's face.

"And fast hands," Stapleton countered.

"So stick and move. Make him throw punches at where you used to be."

The bell rang.

Stapleton agreed with Williams' assessment. Samson had no flaw in his glove work. If he was to be beaten, it would have to be with footwork. Stapleton resumed bouncing on the balls of his feet as he circled his foe.

"What is this, a dance?" a leather-lunged soldier at ringside called out. "Throw a punch, Flyboy!"

Samson refused to be drawn out. Stapleton feared that the wetback, with his marginally greater reach, would outpunch him if he advanced. He also knew that if the two didn't produce some action soon, they'd be dodging rotten fruit as well as punches. Time to see who could take the most punishment.

On his next bounce step, Stapleton leapt forward and threw a left jab. Cruz simultaneously counterpunched, and their gloves bounced off each other. Stapleton stayed in close, punching with both fists. Samson covered up, allowing Stapleton to waste energy pounding his opponent's arms and gloves instead of his face.

Stapleton tried to move down and throw body punches, but he couldn't get an angle. Samson's elbows were in the way. He moved back, and as he did, the Spic landed a glancing blow on Stapleton's left cheek, triggering a starburst behind his eyes and drawing a cheer from the ground crew members in the crowd.

The boxers continued to fence, landing an occasional blow, parrying many more, for the next three rounds.

Someone who had only experienced boxing by watching the movies, or even by watching a fight from ringside, wouldn't know how much a head or body blow cost its recipient. Fifteen minutes of boxing didn't seem like much, but by the end of round five, Stapleton's legs were rubber, thanks primarily to that punch Cruz had landed in the second round. And his arms seemed to weigh as much as one of the quarter-ton bombs the *Reba Jean* carried.

He dropped onto his stool, and Williams used a soaked sponge to fling water on his face. Fortunately, Stapleton's face was uncut. Unfortunately, the same held true for Cruz.

"I don't see that guy's body laying out on the canvas," Williams grumbled over the even louder grumbling of the crowd.

"You want him there, you put him there," Stapleton countered. "The sumbitch won't go down." He slugged down half a glass of water.

"I think you bruised his rib. He's dropping his left hand some."

Stapleton nodded. "I saw that. Maybe I can get a right hook over the top."

The bucket clanged, and Stapleton stood. He tried to bounce on his toes, to show Cruz he still had plenty of juice, but his legs just wouldn't cooperate.

He met the Spic in the middle of the ring and the two began a cautious shuffle around each other.

"C'mon! C'mon!" some brass-voiced GI in the crowd shouted. "Look alive, would ya?"

Stapleton feinted a left jab to the body, hoping to get Cruz to drop his guard and open himself up for a haymaker. Instead the wetback threw a right hook of his own. In the split-second before it landed, Stapleton realized Cruz's dropped left was just a bluff and Stapleton had bought it. That was the last thing Stapleton remembered.

He woke on the mat, with Williams kneeling beside him, bathing his face with the wet sponge. He must have been unconscious only long enough to get counted out, because a blurry Cruz was still prancing around the ring, both hands raised high. The hangar's smell of sweat, gasoline, and motor oil nauseated Stapleton.

"You okay?" Williams asked in a concerned voice.

"Whatta you think?" Stapleton snapped. He tried to sit up, but the ring began to spin, and he lay back down.

"Maybe you oughta go to the infirmary," Williams said. "That guy clocked you pretty good."

"No infirmary." Stapleton managed to sit up on his second try. Dimly he heard the cheers of the ground crew as they congratulated Cruz, and the curses of the airmen as they walked away.

Stapleton struggled to his feet.

Cruz came over. "Hey, good fight, man."

"Yeah, yeah. Get outta my face," Stapleton snarled.

Cruz didn't act insulted as he moved away. *Probably not the first sore loser he's met,* Stapleton thought.

There were no others to offer consolation.

Williams gave Stapleton a drink of whiskey from a tin canteen; he coughed as the burning liquid went down.

"Too strong?" Williams asked.

"It's okay."

Williams surveyed the almost deserted hangar. "Need some help getting to the barracks?"

Stapleton shook his head and winced as a wave of dizziness overtook him. "You go ahead. I'm going to rest a minute, then take a shower."

"Suit yourself," Williams said. He climbed out of the ring and sauntered out of the building.

Stapleton leaned on the top rope and watched two Williams walk away. Double vision. If he reported to sick call, the doc would probably ground him tomorrow. He didn't want that, not with only four missions to go.

The hangar had a latrine in the back. He went in and washed the sweat and Vaseline off his face and upper body. He showered, retrieved the canvas bag with his street shoes and clothes, and changed into them. He stepped into a stall and puked, then washed his face again. His head felt like a bass drum being pounded in time with his pulse. Sometimes his vision was double, sometimes just blurry.

He decided to skip evening mess. His stomach just wasn't up to food. Win or lose, boxing was tough on the body. But the knockout Cruz had delivered had really done him in. He stumbled back to his barracks and crawled into bed.

"Hey, Stapleton! Whatsa matter, you dead? Wake up!" Lisenbe shook his shoulder, making the room spin around Stapleton's bed.

Stapleton usually woke easily, but not this time; and his sleep had not been restful. He sat up, holding his head in both hands. "Awright. I'm up. Go bother somebody else."

He watched two Lisenbes head out the barracks door. Damn. Still double vision. He decided, for safety's sake, to forego shaving. On mission days, Bishop wasn't too particular about having his crew squared away.

At breakfast mess, he let the cook load his tray with reconstituted eggs, bacon, hash browns, and toast. He got a glass of fake orange juice and a cup of the black liquid everybody called coffee, giving Mike Hilton, who was an eating machine, everything but the toast, OJ, and coffee.

Hilton was also a talking machine. His voice rose above the hubbub of voices in the large room. "The brass isn't saying much, but we and the fighter jocks are making headway against the Luftwaffe, guys. Have you noticed how their fighter resistance is getting lighter with each mission? We're gaining what the HQ boys are calling 'air superiority.' "

"I hadn't noticed," Lisenbe muttered, as he sat beside Hilton.

Stapleton said nothing. He just wanted to get out of this noisy room.

"Well, we are," Hilton grumped, apparently miffed at his crewmates' lack of interest.

Lisenbe noticed the two food trays in front of Hilton. "I swear, Hilton, you must have a tapeworm. All you do is eat, and you don't gain a pound."

"It's all this nervous energy I got," Hilton responded. He pointed at Lisenbe's hash browns. "You gonna eat that?"

Stapleton rose and stumbled out of the mess, before he puked again.

The air was cold and the frosty grass crunched underfoot, but the sky was clear. Unless Europe was socked in, the mission would be a go. The non-coms wouldn't know their destination until the officers finished their briefing.

He passed the *Hoosier Haymaker* sitting on its hardstand, as he walked to the *Reba Jean*. Charlie Williams and a few of his crewmates stood nearby.

"Stapleton, how're you feeling?" Williams asked.

Stapleton forced himself to smile. "What round is it? I keep hearing a bell, but I can't find the ring."

Williams laughed, thinking Stapleton was kidding. The *Reba Jean*'s engineer walked on, head still pounding.

Stapleton eventually reached his aircraft. The other non-coms had ridden a bus, and were already there. The officers arrived by jeep a few minutes later.

Bishop assembled the crew. "Our mission is the sub pens at Kiel, Germany. Almost all of our trip will be over the North Sea, so we shouldn't hit anti-aircraft resistance until we reach our target.

"The Luftwaffe will be there, so I'll need you to look sharp," Bishop smiled, "as you always do. For your information, the bomb group is going to be led by a couple of B-17s equipped with the new Pathfinder radar navigation system. But Lieutenant Cannon will still direct the bomb drop."

The crew cheered, which caused Stapleton to wince, but no one noticed. He considered gigging Hoffman about just going along for the ride this time, but he didn't feel like stirring anything up.

"Okay, guys. Let's load up," Bishop concluded.

You might think, Stapleton mused, that in January, with ground temperatures at winter levels, the temps at altitude would be comparatively colder. Not so. Not that it made any difference. At twenty-five thousand feet, forty below was forty below.

The *Reba Jean* took off from RAF Molesworth and slipped into routine formation with no problems. The non-coms, except for Hill and Stapleton, had little to do, so they huddled in their usual spot behind the bulkhead that separated the bomb bay and gunners' stations from "officer's country." Hill was tucked away in the radio shack, monitoring broadcast communications.

Stapleton hung around with the other non-coms, waiting for his head and stomach to settle down before he started his inspection.

Waits passed around a new picture of his pregnant wife, crowing about how wonderful it would be to see her and their new baby when they got home.

"How far along is she?" Lisenbe asked with a smirk on his face. "And how long have you been here in England?"

Waits jerked the cloth cap off his head and threw it at the waist gunner. "I been here six months, and she's seven months along. So shut your trap, unless you want a knuckle sandwich!"

Lisenbe laughed. "I'm just pulling your leg, Waits. Settle down."

Their banter continued, but Stapleton hardly heard it. The vibration of the engines caused the ship to tremble, and his nausea won. He vomited his meager breakfast into the piss bucket.

"Hey, man!" Kyle Waits complained, his debate over his wife's faithfulness forgotten. "Now that's gonna stink like hell."

"No, it won't," Stapleton rejoindered, still fighting the nausea. "It'll freeze in a few minutes."

"Well, throw it out anyway," Waits demanded. "Use one of the waist gunners' windows."

"And get puke all down the side of the fuselage? Not on your life." Stapleton thought Waits might push it, and he didn't feel like a confrontation. But he also didn't feel like getting bossed around by a runt like Waits.

The ball turret gunner looked sulky, but he didn't say anything else.

Stapleton put the bucket down, and rinsed his mouth with water from a tin canteen. Time to make his rounds, anyway.

He began a slow walk, or crawl, around all the areas of the aircraft that he could reach. He studied the engines through the waist gunners' firing windows, looking for smoke, or telltale ribbons of leaking fuel. He checked the hydraulic pumps and motor actuators on the bomb bay doors, and the landing gear. He checked the flight control conduits for any indication of wear and tear. Everything looked copasetic. He reported as much to the captain.

When the *Reba Jean* ascended above ten angels, Stapleton went to his top turret station. Bishop followed him up. "Do you remember that copy of the Uniform Code of Military Justice I gave you, and how I ordered you to study the sections on respect for officers?"

Stapleton's queasy stomach clenched. Even more shit to deal with. "Yes, sir. I studied it, like you ordered. You said you was gonna test me on it."

The Captain canted his head to one side. "I said I *might* test you. I didn't like the way you were treating Lieutenant Hoffman."

Stapleton scowled. "Accused me of tryin' to kill him, was my memory."

"I wanted you to think about your responsibility toward your officers and fellow crew members. Since that time I've been pleased with your behavior toward Mr. Hoffman. So, I'm not going to test you. Just keep your behavior on the up and up. Okay?"

"Okay, sir." It grated Stapleton to say the words, but that's what Bishop wanted to hear. Bishop's threat had been a wake-up call. Stapleton had made it a point to avoid Hoffman as much as possible, and when he couldn't avoid him, to treat him with at least a semblance of courtesy.

After Bishop left, and before he put on his oxygen mask, Stapleton emptied the contents of a BC powder into his mouth, and washed it down with more water. He then connected into the aircraft's oxygen system, and tucked his canteen inside his flight suit so his body heat would keep the water from freezing. Finally, he donned his headphones so he could track the chatter, and know when the bogeys showed up. He sat back and closed his eyes, hoping a nap would ease his aching head.

It didn't work. The vibration and drone of the four engines, along with the interphone talk, foiled his effort to sleep. From the conversations coming over his headset, it seemed that the Pathfinder navigation equipment had malfunctioned, and the planes with that specialized equipment were turning back.

"Looks like we'll just have to do it the old fashioned way," said the navigator, Aaron Hoffman, who didn't sound disappointed.

"Why don't they keep on going, and drop with us?" Captain Cannon griped. "They're carrying bombs, too, aren't they?"

"Air command doesn't want to risk having them shot down. They don't want the Germans to get a look at that technology," Captain Bishop explained.

Cannon snorted. "Equipment that doesn't work? I say let 'em have it."

"Now, now," Bishop warned. "Let's be nice."

Nicky Hill, the radio operator, broke in. "Lieutenant Hoffman, meteorology reports a crosswind over the target. Oh-oh-seven degrees at eighty knots."

"Acknowledged," Hoffman said.

"A cross wind." This from Lowery. "That'll make things interesting."

"Not the first time," Hoffman responded. "We'll be okay.

"They're also reporting heavy undercast," Hill added.

"That will make it hard to see the target," Cannon mused. "That's worse than a cross wind."

"And the navigation waypoints," Hoffman added.

"You guys are talking like this is your first dance," Bishop said. "You can do this. So suck it up."

"Why don't we just scrub, and try this another day?" Stapleton asked. He badly wanted to be back on base and in his bed.

"Not our call," Bishop explained.

* * * * *

The first Luftwaffe fighters appeared shortly before the bomb group reached the German coast.

"Bogeys at four o'clock low," Mike Hilton sang over the interphone.

Stapleton had finally begun to doze, and hadn't been watching. He scrambled to his feet and manned his gun. He swung to the announced direction, but, since the enemy aircraft's approach was "low," he couldn't spot it. He scanned the upper ranges of sky above the *Reba Jean*. With his blurry vision, he had no confidence he could spot a bogey at distance. He would have to rely on the other bombers in formation to cover his ass.

Uncle Sam had added a couple of new wrinkles in the air combat strategy in the past weeks. The first was the introduction of the P-51 Mustang. In silhouette, it closely resembled the Brits' Supermarine Spitfire. The Mustang's supercharged engine and nimble maneuverability gave it equality with, if not superiority over, the German Messerschmitts.

The Allies had also added drop tanks to the new P-51s and the older P-47s. The egg-shaped containers looked like tumors hanging under the pursuit planes' fuselages. The smaller aircraft drank the fuel from the drop tanks until they were empty, or until the bad guys showed up. Then, earning their name, they were dropped into the ocean, or onto the land below, to allow the aircraft maximum ability to juke and stunt in their dogfights with the Krauts.

The extra fuel doubled the pursuit aircrafts' range, allowing them to take their protective cordon into Germany, shielding the B-17s much longer. The bomber crews loved them. If a bomber guy ran into a fighter guy in a British pub, the fighter pilot was guaranteed a free pint.

Though his vision seemed to be clearing a bit, Donnie Stapleton chose not to put his clouded judgment to the test. He didn't fire at an approaching aircraft unless it fired at the *Reba Jean* first. He also discharged a few rounds into the empty sky above the formation so he wouldn't arrive back at Molesworth with too much ammo on hand, and thus raise suspicions.

Meanwhile, Lieutenant Hoffman and Captain Cannon were having their own problems.

"I can't find any recognizable landmarks," Hoffman reported over the interphone. "That damn crosswind blew us off course. I don't think I can hit the IP."

Captain Bishop was silent for a moment. "Do you recommend we go for the alternate target?" he eventually asked.

"Stand by," Hoffman answered.

Stapleton knew he was working his "whiz-wheel," the E6B Navigation calculator, re-computing his course. The device looked and worked like a circular slide rule, only the variables Hoffman used were wind speed, wind direction, air speed, and current course.

"Set your heading for zero-zero-five degrees true," Hoffman said. "I believe that will get us to our IP."

"You *believe?*" Stapleton blurted.

"Setting course to zero-zero-five true," Bishop responded, ignoring Stapleton.

Stapleton cursed silently. That damned kike was going to have them flying around in blind circles.

Within moments, the Luftwaffe fighters peeled off, abandoning the fight. The American Mustangs and Thunderbolts turned for home, too. No doubt they knew what was coming next.

The anti-aircraft barrage began. Since the German 88s were positioned near the militarily significant sites, it meant Hoffman had found his primary target.

"Two minutes to initial point," Hoffman intoned.

"Good work, Lieutenant," Bishop said.

Stapleton hunkered down and gritted his teeth. Each exploding Ack-Ack shell made his head throb as if it had been hit with a hammer.

"Initial point," Hoffman intoned.

"Bombardier has the aircraft," Bishop announced.

"I have the aircraft," Cannon acknowledged. "Opening bomb bay."

The plane flew as straight and level as the turbulent air around it would allow. The wind noise and cold increased with the opening of the bomb bay doors.

A few minutes later, Cannon shouted, "Bombs away!" and the deafening rush of air diminished as the double doors closed.

"Pilot has the aircraft," Bishop said, followed by Cannon's acknowledgement.

"Looks good," Cannon reported over the interphone.

"Okay, boys," Bishop said. "Let's go home."

The bomb wing made its turn for southeastern England, and Stapleton prepared himself mentally for the return leg. They would have a few more minutes of anti-aircraft fire, then the Luftwaffe would be back. If they were lucky, a squadron of American fighters would meet them not far outside of Kiel to hold the Germans at bay.

Without warning, the *Reba Jean* seemed to jump, as if it had hit a sudden updraft. Stapleton's body was thrown upward, and he banged his already sore head on the turret canopy.

"What the hell was that?" Somebody said over the interphone. It sounded like Waits.

"Keep quiet, boys" Bishop ordered.

The *Reba Jean* nosed over just after the shock wave. Stapleton guessed Bishop was making an adjustment to bring the bomber down and back into formation, except that the plane stayed in its nose-down position. The dive was not steep, but the gradual descent had already pulled the aircraft below the bomb wing's formation altitude, and its descent continued.

"That was flak. It went off just under the *Reba Jean*'s belly. Waits, are you okay?" Bishop said.

"Yeah," Waits responded. "I just got walloped by the biggest damn firecracker I've ever seen, but I didn't catch any shrapnel, and my turret still works. So, chalk one up for my guardian angel."

"Good," Bishop continued, "but I think it damaged our aft flight controls. I can't pull up. Stapleton, see if you can find the problem."

"Roger, sir," Stapleton answered, trying to clear his foggy brain. He unhooked from the B-17's internal oxygen system, grabbed his tool box, and clambered out of his top turret position, walking right past his portable oxygen bottle.

The waist gunners had already picked up targets, and he had to waltz around their movements as they tracked and shot.

The plane was in a shallow dive. If the rate of descent was a thousand feet per minute, and they started at twenty-five thousand feet, it would take—the number wouldn't come—a long time to reach sea level.

Stapleton worked his way back to the tail of the aircraft. Behind him, he heard the top turret gun begin to chatter. Lowery must have left his co-pilot seat to keep the Krauts off the *Reba Jean*'s head. So, everybody was occupied. He'd have no help in finding and solving this problem, whatever it was.

"Hey, O'Hara," Stapleton shouted over the wind noise, "see anything? Damage, I mean."

"I can't see the elevators," O'Hara answered with his thick Boston accent. "But I've seen no debris, either, and no sign of leaking hydraulic fluid." The tail gunner hadn't looked at Stapleton, his focus was on the area behind the aircraft.

"Okay," Stapleton said, and turned back toward the nose of the B-17. He looked up toward the fuselage's interior ceiling. Two sets of linkage cables ran inside conduits to the aft flight control surfaces. These cables allowed the pilot—first set, or co-pilot, second set—to move the two elevators on the horizontal stabilizers up or down, and to move the rudder on the vertical stabilizer left or right.

However, for some reason, the elevators were stuck in the slightly down position—or so it would seem.

Stapleton began to crawl forward, inspecting the cables as he went. He immediately spotted the problem. The flak explosion just underneath the *Reba Jean* had caused the aircraft to bow slightly in the middle as the force of the concussion pushed upward. Bishop would have quickly pushed the elevators down to bring the aircraft back to its allotted altitude. While the elevators were in the marginally down orientation, the torqueing stress popped one end of a support strut loose, throwing it against the conduit housing the pilot's elevator cable, and pinching it, freezing the movement of the cable inside. As long as the strut stayed where it was, neither the pilot nor co-pilot could move the controls.

For some reason, Stapleton seemed to feel better, almost giddy. He grabbed the guilty strut and pulled, planning to move it out of the way, freeing the cable. No such luck. It was firmly stuck. When the plane "untorqued," it lodged the strut in place. That explained why it was applying enough force to bind the cable even through the protective conduit.

"I'll have to cut it," Stapleton muttered to himself.

He pulled his jackknife from his pants pocket, opened it, and placed the sharp edge against the elevator conduit. He stopped and frowned. That wasn't right. "Ah," he said, and smiled. He moved the knife blade to the strut and began to saw. After a moment, he frowned again and stopped. That still wasn't right. He felt better, although considerably light-headed, but he still wasn't thinking any clearer.

Stapleton dropped the knife and stroked his chin. He pulled an oxyacetylene torch from his tool box and lit it using a friction sparking device. The torch had two small canisters, one for acetylene and one for oxygen, since there wasn't enough O2 at this altitude to keep the acetylene burning. He then tweaked the flame until it was a fine blue point. When he held it to the strut, his solution finally felt right.

Stapleton had no concept of how much time had passed. He didn't know what altitude the *Reba Jean* had fallen to. He only knew that every gun on the ship was firing, and he had a job to do. The strut glowed pink, then red, and a seam opened behind the flame along the width of the metal bar until the end pushing against the conduit dropped away. He grabbed the amputated end of the strut to pull it back, but hissed in pain and quickly released the hot metal.

Where he had felt light-headed and euphoric a few minutes ago, and his damned headache had gone away, now he felt dizzy, and his vision had gone blurry again. But he could still see that the strut's pressure had put a crimp in the conduit. The cable inside might be able to move a little, but not much, and not easily. Ignoring the pain in his hand, he grabbed a set of pliers from his tool box, and even as his vision grayed out, he squeezed the sides of the conduit to un-crimp the cable and relieve the pressure.

He thought maybe the downward pitch of the aircraft had begun to change into a climb, and he thought maybe he heard cheers as he lost consciousness.

Tom Hooker

INTERLUDE B

The Navigator's Tale Continued

As the *Reba Jean* climbed back into formation, and the Luftwaffe fighters that had been harassing them disengaged in apparent disappointment, Hilton called Hoffman's name over the interphone. "Better get back here if you can, Lieutenant Hoffman. I think Donnie's dead."

"What?" said Bishop and Hoffman in unison.

"It's Donnie," Hilton repeated, a hum of panic in his voice. "He's not breathing."

Usually the radio operator acted as medic on a B-17 crew, but Hoffman had some medical training, so he inherited the job on the *Reba Jean*. He grabbed his first aid kit and stuck his head up between Bishop's and the empty co-pilot's seat on the way. "Just stay in formation, Captain, and you'll be okay."

"Roger," Bishop responded. "Now go take care of Stapleton."

Hoffman reached Stapleton's supine body, and knelt beside it. Hilton was already there, along with Lowery. With the Germans gone, the co-pilot was no longer bound to man the top turret. He was already putting an oxygen mask on the engineer.

"I found his portable oxygen bottle in his compartment," Lowery said. "He must have forgotten it."

Hoffman checked for a pulse. Nothing. Stapleton's skin had a blue tinge. The lieutenant began chest compressions. "Hypoxia. Lack of oxygen," Hoffman announced. "Hilton, get all the blankets you can find. We need to get him warmed up. Wayne, ask Captain Bishop to descend to below ten angels as soon as it is safe to do so."

Hilton and Lowery moved off to accomplish their errands.

Hoffman continued his chest compressions, hoping the flexion of the diaphragm would keep some blood flowing through Stapleton's veins, and move a little oxygen into his lungs.

Hilton returned with several olive-green, wool blankets, and the officer and non-com wrapped the engineer up like a mummy. The chest compressions continued.

The *Reba Jean* began a gradual descent, controlled this time. Hoffman was too busy to look, but he assumed a couple of Yankee fighters had followed the B-17 to provide cover.

Stapleton's skin slowly regained its pink glow. After a while, Hoffman paused in his compressions, watching. The engineer's chest continued to rise and fall on its own.

Hoffman exhaled softly. He thumbed his interphone throat mike, "Captain, Sergeant Stapleton is breathing again."

All the non-coms except Nicky Hill were clustered around. They lifted a relieved cheer.

Stapleton's eyes flickered, then opened. He seemed disoriented.

Lowery returned from the cockpit. "We're below ten thousand feet."

Hoffman nodded and removed his own portable oxygen tank. "Let's leave Stapleton's mask on for a while. The air is still thin up here."

Stapleton's eyes settled first on Lowery, then on Hoffman. He seemed to recognize the two.

"You must have forgotten your portable oxygen bottle when you left your gun turret. The air was too thin, and you didn't have enough oxygen to breathe, so you passed out. You were unconscious for a while," Hoffman explained. He decided to overlook the not breathing part.

"And you weren't breathing," Lowery added, unaware of Hoffman's decision. "Lieutenant Hoffman got your ticker started back up."

Stapleton reached up and removed his oxygen mask. His expression was dark. "Don't expect me to thank you," he said to Hoffman.

Hoffman flipped his hand dismissively. "I don't. I've heard that people who drown in extremely cold water can go without breathing for an extraordinarily long time before being successfully resuscitated. I assume that works in cold air, too. I don't know how far we descended while you were working on our problem, but the air was still super cold. That probably helped. When you got warmed back up, you started breathing on your own." He paused before continuing. "Besides, I should be thanking *you*. If you hadn't freed up that elevator cable, we'd all be swimming by now — *again*."

Stapleton couldn't seem to find anything to say.

The Ball Turret Gunner's Tale

January 29, 1944
Frankfurt, Germany

Stapleton was awake and alert when Captain Bishop brought the *Reba Jean* down on the runway at Molesworth, so Lieutenant Hoffman chose not to fire a flare requesting emergency medical attention.

He did insist that the flight engineer go to the infirmary to get checked out, and he accompanied him on the trip.

Later the navigator came by the barracks to give the non-coms a report. "Sergeant Stapleton has a concussion, although the doctor couldn't find evidence of a blow to the head."

Kyle Waits figured Lieutenant Hoffman probably knew about the boxing match the day before. Secrets of that kind were notoriously hard to keep on an Army base, but he had apparently elected not to acknowledge that he knew. He could have probably gotten Stapleton in trouble if he'd charged him with flying a mission in an impaired condition.

"Nobody knows how long Sergeant Stapleton went without oxygen," Hoffman continued, "so the doctor is going to keep him for a day or two to make sure there isn't any brain damage."

Waits wondered how the doctor could tell . . . about damage to Stapleton's brain, then felt guilty for the thought. Stapleton was a good gunner and a good mechanic, and he had just saved their bacon. Waits couldn't help it if he was a redneck and a fool with a chip on his shoulder.

For some reason, the brass didn't schedule a mission for the next day. The *Reba Jean* and her crew would not have flown anyway, but the mysterious stand-down put the rumor mill into overdrive. Waits thought about going to visit Stapleton at the infirmary. *Later*, he decided.

After breakfast, several games of chance started up: the universal time-killer. Some guys, like Lisenbe and O'Hara, played for serious money. Since a deck of cards had stopped a German bullet and saved his life, Lisenbe played poker like the lucky dog he was. Not Waits. Those games were cutthroat. Waits just wanted to pass the morning, and have some fun doing it. He found four other guys, all from other crews, who were up for seven-card stud.

"Penny ante," Bernie Lockwood intoned. "Nickel maximum raise. If anything's wild, it'll be the hair in your ass." Nobody objected. They all formed a circle on the floor between two bunks.

Lockwood dealt two face-down cards to each player, then a round face-up. "Shannon gets a five-spot. A pretty lady for Ellis, a bullet for Waits—and a baby, so I hear." He continued with the deal. Shannon raised a penny and everybody else saw his raise.

"By the way, Waits, you owe everybody a cigar. That's what new papas do," Kenny Shannon said.

"Not yet, doofus," Waits answered. "Lucy's still got a couple of months yet. Don't jinx me. You'll get your cigar when the baby comes."

"Just don't forget," Shannon warned, but he smiled when he said it.

Lockwood finished the deal.

Waits' hand was a satisfying all red color, but a closer look revealed a mix of hearts and diamonds.

"Woo hoo," Jason Ellis crowed. "Waits is looking kind of flushed." He stacked his cards, and dropped them face down on the floor. "I'm out."

"I sure hope that baby looks like its mother," Tom Gann said. "Especially if it's a girl. Otherwise you'll have to pay the neighborhood kids to play with him, or her."

Waits made a kissing motion toward the tall man. Ribbing came with the territory. He had no flush. Nevertheless, he bluffed everybody out and won the whopping four-bit pot.

Play continued.

"I heard that General Eaker is out," Jason Ellis said. "Jimmy Doolittle, that guy that led the B-25 raid on Tokyo back in '42, he's the new Eighth Air Corps boss."

"Where'd you hear that?" Waits asked.

"Some guy at G-2 told me."

"No shit? That guy oughta have his tongue cut out!"

"What are you, OSS now?" Ellis asked with a smile. "That's old news, anyway. Doolittle's already met with the bomb wing and fighter wing commanders. That's why no missions today. All the brass is implementing the new policy changes."

"What changes?" Gann asked.

Ellis leaned in, speaking in a conspiratorial whisper. "You've seen the troop buildup? I bet there's more American soldiers in England than there are in the States." Ellis had everybody's attention, and he seemed to relish it. "There's going to be an invasion. That's no secret. Rommel knows it. Hell, even Hitler knows it. But nobody knows where or when."

"Not even *you*?" Waits couldn't resist a dig.

"If I knew, Papa Waits, I wouldn't be telling it. I wouldn't want anybody cutting my tongue out, or shooting me for treason, which would be more likely."

Everyone was silent for a moment, contemplating that statement.

"Anyway," Ellis continued, "Eisenhower put Doolittle in charge of the Air Corps, and his job is to make sure that whenever and wherever the invasion occurs, there are no Luftwaffe around to bollix things up.

"What does that mean for us?" Lockwood asked.

Ellis leaned back on his haunches. "From now on, the fighter wing's number one priority is to shoot down enemy aircraft."

"Hasn't that always been their priority?" Bernie Lockwood asked.

"No. Up until now, their priority has been to protect the bombers. That usually involved shooting down Germans, but if a fighter pilot had to choose between going after a Kraut or providing cover for the bombers, he maintained cover. Now, if he gets the same choice, his orders will be to abandon the bombers and get the Kraut."

"So that means us gunners will be on our own," Gann mused aloud.

"You got it."

The card game was forgotten, as the airmen debated the effect this would have on their missions. Kyle Waits felt thankful he had only three sorties left.

After lunch, Waits strolled over to the infirmary to check on Stapleton. He found the flight engineer sitting up on one of a row of cots, each occupied by a soldier. Some were bound in bandages, some were asleep. Everything was white, albeit dingy white, so much so that Waits seemed to be walking in a cloud among the heavens. Only the muted cough or clink of some medical instrument intruded on the silence.

Stapleton was playing solitaire. A slender pole held an upside down bottle of clear liquid with a small tube running from its neck to a needle in the engineer's arm.

Stapleton saw Waits' look. "The nurse called it 'Ringer's Lactate,' but it's really just salt water. I think they decided that if they were going to pretend I'm sick, they should stick some pretend medicine in me."

Waits noted that Stapleton's solitaire array followed the rules. An indication that his brain seemed to be in working order.

"How ya feeling?" Waits asked.

"Bored outa my gourd," Stapleton responded without hesitation. "That's a good sign, according to another nurse. She says when a patient gets restless, it means he's ready to leave. Anyway, they're going to let me out tomorrow morning. Are we up for a mission?"

"Nope. All of today's assignments got scrubbed. So everything got pushed back a day. We won't fly until day after tomorrow at the earliest."

"Scrubbed? How come?"

Waits brought him up to date on the grapevine news.

Stapleton scratched his nose. "Won't make any difference. SOP for us. If a Kraut comes close, we'll just shoot him — like always."

"I suppose you're right. Anyway, I wanted to say thanks for yesterday. Our goose would have been cooked if it hadn't been for you."

"Just doin' my job." Stapleton looked uncomfortable being the focus of somebody's good will.

"How come you didn't take your oxygen bottle with you?"

"Forgot it." Stapleton peered around before adding, "I think that punch I took in the ring scrambled my brains a bit."

Waits nodded. "Good thing Lieutenant Hoffman was there to get your ticker started back up."

Stapleton scowled. "He said I'd probably started breathin' again on my own, once I got warmed up."

"Yeah, he was probably right." Waits had forgotten that Stapleton held no love for Hoffman. "Well, I'd better get going. See you tomorrow?"

"That's a deal."

* * * * *

In fact, the *Reba Jean*'s crew's twenty-third mission was on January eleventh, thanks to several days of inclement weather over Europe—typical in January. Their mission was to bomb a Focke-Wulff assembly facility in Oschersleben. Stapleton was back on duty, and seemed none the worse for wear.

The mission, while successful, was a bloodbath—as bad as Schweinfurt. Some bomb groups suffered losses as high as twenty-five percent.

Waits didn't think the new policy made much difference, just as Stapleton predicted. The Yanks went where the Krauts went, and the Krauts went for the B-17s. So the bombers had pretty much the same cover as before. Nevertheless, Waits assumed General Doolittle would get the blame for the tragedy, since he had re-tasked the fighters. According to scuttlebutt, the guys with stars on their collars were doing a lot of finger pointing, but the scapegoat seemed to be General Bob Travis. Gossip said that the Germans knew the target and were lying in wait, and that Travis knew they knew, and he green-lighted the mission anyway. Waits had trouble believing this. But it didn't matter. The *Reba Jean* survived again.

Waits concluded that, with the invasion imminent, the air corps brass was under a lot of pressure to weaken German defenses as much as possible. A lot of Allied ground-pounders were about to die on some French or Belgian beach, so a few flyboys were expendable if that's what it took to make the endeavor a success.

On the way to his barracks, Waits stopped by the base post office and discovered he had a letter from his wife. He carried the blue envelope in both hands as he hurried to his bunk, occasionally lifting it to his nose to inhale the soft vanilla scent of Lucy's perfume.

Everyone understood that if a soldier sat or lay on his bed with a letter, he was to be left alone. So, Waits had his required privacy when he unfolded the paper and began to read:

December 15, 1943

My Dearest Kyle,

Well, here it is, ten days before Christmas, and my belly is beginning to resemble Old Saint Nick's! I know you can't tell me anything about where you are and what is going on, but I hope you can write me and tell me how you are doing. Maybe you can find a Christmas tree somewhere, look at it and think of me, knowing that I will be doing the same and thinking of you.

She won't have thought about her letter arriving after Christmas, Kyle thought. Even so, he searched his memory for someplace a Yule tree might still be standing. No luck.

> *I've begun to feel our little one move inside my stomach. Grandma Marshall calls that "quickening." I wish you were here to feel it.*

(Kyle wished he were, too.)

> *Have you thought about names? I thought maybe Kyle, Jr., if it is a boy, and Wanda, after Grandma Marshall, if it is a girl. When you write, please tell me your thoughts.*
>
> *I'd better go. The family is going to gather and sing carols after dinner. I'll make sure we sing, "O, Holy Night." I know that is your favorite.*

With my undying love,

Lucy (and child)

The words got blurry at the end, and Kyle had to wipe his eyes. After taking some time to collect himself, he opened his footlocker, and took out a sheet of plain paper and a pencil.

12 January, 1944

Lucy, My Love,

I received your letter of 15 December. Thank you. It really lifted my spirits.

Kyle chewed on his pencil and tried to acknowledge Lucy's growing belly without risking hurting her feelings. He finally chose to skip that part.

Christmas has come and gone, and there are no trees still up, but I will find one somewhere and decorate it, just so I can look on it and think of you.

I haven't thought much about names for our baby. Kyle, Jr. and Wanda seem okay. If I think of something else, I'll write you (or telegraph you, if your time is close).

When an airman reached twenty missions or so, he often developed a case of nerves. He became obsessed with surviving the last missions, sometimes to the point that it impaired his effectiveness.

Kyle hadn't had that problem until this moment. As he tried to find some words to tell Lucy he had only two missions left in a way the censors would let through, he began to tremble. Suddenly, he couldn't envision surviving these next few days, and making it home to his wife and child. He had to wait a few moments to allow his wavering hand to steady. It wouldn't do to reveal his state of mind to Lucy.

As I write this, by my count you have two months to go until your journey is ended. Please understand that the number two is important to me, too.

I also have to go. I have duties to perform.

With all my love,

Kyle

Waits wiped his eyes again, addressed an envelope, and left the barracks. His first stop would be to post the letter. Then he would collect some bottle caps and other shiny objects, and find a tree to decorate.

The *Reba Jean's* next mission saw two new captains on the crew. Former lieutenants Lowery and Hoffman now sported captain's bars. This would be the twenty-fourth mission for all but Captain Bishop and Sergeant O'Hara. The objective was a V-1 buzz bomb facility at Pas de Calais, France: a milk run, except for the fact that the bomb group dumped their payload from twelve thousand feet. At that altitude, in the ball turret, Waits felt like he was in danger of scraping his ass on the ground.

The tactic worked. It befuddled the anti-aircraft batteries, and their accuracy was atrocious. Waits knew that a trick like that would only work once. The Luftwaffe could fight at any altitude, so their strafing runs were just as vicious as ever. If General Doolittle's (Stapleton had begun calling him General "Do Little") attrition strategy was working, Waits couldn't tell it.

Another extended spell of bad weather gave the 303rd bomb group an unexpected — and in Waits case, undesired — break. He wanted this last mission to be done and gone. By the time the weather began to clear, every scrap of paper on base had been policed, and every other make-work chore the higher-ups could think

267

of had been performed. Who knew you could, or should, rake a gravel sidewalk?

Twenty-nine January. This was it. The NCOs assembled at the hardstand. The officers arrived via Jeep. For some unknown reason, Waits remembered how the vehicle got its name. It had been designated as a General Purpose vehicle—GP in Army speak. Only when everyone said the letters, "G" and "P" aloud, it came out close to "Jeep." So that's what it was called.

While everyone milled around getting their gear ready, Waits approached Captain Bishop. "I'm sorry you still have to make another mission after this one," the belly gunner said, hoping he didn't seem to gloat. That wasn't his intent.

The pilot smiled. "That's the way the cookie crumbles, Sergeant. I guess O'Hara and I will get lumped in with some other guys who missed a mission. Who knows, we might even go on the *Reba Jean* here." He gestured toward the aircraft. "O'Hara has more missions than me to make up, I guess."

"Just wanted you to know I wish this was your last one, too, Skipper."

"Thanks."

The crew loaded themselves and their equipment into the B-17. They went wheels up at 0750 hours.

"Target is Frankfurt," Bishop reported over the interphone. "We'll be dropping incendiaries."

Everybody had known that as soon as they boarded and got a look at the bomb rack. Incendiaries were smaller and slimmer than the other high-explosive bombs. The qualms some airmen had expressed earlier about fire-bombing had faded away. The mindset now seemed to be: whatever it takes to end this war.

"Since we aren't going after a specific military target," Bishop continued, "we can hope for light anti-aircraft fire. But let's take nothing for granted."

After the bomb group formed up and crossed the European shoreline, an array of P-47 Thunderbolts, P-38 Lightnings, and P-51 Mustangs joined them.

The inbound flight to the target was routine, as missions go. Waits shoehorned himself into the ball turret.

When he'd gone to volunteer after Pearl Harbor, he'd been afraid the recruiter would reject him as too short. He was only five feet three inches tall. He'd always thought of his size as an advantage in achieving his dream of becoming a jockey at Pimlico. It had never occurred to him that it might be a barrier to his service in the Army.

The burly guy with chevrons on his biceps had paused in the middle of his "too bad, son," speech, plucked at his lower lip and asked, "What do you think about flying in an airplane?"

"You mean being a pilot?"

"Shit, no," the sergeant laughed. "There is a slot on B-17 bomber crews for a ball turret gunner. He needs to be short and light, like you. Whatya think?"

"Sign me up." Waits declared.

The recruiter had conveniently failed to mention that the ball turret would be on the belly of the bomber, or that the bomber would be flying at twenty-five thousand feet.

He'd quickly learned not to look at, or think about *down*. He'd trained himself to look *out* or *low* for his targets, most of which, for him, were below the *Reba Jean*. But he looked at the enemy planes, not beyond them.

Once in the ball turret, Waits was essentially sitting on his lower back, with his knees up around his ears. His fifty-cal, double-barreled machine gun hung from a mount between his thighs. He had a joystick control that allowed him to gimbal in a full circle so he could fire in any horizontal direction, and could pivot the turret from horizontal to almost straight down. The only direction he couldn't shoot was up, since that would be into the plane that carried him. The ball turret wasn't a spot for a claustrophobic.

The bomb wing made it through the gauntlet of Luftwaffe fighters on the Frankfurt approach with only moderate resistance. Once the fighters disengaged, the anti-aircraft fire began. It, too, seemed light, and Waits allowed himself to feel a sense of optimism that his farewell voyage might be a milk run, even if it was deep into Germany.

That's when the *Hell'N'High Water*, flying to the left and slightly below the *Reba Jean* turned into a ball of fire so big Waits could feel the heat through the metal and Plexiglas of his turret. Immediately after, the *Reba Jean* was peppered with debris from the no longer existent airplane.

"Holy shit!" Waits exclaimed.

"What was that?" asked O'Hara from the tail gunner's position.

"One of our guys just went up like a Roman candle," Waits said.

"That's what happens when an incendiary gets hit by a piece of hot shrapnel," Captain Lowery observed.

"Waits, are you okay?" Captain Bishop asked.

"Wait one . . ." Waits conducted a thorough examination of himself and his turret. He'd heard stories about people who'd been injured and didn't even know it. "I'm okay," he said after a moment.

"Good," Bishop continued. "Stapleton, take a look at the bomb rack and bomb bay doors. We need to know if we can drop with no problems."

"Will do," Stapleton answered.

"And hurry. We're almost to the IP," Cannon added.

"Waits, survey the underside of the plane. Do you see any damage?" Bishop asked.

"Stand by," Waits said. He pivoted his ball turret in a full circle, looking carefully at everything he could see. "The left wing took a hit from something. It looks like the left landing gear mechanism has been badly damaged. My guess is it won't deploy. And there's oil or something leaking from the number two engine."

"I confirm number two's oil pressure is dropping," Lowery added.

"Captain, the bomb rack is good to go," Stapleton interposed.

"Acknowledged to all reports," Captain Bishop said.

The chatter dropped away as the bomb wing hit its initial point and began the bomb run.

Waits swiveled his turret around so he could watch the bomb bay doors open and the incendiaries drop away. As Stapleton had predicted, everything worked perfectly. The belly gunner had some time to think about the *Reba Jean*'s return to base. The plane would have only the right landing gear wheel and the small wheel on the tail. He didn't see any way the aircraft could land in one piece. Many other B-17s had dealt with similar problems. The crews seemed to have a good chance of survival if they sat on the deck with their backs against the bulkhead behind the cockpit. Or the captain could have everyone bail out over the base, except himself — the pilot.

The bomb run ended, and the captain retrieved control of the aircraft. Now they had to prepare to run the Luftwaffe gauntlet again on the return leg.

"Sergeant Waits," Captain Bishop said over the interphone, "I want you to vacate the ball turret. We can't let you get trapped in there if we don't have functioning landing gear."

"But, Captain," Waits protested, "the ball turret is fine."

"I'd rather have you out, just in case something happens."

Waits sat for a moment, silent. Then he pivoted the turret to its home position, the only position from which he could exit the sphere, locked it in place, and disconnected his harness and internal oxygen. He opened the hatch, grabbed an oxygen bottle and clambered out.

Working his way around the bomb rack, Waits climbed the couple of steps that allowed him to poke his head up into the space between and behind the pilot and co-pilot.

"Captain, I understand that you're trying to protect me, and I'm grateful for that. But I have a job to do. I have to protect the *Reba Jean* and the rest of the bomb wing from attack from below. There isn't another gun on board that can do that."

Captain Bishop opened his mouth as if to speak, but Waits barged on. "With the fighter wing's new priorities, coverage by the bombers' guns is even more important."

"But what if you get stuck?" the pilot asked.

"We all take risks, Captain. That's our job."

A bevy of expressions crossed the captain's face. Waits assumed he was thinking through the possibilities, including the danger to the crew if the ball turret guns went unmanned. "Very well, Waits. But I want you out as soon as the Krauts break away."

"Roger that, Captain," Waits said with a grin, and hustled back to his post.

"What the hell am I doing?" Waits asked himself aloud as he buckled himself back into his bubble. "Asking to come back here? Now I know I'm certifiable." But he also knew he couldn't abandon his post, even under orders, while his crewmates put their lives on the line.

Just before they cleared the anti-aircraft fire field and re-engaged the German fighters, Captain Bishop reported, "I'm shutting down number two engine. It's out of oil. We'll be hard pressed to keep up with the bomb wing, so stay alert, guys. When the Krauts see that one of our props isn't turning, they'll swarm all over us."

Flying east to west usually increases the headwind, and as the firefight with the enemy progressed, the *Reba Jean* gradually slipped farther and farther back in the formation.

Things were bad, but not as bad as Schweinfurt or Oschersleben. Even so, Waits had his hands full. On a couple of occasions the belly gunner fought off charges by determined German fighters.

Even with the game wing, the *Reba Jean* had better luck than some of the others. The number three engine, the inside one on the co-pilot's side, on the *Sparrow Hawk*, flying to the right of the *Reba Jean* caught fire. The heat must have softened the steel, or something, because the right wing just folded up. The plane seemed to be trying to fly with one wing, but no go. It canted over and began a weaving spiral to earth. No parachutes. Waits guessed the G forces of the spiral wouldn't let anyone get to an escape hatch.

A Messerschmitt Me-109 approached the *Reba Jean* from below in a swooping climb. It came from forward, so the closing speed of the two aircraft was about six hundred miles an hour or more. Waits pivoted his turret around and fired, using the red tracers from his guns to walk his stream of fire into the body of the plane. Even as he saw pieces of debris fly away from the '109s engine cowling, he heard and felt the German's thirteen millimeter bullets thud into the underside of the turret and the bomber itself.

This SOB is going to fly into us, Waits thought. But, no. At the last second it veered off. If its wing had been two inches shorter, it would've just been a close call. Instead, the tip of the wing clipped the underside of the sphere enclosing Kyle Waits—at a relative speed of six hundred miles per hour.

The blow knocked the turret askew, dislodging it from the track that allowed it to pivot and swivel.

Waits didn't have the presence of mind to watch the Messerschmitt fall away in a cartwheeling spiral. He was too busy grabbing his balls and other parts of his anatomy, to make sure he was still in one piece.

"Jeez, Louise," he muttered aloud. "That was close."

"Sergeant Waits, are you all right?" Captain Bishop asked over the interphone.

"Stand by," Waits responded, thankful he hadn't thumbed his own interphone mic when he uttered his earlier outburst.

The belly gunner tried to swivel his turret, but nothing happened. He only heard the grind of the actuator motor in its futile effort to rotate the sphere.

The entire mechanism rattled loosely in its housing. Waits had the queasy feeling that it wouldn't take much to shake it free from the aircraft and send it on a twenty-five thousand foot drop. He wondered if he could open the hatch, get out, and deploy his parachute before he reached the ground.

The turret's "home" position was with the gun barrels facing aft. This way, the barrels wouldn't be facing the direction of travel and endanger the airplane if they caught on the ground during landing. This position also was the only one that allowed the hatch to open and the gunner to exit the station. At the moment, the guns were stuck facing just to the left of forward, and the ball wasn't going to move.

"Uh, Captain," Waits said over the interphone, "you should take up fortune telling. I'm stuck."

The pilot didn't speak for several seconds. Waits assumed he was thinking. "Water under the bridge," Bishop said. "I'm sending Stapleton down to take a look."

"Okay . . . uh, Captain, you might want to try flying real smooth. This turret is so loose, it feels like it could fall off the plane."

Waits expected a chuckle at his impossible request, but Bishop's response was solemn. "I'll do the best I can."

A few minutes later Waits heard someone knocking around the area where the turret fitted, ball-bearing-like, into the B-17's fuselage. Not long after, Stapleton's voice came over the interphone, "You can relax Captain—and Waits—the ball turret isn't going anywhere, but it'll take more leverage than I've got to move it so Waits can get out.

"I also don't have enough oxy-acetylene to cut him out. Even if I did, the sparks would probably burn him badly."

"Better burned than the alternative," Captain Bishop mused.

"True," Stapleton responded, "but I still can't cut him out."

Waits had nothing to say to this news.

"Sergeant Hill, encode and send a message to Molesworth advising them of our situation. Ask for suggestions for resolution," Captain Bishop ordered.

"Roger, sir," Nicky Hill, the *Reba Jean*'s radio operator answered.

More silence. Only the chatter of the ball turret in its loose housing, and the subtle *whoosh* of the wind flowing around the plane provided company for Waits.

The interphone clicked, followed by Captain Bishop's voice. "I've ordered everyone to disconnect from the interphone. I'm just above you, Kyle, in the fuselage. We haven't given up. The best ground crew engineers at Molesworth are working on finding a solution . . . in the meantime, I'm going to have each crew member come down to speak to you privately. No one else will be listening in."

"Thank you, sir," Waits said. He got the message. The captain was giving everyone a chance to say goodbye.

Shortly, Waits heard a knock on the metal of the turret, and Stapleton's voice came over the interphone. "I just wanted to say thanks for coming by the hospital the other day."

"Welcome," Waits said. He could think of nothing else.

After an awkward silence, Stapleton spoke again. "They'll probably give you a medal. To your wife, I guess."

Waits bit back a sharp response. He didn't want to hear this.

Another awkward silence.

"Look," Waits said after a while. "I know there's bad blood between you and Captain Hoffman. I think the two of you should set things right. It's no good being bitter like you are."

"Here's a thought," Stapleton snapped. "Mind your own beeswax."

"It was just a suggestion," Waits puled.

"I'm just going to finish my mission, end this tour, go my own way, and let Hoffman go his."

Waits held his tongue. Stapleton couldn't understand what talking about his own future was doing to Waits.

A parade of crew members followed Stapleton: Hilton, Lisenbe, O'Hara, Hill and the officers, Cannon and Hoffman. Each said meaningless words intending to be comforting, some so soft and weepy Waits could barely hear them above the wind noise and rattle of the turret.

Despite the winter season, the sky was a crisp, clear blue. It didn't seem fair to have to die on a day like this.

The pilot would be last, Waits knew. That left only Captain Lowery in a parade that had become more torture than comfort.

"Kyle, how are you doing?" Lowery asked over the interphone.

"With respect, how do you think?" Waits asked.

"Yeah. Dumb question. Sorry."

"Me, too. This is getting on my nerves."

The two were silent. There had been a lot of awkward silences in the talks with the crew. How do you say goodbye to a breathing dead man?

"Say Captain, didn't you say you had a ranch out west, somewhere?" Waits asked.

"Sure did. In Colorado. Only it belongs to my parents. I grew up on it."

"So you rode horses?"

"All the time," Lowery answered.

"You know, I was a stable hand at Pimlico, the racetrack, before the war."

"Yes," Lowery said, "you mentioned that one time."

"I was going to become a jockey after I got discharged. Maybe ride in the Preakness."

"That would have been a dream come true," Lowery's voice sounded thick.

"Did you ever race horses, Captain?"

"Most of my riding involved herding cattle, but yes, my buddies and I raced a few times—when the grown-ups weren't around."

"Sometimes one of the trainers would let me give a thoroughbred a workout," said Waits. "That was fun. My favorite was a bay stallion named Knockabout."

In the background, the *Reba Jean's* three engines droned, accompanied by the rush of wind and the occasional rattle of the loose turret when the plane hit a patch of rough air.

"We'd start out slow. Just a canter," Waits continued, "to get the muscles warm. This would be in the morning, about dawn. The dirt track would be soft and loose. You could play music to the beat of the horse's hooves.

"After a half mile or so, we'd pick up the pace. The breeze would feel so cool on my face. Knockabout would be antsy, ready to run.

"I wouldn't even have to use the crop. I'd just lift my butt out of the saddle. My weight on the stirrups, my knees forward, against the withers. And that horse's ears would perk up." Waits voice rose, carrying the thrill of his memory. "I put my head alongside his neck, so the mane wouldn't be in my eyes. And I could feel his haunches bunch up, 'cause that horse knew it was go time. And boy, did we go! I tell ya, Captain, I knew what flying was like before I ever got in an airplane."

"I don't think I've got a memory that can match that," Lowery said.

Waits cleared his throat to move the lump in it. "Yeah, well. That's what kept me going. The idea that I would get back to Pimlico someday."

Lowery didn't say anything.

"Say, Captain, do me a favor?"

"Anything."

"Will you visit my wife when you get back to the States? And my kid? My kid ought to be born by then."

"Of course I will, Kyle," Lowery said. "I'm sure Captain Bishop will visit them, too. Anything you want me to tell them?"

"Just that I was thinking about them . . . at the end. You don't have to tell her about the horses."

Lowery laughed a bit. "Yes, I'll tell them, but not about the horses."

Waits heard a clatter from the space above him.

"Stapleton's here," Lowery's voice said. "He's plugging into the interphone."

"I've got a pipe," Stapleton said. "I'm going to try to jimmy this turret around so we can get this hatch open."

"Just be careful," Waits answered, a note of anxiety in his voice. "I don't want this thing to fall off."

"Don't worry. It's not going anywhere, except in a circle, I hope," Stapleton replied. "Who was it said 'Give me a long enough lever and I'll move the world'? Ben Franklin, wasn't it?"

"Uh, Archimedes, actually," Lowery said, "but I think you're onto something here. I'll help."

Everybody fell silent, and the sound of metal scraping on metal was added to the engine and wind noise. Occasionally the turret would shift slightly, causing Waits's gut to clench. Then the sphere would drop back into its original position.

After a few minutes, Stapleton's voice came back on the interphone. "Either that sumbitch lied, or this lever ain't long enough. Sorry, bud."

"That's okay, Donnie. Thanks for trying."

"Listen, Kyle, we're approaching the English coast. I'd better get back to the cockpit," Lowery said.

"Okay, Captain."

"Yeah, sing out if . . . if you need anything."

"Okay."

"I got some stuff to do, too," Stapleton said.

"Okay, Donnie. Good luck."

Stapleton didn't reply.

Kyle's interphone crackled, and Captain Bishop's voice said, "We've dropped to the rear of the formation. The other planes will land first. Then all the crew except you and me will parachute out.

"The guys at Molesworth haven't come up with any solutions. I'm sorry. We talked about taking the *Reba Jean* out to the beach and ditching in shallow water, but we don't think we'd be able to get you out before you . . . drowned." Bishop drew a deep breath. "So we're going to make a belly landing in that open field beside the base. I wish that meant you had a chance, Kyle, but even that soft ground won't make any difference when several thousand pounds of aircraft come down on top of you. We're going down in the field to avoid tearing up the runway."

"I understand, Captain," Waits said.

There was little conversation over the next half hour while the other planes in the bomb wing made their landings. The crew members made one last round of goodbyes, blessedly brief, some tearfully. Waits couldn't see aft, but he heard the metallic resonance when the rear hatch opened, and knew that eight parachute blossoms were now trailing the plane.

Waits looked down upon the scattered buildings of RAF Molesworth. He saw ant-like figures begin to migrate across the runway toward the fence that separated the airbase from the open field. The grapevine had done its thing. The *Reba Jean* would have an audience.

"I'm going to orbit the field a couple of times while I purge most of our remaining fuel. We don't have much left, so it won't take long. We'll keep just enough to come in under power. That way we'll be less likely to start a fire," Bishop reported.

Waits didn't trust himself to speak, so he double-clicked his interphone mic button, the non-verbal acknowledgement signal. He wondered about the Captain's chances. His survival wasn't guaranteed. But probably better than even odds.

The plane leveled out, and the trees seemed to grow larger. The *Reba Jean* was descending. A mile or so in the distance Waits could see the field where he would meet his fate. He thought of the thousands—tens of thousands—of airmen who had died on impact with the soil of Europe. Some might say it was better to die in Allied territory, but it didn't seem that way to Kyle.

Waits keyed his interphone. "Captain, will you visit Lucy, my wife, and my kid, and say something nice about me?"

"Say it yourself," Captain Bishop responded.

Waits felt his center of gravity shift as the *Reba Jean* began a slow half-roll. "Captain. What're you doing?"

"Giving you a chance. When you see your wife and baby, give them a kiss for me."

The plane completed its maneuver and now flew inverted. Waits' ball turret was now on top, and the body of the plane was under him. Waits' didn't have the

Captain's know-how, but he knew a plane this big wouldn't be able to fly upside down for long.

It wouldn't have to.

The *Reba Jean*'s vertical stabilizer hit the ground first, plowing a furrow in the soft loam of the vacant field. This drove the nose of the plane into the ground, shattering the Plexiglas bombardier's nest and collapsing the roof of the cockpit in on the pilot.

Waits, securely harnessed and hanging upside down in his bubble, was shaken like the pea in a baby's rattle. Around him, chaos reigned. The B-17's wings sheared off. The fuselage cast off debris as it plowed a furrow the length of the field, slowing from one hundred eighty miles an hour to zero in a matter of seconds. Everything went black.

Twenty-Five Angels

POSTLUDE

The Ball Turret Gunner's Tale Continued

March 19, 1946
Buttermilk Springs, Taliposa County, Mississippi

Sergeant Kyle Waits, wearing his dress uniform, stepped onto the porch of a plain house with dingy whitewash paint, his limp hardly noticeable. He rapped his knuckles sharply on the door jamb. His wife stood beside him in a flower print dress that bulged slightly between the buttons. Despite almost two years, she'd never quite been able to shed her baby weight. She held their son in her arms. Kyle knocked again.

Waits knew the woman who answered the door was only about four years older than his own age of twenty-two, but she looked much older.

He recognized her strawberry blond hair and freckles from the image that had adorned the nose of the *Reba Jean*, but she had wrinkles that shouldn't have been on a face so young. And she had eyes that only grief could shape.

A double-framed display hung on the wall of the entryway behind her. The left side of the frame held a photograph of Captain Ray Bishop, and the right side held a star-shaped medal suspended under the V shape of a powder blue ribbon. His parents must have given her that, Waits thought.

Kyle removed his hat, tucked it under the stump of his left arm, and looked into the woman's sad eyes. "Miss Reba Jean Carwyle? I'm Sergeant Kyle Waits. I had the honor to fly with your fiancé. I'd like you to meet my wife, Lucy, and our son, Raymond Bishop Waits. We call him Ray."

Bibliography

Robert Morgan and Ron Powers, *The Man Who Flew the Memphis Belle: Memoir of a WWII Bomber Pilot.* © 2001, Dutton

Brian D. O'Neill, *Half a Wing, Three Engines and a Prayer,* © 1998, McGraw-Hill

Acknowledgments

I'd like to thank Joe Perrone, Jr. of Escarpment Press for helping me get Twenty-Five Angels airborne. His help was irreplaceable.

I'd also like to thank Bob Brooks, Frank Robinson, Jerry Mandel, Rob Jacoby, and the late Lenny Bernstein—collectively known as the Appalachian Round Table—for their concise editorial assistance in getting this manuscript in shape.

In like fashion, my thanks go to Pat Vestal, Sam Stone, and Gary Ader—the Write On Writers—for their input and encouragement.

And lastly the myriad members of the Blue Ridge Writers' Group for their input.

As with any such project, all errors are my responsibility, and not that of the above-referenced advisors.

About the Author

Tom Hooker was born and raised in North Mississippi, receiving a degree from the University of Mississippi. He and his family have lived in Hendersonville, North Carolina since 1988. Tom has had short stories and poems published in a number of literary journals across the nation.

In addition to *Twenty-Five Angels*, Mr. Hooker has authored a non-fiction work entitled, *Calvary's Child: The Life of Amanda Carol Hooker*, and co-authored, along with Gary Ader, a novel entitled, *The War Never Ends*.

A Word about Reviews

As you all are probably aware, reviews are the life blood of any author. They are what readers look at when selecting a book to purchase. I hope you've enjoyed *Twenty-Five Angels,* and, if you have, won't you please take a moment to write a positive, descriptive review? Please cite what it was that you liked about the book (plot? characters?), and why you would recommend it. Your review doesn't have to be fancy, or long, just honest and positive. Then, post that review anywhere you think it might be helpful, beginning of course with Amazon. Thank you in advance for your review.

Tom

Made in the USA
Monee, IL
23 September 2021